The Devil in the Dust

The First Book
of
Outremer

The Devil in the Dust
The First Book of Outremer
Chaz Brenchley

WIZARD'S TOWER

Wizard's Tower Press

Trowbridge, England

The Devil in the Dust
The First Book of Outremer

Text © 1998, 2003, 2022 by Chaz Brenchley
Cover art & design by Ben Baldwin
Book design by Cheryl Morgan

First published in Great Britain
by Orbit as part of
The Tower of the King's Daughter,
October 1998

First published in the USA by Ace,
May 2003

This edition by Wizard's Tower Press,
April 2022

Paperback ISBN: 978-1-913892-32-6

http://wizardstowerpress.com/
http://www.chazbrenchley.co.uk/
http://www.outremer.co.uk/

Contents

The Bright Dead of the Day   11

The Devil in the Dust   24

No Daughter, No Door   45

How High, How Far Below   71

These Things Happen   97

Heights of Folly   123

What They Carried   152

The Hidden and the Lost   181

Brothers in Arms   209

In the Dark   240

The Living Bleed   254

The Lights of Judgement   274

Best things come in big packages.
The start of something this big,
it has to be for Ian.

Cher a tort unt ses fieuz saiziz;
Bien en devums aveir dolur,
Cher la fud Deu primes servi
E reconnu per segnuur.

—CRUSADER SONG,
ANON, c. 1143

Praise for
The Devil in the Dust

"Along the way there are all the adventures a discerning fantasy reader could wish for and Brenchley's concise, muscular prose makes the story flow, free of genre clichés" – *SFX*

"Brenchley's grasp of his colourful narrative never falters, and his descriptive powers are exemplary." - *Orbit*

"Chaz Brenchley's striking new epic fantasy series [is] a revelation. The atmosphere is so well described you can almost taste it." – *Starburst*

"Brenchley the horror novelist and Brenchley the fantasist come together in perfect alignment...the kind of dark, painful power rarely seen in the literature of heroic fantasy."
– *Cemetery Dance*

"If you like slow tension and intrigue and well-developed world-building, this is recommended. Brenchley's prose is crisp and descriptive and his characterizations are nicely done. The last quarter of the book finally cuts loose and the ending left me wanting to see what will happen next in the second volume" – *Sigma*

"Brenchley has created a fascinating alternate-world version of the Crusader kingdom and has set up a bunch of interesting plot strands. The addition of Arabian Nights-style magic is a very clever touch that promises much to come."
– *Emerald City*

CHAZ BRENCHLEY

"As with all Brenchley's novels, the prose is beautifully crafted and a joy to read ... I can't wait to see what happens next." – *Northern Review*

"Compelling reading" – *Locus*

THE DEVIL IN THE DUST

DESPITE WHAT THE church claimed and the people believed, this was still a kingdom born of younger sons, the land-hungry and the dispossessed.

And those sons were fathers now, they had sons of their own; and their landless younger sons were looking north and east and south themselves, finding this realm of Outremer too tight a glove, seeing no border—internal or outward-facing—invulnerable to change.

The Kingdom of the Hammer they called it, drinking late and talking, always talking in the halls of their fathers: from its shape, and from their own aggressive yearnings to see that hammer fall and crush, beat out new territories for the needy.

But the church preached contentment, as ever, *we have what we came for*; and their fathers preached security and caution, *we have all that we can hold.*

And the wisest among them, churchman or father or younger son—or daughter—looked at the land unblinkered, and saw that in truth this was not even one kingdom, for all that it had one king and many public oaths. Too quarrelsome, these exiles, these families far from kin; they were four states—four and one, but that one closed, that one Folded and never now to be named, torn from maps and memory both—and always in contention, always wrangling each with the others. And of course always, always at war with the world around.

No, the wisest said, *this cannot last. It cannot live.* A hundred years, perhaps, they gave Outremer; no more than that. Certainly, no more.

ONE

The Bright Dead of the Day

NOT THE FIRST, Marron knelt in the Chamber of the King's Eye and thought, *what need Ascariel?* Why had his father, had so many fathers fought and died to win possession of the golden city, that dream of priests and kings, when it seemed that they had it all already? When the dream and the deaths and the very Mount itself could be contained within a bare room rock-hewn and chilly, where the walls sweated sour-tasting water and it needed only a single plaited candle and the words of a fat and sour-sweating brother to bring forth miracles?

The thought, of course, was heresy. It should be confessed, and due penance paid. But Marron was fresh come from far away, gentler country where he'd seen no more true magic than the seasons' changes, the hand of blessing laid upon the land. Here his mind was dizzy with wonder, and it was from that unaccustomed whirling strangeness in his head that the words and the idea—*what need Ascariel?*—had been flung up, all unintended. He thought both souls of the God would understand him.

Besides, his troop had burned a village for heresy only the day before, and he was afraid of his confessor.

I T HAD SEEMED like a celebration, he remembered think- ing even at the time, in the heat and the hard light and the hurry, hurry urgency of it all. Not the human arm of the God's justice wielded, but only something done in madness to mark the end of a long march and their new home almost in sight now, very much on their minds. They'd been too many days in the saddle, a storm had forced them ashore too soon; days and days of eating tack and sleeping on dusty earth and riding, riding. The sun savage above the alien hills, their bodies baked as dry as the road they followed, vows resurgent in their minds and untried steel impatient at their backs, seeming as hot and as thirsty as they were themselves.

And Fra' Piet had led them away from the road one morning, promising them the castle by tomorrow sunset and the God's work now; and they had followed a track high into the hills till they came at the bright dead of the day to close-shuttered huts with domed roofs and ragged mud-mortared walls, two dozen such and a well, and a temple of dressed stone at the heart of the village. And the heresy was there, clear to be seen on a weathered board above the temple's door: the Blinded Eyes, the double loop that was the sign of the God Divided, but with the hollow spaces filled as though to say His unremittingly watchful eyes were closed, for now and always. Fra' Piet had warned them of worse in these hills, of the sign painted with a fringe of lashes below, to say that the God slept; but that was deliber- ate defiance, a sign of Catari revolt. This, these blank circles were something entirely other.

The Heresy of Korash: that the God moved indeed on His doubled path but that He gave no heed to mortal men, that He cared not a whit for their deeds on the earth. Though Korash had been redeemed by fire and his bones crushed to

CHAZ BRENCHLEY

powder two hundred years ago, he still had his adherents,
here particularly, in these hills long lost to the voice of the
true church. So they had been told, Marron and his new-
sworn brothers, and so it had proved.

They had ridden into that hilltop village, three dozen
men with the ache of their weary road still on them,
hungry for more than food. Fra' Piet's disfigured hands had
swung the axe that smashed that sacrilegious sign, it had
been his hoarse voice that called down fire and steel and his
own weapon again that hacked the black-robed priest on the
temple steps. After that, though, he had only sat his horse
and watched. It had been a test, Marron thought later, or a
challenge. Perhaps a baptism.

ONE HALF OF a baptism, he thought now, the opening
rite. This was the completion, here under the castle, a
gift of marvel from the King's Eye.

They had been mad that day, young men crazed by the
sun, drawn and deadly. They had screamed, he remembered,
louder than the women and the children both; now they
were mute, transfixed. In themselves emblems of the God,
turning and turning, each one a traveller on two paths: to the
savage, to the serene. Looping always to the centre, to the
Godhead, and always passing through.

Not an hour had passed since their arrival. They'd ridden
up the precipitous hill and through the gate of the massive
castle, up the broad shallow steps and the long covered ramp
that followed, as weary as their horses and stained with more
than travel now. In the courtyard by the inner moat, their
packs and mounts had been taken from them by thin black-
haired boys, Sharai slaves, someone said; and without even
the chance to change their habits or rinse the caked dust
from their skins, they had been ordered to silence although
they were silent already, and led up another ramp too

narrow for horses and so into the castle proper. Then down: down and down they had come, soon confused by the winding stairs and the ill-lit passages, shivering in the sudden chill and the uncertainty.

At last a door, cedarwood bound with iron; and beyond that, this. Nothing like the great halls and pillared spaces they'd heard of and not yet seen, caught like bubbles of air within the mass of rock and stone above their heads. A troop of men made this small chamber crowded. Where they knelt in a rough circle, each brother's legs and shoulders brushed his neighbours' on either side, but the touch of another human was nothing but relief here. Even the smell of his brothers' bodies and his own too long unwashed, the rank heavy odour of woollen habits damp with sweat, even those gave Marron something to cling to, something to root him to the known world in a place of wonder and terror strangely mixed.

What is this? was the question they must all have been asking silently as they had filed in behind the brother with the torch. None had spoken it aloud, but Marron had seen it in their eyes as they'd glanced at each other and at the crudely rounded walls and the uneven floor, as some few of them had reached to touch damp rock and carry the wetness on their fingers to dusty lips. He had done that himself, and then had wanted to spit, had swallowed instead though his mouth had twisted at the rancid taste of it.

The brother with the torch, Fra' Tumis had gestured them into a circle and then onto their knees, his heavy-jowled face frowning with suspicion as his narrow eyes flickered around watching for any semblance of disobedience. Denied that, he did finally speak himself, though only to say, "This is the Chamber of the King's Eye," which told them nothing. Then he went to the only furniture in the chamber, an iron tripod holding a four-wicked candle, two white and two black tapers plaited and twisted into a single column.

He lit the wicks from his torch before handing that across
the kneeling circle to Fra' Piet, who had carried it outside
and closed the door behind him.

Somehow the click of the latch set a shiver to run down
Marron's spine, nothing to do with cold or rank wet air. Fra'
Piet scared him, to be sure; but it was a fear born of knowledge and witness, many weeks in the man's company and
one frantic hour caught in his madness, when they'd been
brought by him into the pitiless possession of the God.

That fear Marron could understand and deal with. It was
good sense, to be afraid of Fra' Piet.

This was different. Here he was ignorant and bewildered
and his brothers the same, strangers both to the land and
to the life. Only a few short months since, they had been
yeomen or artisans or peasants in another world. Fra' Piet
was their bridge from that to this. He was their mentor, albeit
harsh in his demands and obsessive in his duties; he was a
rock in an ocean, craggy and dangerous and sure. And he
had left them suddenly in the hands of an unknown, in this
bare hand-hewn cave of a chamber, and Fra' Tumis seemed
bored or contemptuous or both, but not at all fearful and yet
Marron was fearful of him, or of what he meant to do.

What Fra' Tumis meant was a mystery; what he did had
been hard enough to see, in the moving shadows of the
candle's light. Harder still after he'd glared around the circle
and stabbed one hand sharply downward, redirecting their
nervous, curious stares to laps or folded hands or the dark
damp stone they knelt on.

Marron had lowered his head obediently, but no will of
his or any other's could have stopped his eyes from spying,
as best they could. It seemed to him, in what bare glimpses
he dared risk, that Fra' Tumis held his hands above the bend-
ing flames of the candle, to cup the light within his fingers;

it had seemed as if that pudgy flesh went too close, there should have been a smell of singeing and a yelp of pain.

But Tumis had chanted softly, and his voice at least was sweet. The words, the language Marron didn't know. Nor did he know how there could have been more light suddenly in the chamber and not less, when Tumis' hands guarded the candle so nearly. Light there was, though, fierce white light that made him squint, that drew hisses of breath from all around the circle, that made his neighbour—*Aldo, for the love of your skin, be still!*—grunt and draw his hood up over his head, to shade dazzled eyes within it.

*L*IGHT, THEY HAD been taught, *is the chief token of the God's even-handedness, that we walk half our time in the sun and half in darkness. It is His gift to us, that we may see our way to virtue; it is also an instrument of His justice, that others may see our sin.*

This was light as Marron had never known it, though, light they had made no space for in his theology. This light drew lines of gold and fire in the air, and not only Aldo was moving now. Men were making the sign of the God against their brows, more in superstition than in prayer, Marron thought; but he gave them only a glance, only a moment before his eyes and his mind were gripped again.

This hard light came, it seemed, from the candle: flames rose above it like glass, like white-hot rods of glass, so rigid and so still. The walls of the chamber were in shadow, though Tumis had snatched his hands away now; Tumis also stood in shadow, though he stood only a pace back from the candle. Fragile and strong as skeins of silk drawn taut, all the light there was struck down to the heart of the brothers' circle, and there it showed them wonders.

You will see miracles, they had been told before ever they set out for the Sanctuary Land, you will see miracles and monsters; be prepared.

16

But how could they ever have prepared their minds for this?

"This is the King's Eye," Fra' Tumis intoned, against their staring, straining silence. "It is the God's benediction upon the king, that he may watch over all this land in the God's name, to guard the borders from the God's enemies and the heartlands from heresy. It is the king's kindness to his subjects, that he gives this blessing also to the Church Militant, that we may serve the better."

Was this kindness? Marron was unsure. He sweated cold in that cold place, his fingers trembled with the beat of his blood; this was the second time in two days that he had been stricken to the core of him and the blade in his heart was not more than half of wonder. The rest was sheer terror.

The light drew lines like golden wires, and planes like sheets of gold. It drew walls and domes and minarets; it built a palace or a temple in miniature, like a princess's golden toy only that this toy burned his eyes, its making burned his mind like a brand, and it lay still in the air a hand's span above the floor.

"This is the Dir'al Shahan in Ascariel," said Tumis, "that was their greatest temple when the Ekhed governed the city. It would have been destroyed," *it should have been destroyed,* his voice seemed to say, "when the God gave us victory there; but the king decreed otherwise, and took it for his own. Now it is his palace, and the seat of his power."

And it turned in the air and seemed to move further off, from all sides at once; and as it moved so other buildings flowed into the light, and streets, and vast gardens on steep slopes and a river below, and...

"This is Ascariel," said Tumis, when all the city on its high hill was before them, gleaming golden in that foetid air; and Marron thought, *What need the real world, then, what needed all those deaths?*

17

MARRON HAD SEEN maps, in the library of the great abbey where he had made his profession. He had even seen a map of these lands, though that had been Sharai work looted at the fall of Ascariel and sent back as a gift to the abbot, and he could not read it. He had been shown the holy city by an elder brother there, who understood the strange writing. Only a mark of coloured ink on parchment, but still he had felt a thrill to lay his finger on it and murmur the name, *Ascariel!*

This, though—this was more than a map, more even than a map of light and magic. This was the blessed land itself, brought forth in glory. It seemed to him that he had seen guards around the king's palace, figures in the streets, horses and wagons and a busy marketplace. Even now there was a shimmer of gold, like a string of beads being drawn slowly through a tiny gate in the outer wall, and he thought that was a merchant's caravan come to trade in the city.

Fra' Tumis brought his hands close to those glassy pillars of light rising from the candle, and chanted words that Marron could distinguish but not comprehend. White faded to yellow, pillars shrank to normal flame and Ascariel was gone.

Like men waking from a dream, Marron and his brothers stirred and shifted, worked their shoulders against a dying tension, gazed at each other's awestruck faces and knew they saw there reflections of their own.

Looking at Tumis, Marron saw him pale and sweating, trembling, rubbing wet hands on his habit. No shell of supercilious boredom on him now, and no contempt.

"Go," he said, his voice also drained of its strength and self-content. "Go out. Fra' Piet will show you where."

THEY FILED OUT as they had filed in, in silence. Fra' Piet was waiting in the corridor, thin-lipped, grim-lipped as ever, but nodding in satisfaction as he read their faces. There was a man, Marron thought, who would never need to see the miracle twice. A vision once witnessed would live in his sight forever, a burning testament to faith and a private covenant between himself and the God. This might have been how it began for him, Marron thought: that he had come to Outremer like Marron himself, a young man no more than ordinarily devout, impelled as much by family history as by religion; that he like Marron had been shown Ascariel in that dank dungeon, like a sending; and that for Fra' Piet at least the fire had never dimmed since, that he had discovered a true vocation then and sought only the direct path since, the glory of a golden city blinding him to pleasures of the body or the mind, or any earthly glint of light.

Numbed and dazzled, Marron could see that path threatening for himself also, could feel it almost opening like a pit beneath his feet, waiting only for his mind to lose its hold on anything but wonder.

But Fra' Piet brought them no sermons, nor—thank the God!—another miracle; he only led them back the way they'd come, up to the moat and the courtyard and the dry hot dusty wind. There were the stables, where their horses dozed now in wooden stalls in cool stone shadow, groomed and watered and revived. Here blessedly was the bath-house, here boys in white tunics fetching water in leather buckets from the moat. Here at last was the time to jerk and wriggle free of the heavy habit, to kick off stiff riding boots, to leave all in a heap in a corner and fight to be first to a bucket; and then to shudder under the sluice of chill water down his back and through his matted hair, to chase the shudder with a laugh and earn Fra' Piet's scowl for laughing. To turn away, rubbing at wet skin, catch Aldo's eye and share a private grin; and in that moment to feel the spell fade, not leave him but recede into the secret spaces of his mind, where it could be kept safe and treasured but not allowed to rule his thinking beyond reason.

Pushing his fingers through his hair and looking around, impatient for another bucket, Marron saw a boy carrying a wooden box. He took it first to Fra' Piet, who grunted and dipped his twisted fingers in, scooping out a handful of something soft and greyish. Marron watched him massage the paste across his lean, scarred body, raising a froth which he rinsed away with fresh water. Looking away, the boy caught Marron's gaze, took it for a summons and came to him.

Marron peered uncertainly into the box, and asked, "What is this?"

"Soap," the boy said in a light singsong. "For washing."

The word meant nothing. The paste felt greasy between Marron's cautious finger and thumb, but Fra' Piet had shown him its use; he took a dollop on his fingers and stroked it onto his arm, rubbing at it till he raised a thin grey lather, as on a horse after hard running. When he wiped it away, a swathe of skin showed startlingly pink, in a place he thought he'd washed already. He gave the boy a grin, received a shy smile in return and took more of the soap, working that across his shoulders and neck and into his hair, feeling it foam more stiffly there.

"Not for the eyes!" the boy said urgently, too late. Marron had already rubbed his face with frothy fingers.

His eyes burned suddenly; he gasped, pressing the heels of his hands against them, barely hearing the boy call out in a liquid, foreign tongue.

Searing pain, and then the cool flow of water over his head again. He reached to cup it in his hands and rinsed his eyes as best he could, blinking hard. Two boys there were now, one with a bucket; Marron scooped out handfuls of water and splashed his face until the burning eased.

"Not for the eyes," the first boy said again, trying another smile.

"No," Marron agreed wholeheartedly. And not for the mouth either; he'd had a taste of that lather, and his tongue and lips were burning. He rinsed his mouth and spat; but still took more of the paste—*soap, remember the name of it*—before the boy was called away to another curious brother. It hadn't burned his skin, at least, though it made his fingertips pucker; and he felt scoured clean where he'd used it, cleaner than he could remember.

DISCIPLINE SEEMED TEMPORARILY in abeyance, within the Order's walls yet; unaccustomed time they were given, to wash themselves. Marron soaped Aldo's back for him and Aldo his, and they fetched more water from the moat to rinse each other, as other brothers were doing all around. They drank also, surreptitiously at first—*obedience is the prime commandment, children: to do what you have not been ordered to do is disobedience*—and then openly, after they'd seen Fra' Piet do the same.

At last the boys brought linen towels and clean fresh habits; and when Marron and all his troop were dry and dressed and once more under the bleak gaze of their confessor, they were taken barefoot back into the castle and up to a chapel for prayers.

THIS AT LEAST was familiar and undisturbing, old words in an old tongue, rhythms and responses ingrained into Marron's mind since he was an infant.

Familiar also was the way his mind wandered from the words, even here in the God's own land, where he had thought he might have been different, more devout. Not even the blinding revelation of a miracle could work magic on his digressing soul, it seemed. He knelt on the bare stone floor of the chapel with Aldo on his left side and another brother, Jubal, on his right. His voice murmured steadily with theirs, with everyone's; and his thoughts slipped free, slipped back to a day, an hour not far in time or distance but far indeed, very far in strangeness.

Aldo, friend of his childhood and friend of his youth, in many ways a brother long before they were brothers in religion:

Aldo with his long-known, long-loved face twisted beyond knowing as he leaned sideways in his saddle to throw a flaming torch through an open doorway; Aldo with his laugh tuned harsh and knowing at the scream that came back, at the sight of a woman running out with her robe and hair afire; Aldo who must have seen the woman in there before he threw, who already had his sword in his hand and used it not to kill quickly but to drive her back, back and burning into the burning hut.

Jubal, an older man and a stranger before this voyage but all his life a monk, sent to Outremer by his abbot as penance for an offence not to be talked of:

Jubal wide-eyed and screaming, no longer containing heavy thoughts behind his heavy brows; Jubal a better soldier maybe than he ever was a monk, swinging a mace with joy, his bare arm blood-spattered as he hacked, as he kicked his horse on and hacked again, as he screamed; and there were words within his screaming, that was the Credo that ran mixed with spittle from his mouth as he declared his belief in the one true God, twin-souled and all-pervading.

And between Aldo and Jubal there was Marron, there was himself; and he had a new image of himself also to wonder at, to shudder at, to come between him and his prayers, him and the God's due worship:

himself on his feet now, slid down from his bucking, frantic horse; himself with a child in his hands, a heretic, a babe snatched from its father's arms and too young yet to be clearly boy or girl; himself gripping its ankles and spinning with the frenzy like a mad priest on the temple steps, stumbling over the body of the priest but catching his balance with a hoarse cry, crazed even to his own ears as he dashed the babe against the stones of the wall there, as he saw its skull split and heard its sudden silence even in all that noise, as he tossed it through the open doorway into the fire within and turned away from the stain, so small a stain it had left on the wall there, a thin smear of red that the first rains would wash away if ever it did rain in this barren, sun-bright land.

TWO

The Devil in the Dust

A BARBARIC HABIT, her father called it, veiling women as the Sharai did. *No practice for a civilised land,* he called it, though that had of course not stopped him sending Julianne into the hands of men whose practice it was.

It was the same with the litter she travelled in. She'd fought against that—why be carried at a slow walk, when she could perfectly well ride her own palfrey, they could mount the whole party and be half the time on the road?—but her future husband had sent a palanquin and the men to bear it, and her father had insisted. Perhaps he'd even been thinking a little of her comfort, she granted grudgingly, though mostly of course it was politics, not to offend either custom or a powerful man.

At any rate, this easy swaying ride on soft cushions was in honesty no burden to her, nor seemingly to the eight black giants whose shoulders took the weight of it. They talked between themselves in soft voices as they went, though she couldn't understand their speech; they laughed often, with a bubbling and mysterious humour. The men-at-arms who walked beside—also sent by her intended husband—found the journey more testing, though they were soldiers and all they had to carry was their own packs. She watched them sweat in the hard sun, heard them curse in hoarse whispers and saw how their shoulders drooped in the late of the day, how their feet dragged in the dust.

That dust was the devil, throat-choking and harsh; even the men veiled themselves against it when the wind lashed it eye-high and stinging. No, she hated to admit it but she was better here in the palanquin than on horseback in such heat, in such a land. Better to conceal her face behind soft silken curtains than behind a veil that would soon be damp and sticking to her face, soon clogged and filthy and stifling with the dust. Better to be shaded, cool and comfortable, though she had stamped and shouted, stamped and wept for one last freedom, not to be confined until she must.

Oddly, she had neither shouted nor wept against the journey itself. It seemed odd to her, at least. She had thought herself shamed by the palanquin, until she'd seen the truths of sun and dust; but being first taken and now sent to marry a man she'd never met, for reasons of politics and power—surely there should be greater shame in that, for her and for her father? And yet she didn't feel shame, only a cold dread and a great weariness that she thought would never lift here-after.

She was sixteen, and the weight of her life to come exhausted her. When she thought about it, when her clouded vision turned that way. *Not yet*, she reminded herself once more. That was another reason to be glad of this slow proces-sion.

THERE WERE PANELS of gauze let into the curtains, allowing her to see out quite easily, though they were small and cleverly offset so that the men would see nothing clearly within.

THE DEVIL IN THE DUST

There was little enough to be seen outside, though she watched for hours, her mind dulled by the swaying of the litter and the slow drift of the endless hills, yellow and grey with dust, studded with dark thorns and what other bushes were tough enough to grow in this hard hot land. A hateful land, she thought it: and wondered what Elessi would be like. So much nearer to the desert, so much worse than this. No land for riding, even were she allowed to ride. A land without shade, without compromise, and its people much the same; and her father the diplomatist, the smooth and subtle intermediary, sending her alone into such a country and for all the rest of her life...

And no, she was not, was *not* going to allow her anxieties and resentments to blight these last few days of travelling. *Deal with what comes, when it comes; you leave the future be.* That had been her milk-mother's advice when she was a child, and it had always seemed nothing less than good sense to Julianne. Why be miserable, when cheerful was always a choice?

Now she felt that choice had gone, or was going. But she determined to keep despair out of her soul, where it had never had a place before and would not be granted one so long as she could fight it.

She turned her gaze forward, only looking for something to distract her suddenly rebellious mind, teetering on the verge of falling into the pit wherein it was forbidden to fall; and *blessed be the God and all His saints and angels*, there actually was something for once that she could look at.

Not that it seemed so very much at first, just barely enough to pique her interest. Not of course what her soul yearned for, a city the like of Marasson to bring colour and life to parched eyes; neither what her father dreaded more than she did, a horde of bandits sweeping down to overmaster this small troop of men and carry her off into slavery or worse. It was only someone else on the road, a local boy to

26

judge by his size and dress. The sergeant of her guard was speaking to him, though, and not simply to order him out of the way. That was sufficiently unusual to make her curious.

When her litter drew alongside the sergeant's horse, she reached to strike the chime that would call her bearers to a halt, but then didn't need to do so because he gestured them himself to stop. Even through the blurring gauze, she could read consternation and uncertainty on his face.

"What is it, sergeant?" His name was Blaise, but he preferred her to use his rank, for the sake of discipline; and she'd grown accustomed to holding conversations like this, through the curtain. If she drew it aside, she'd have to veil her face to spare his blushes. Though he seemed to be blushing in any case, and she didn't understand that at all.

"My lady, this lad... Well, he isn't what he seems to be. He speaks like a noble's son, though he won't give his name or family. And he says we'll find trouble up ahead."

The sergeant's horse danced aside then, to give her a clear view of the boy. Julianne looked, stared, did twitch the curtain aside momentarily to be certain; and then she laughed and said, "Sergeant, that lad isn't a lad either. She's a girl."

Sergeant Blaise gaped. The girl was dark and crop-haired like a boy, certainly, and the dirt on her face was enough to hide her lack of any coming beard. She was wearing the rough burnous of a peasant lad, though her soft boots didn't suit that disguise; she should have gone barefoot, Julianne thought. Nor did the pack she carried seem likely to be local work.

The girl scowled, and spat into the dust of the road; and then shrugged, and threw an easy smile towards the litter's concealing curtains. "Someone has eyes, at least," she said, in a clear voice that certainly hadn't grown up in these hills. Julianne could well understand her sergeant's confusion. "May I know whose they are?"

So Julianne struck her chime after all, for her bearers' attention, and asked them to set the litter down. She lifted the curtain aside—while Sergeant Blaise turned his face away, and cursed at his men for gawping—and said, "I am Julianne de Rance. Will you join me?"

That invitation agitated the sergeant further, but before he could forbid her the girl had stooped and slipped into the litter, settling comfortably cross-legged on the cushions as Julianne made room.

"My name is Elisande. And I could wish that you hadn't made me say that," added with a rueful twist of her mouth.

"Elisande of what family?"

Julianne was trying to learn what Blaise could not, but she had no better fortune, only a shake of the head in response and, "You wouldn't know my grandfather."

"I doubt that," Julianne said dryly. Many of the lords of Outremer had passed through Marasson in the last ten years or so; of those to whom she hadn't actually made her curtsey, she could still recite their lineages for a dozen generations.

"Truly, you wouldn't." Elisande was smiling, enjoying the mystery, irritating Julianne a little.

"Then why not give me his name?" she demanded. "If it will mean nothing to me, it can do no harm."

"Nor any good, either. And he is a very private man," said solemnly, but with dancing eyes. "I think I will keep his privities a little longer, if I may."

"As you wish, then."

"Thank you, Julianne." And that at least was said honestly, no teasing in her now; and Julianne's chilly stiffness melted after just the one moment, the one brief touch of her father's daughter. Trained though she was to haughtiness at need, in a court where the ability to freeze with a glance was almost a survival trait, she nevertheless couldn't sustain it here, with her curiosity burning so hotly.

"So what will you tell me, then?"

"What would you like me to tell you?"

"Why you're dressed as a boy, why you're on foot and alone, where you've come from, where you're going," and a whole host of questions more, indicated with a wide, curtain-brushing sweep of her arm.

Elisande chuckled. "In that order?"

"If you like."

"Well, I'm dressed as a boy because that makes it easier to travel on foot and alone in the places I'm coming from, though not necessarily where I'm going. I suppose," she went on, sighing lustily, "I'll have to go veiled and robed now, if I'm not to scandalise your sergeant?"

"You have already," Julianne assured her, "scandalised my sergeant beyond repairing. But you haven't really answered any of my questions."

"No. Well, the first, perhaps. This," with a brush of her hand over coarse-woven wool, "makes things possible that wouldn't be, else. Some of the villages hereabouts, they'd stone me for walking shameless so far from my house, with no men to watch me. So I cut my hair and wear a burnous and no one looks twice, except to be sure I don't rob them. I keep to the sheep-tracks mostly, and trouble the villagers not at all. Only I saw something was happening ahead, there are camels and wagons standing for half a mile, and they haven't moved for an hour; so I came down to see, and your sergeant wanted to know where the next water was, and got suspicious when I couldn't tell him."

Some answers, Julianne thought, were designed to bury the question, not to resolve it. She wasn't going to be distracted; Blaise would find out what the trouble was, holding people up on the road ahead. Meanwhile, "But why alone, how is this possible? How could your father let you?" And how could she keep the envy out of her voice, given such a difference of fathers?

"Oh, he didn't," Elisande said, with an odd contempt in her voice. "I knew he wouldn't, so I just left."

And had done so some time since, by the baked brown of her skin. She was lucky, Julianne thought, to go so dark and look so natural. And to have black hair, like all the Catari peoples; and to have eyes that could pass for black, though this close they were midnight-blue and startling. Not many would be let this close, she supposed.

"Left where?"

"My father's house," obviously, and back to mysteries carried openly and unashamed.

"To go where?"

Elisande gave her a smile, and a true answer to that one. "Roq de Rançon."

And so was Julianne on her way there, but she felt entitled not to say so. "Why, though?"

If anything, she was expecting to be told of a young man too deeply loved to be let go without a chase; but really she expected nothing, and was given no more than she expected. "I wanted to see the Roq," said Elisande, "and my father wouldn't bring me."

Of course, she wanted to see the Roq and ran away from her family home to do it. What girl would not? Again Julianne felt piqued, almost insulted; again she felt the temptation to draw back from any sign of warmth towards this vagrant tease. Again, though, her impulse failed in the moment of its birth. The ability to make quick and accurate judgements of other people was another necessary gift in the Emperor's palace at Marasson, and very much so for her father's daughter; and all her instincts were saying that she could make a friend here, regardless of secrets kept from

30

her. A friend on the road at least, and oh, she would like to come to the castle with a friend in tow.

"You must be thirsty," she said, thinking of the dust and the dry road and the high hot sun beyond her curtains.

"Parched."

"I have some grape juice here..."

There was only one beaker for the juice, so they shared it; and then Elisande said, "So what of you, Julianne? There are men to protect you here, but none of your family, I think?"

You are as alone as I am, she was saying, and it was true in its way. "My father was with us," Julianne said, "until just yesterday. But he was called away, he had to leave me." And then, to show that she at least was prepared to share more than a beaker of juice, "My father is the King's Shadow."

"Ah. And when the king moves, so must his Shadow, yes?"

A moment of staring, followed by a rising laugh she couldn't choke down for all her years of training. "That's what he says. Exactly."

A shrug from Elisande. "All through Outremer, that's what they say. Where did he go, your father, where did the king send him?"

"He didn't say." He rarely did, and she'd learned early not to ask. Her father kept the king's counsel, the king famously kept his own; few crumbs of information fell her way, and those she hoarded.

Elisande nodded, unsurprised. "Did he say where he was sending you?"

"Yes, of course," though in honesty there could be no certainty about it, for anyone who did not know her father. Many men moved their womenfolk like gamepieces, valuable perhaps but not to be consulted, only summoned or sent according to value, desire or whim. Julianne should, she supposed, feel grateful to have had her future explained to

31

her, with reasons and even an implicit apology. "We were travelling to Elessi; I am to be married to Baron Imber."

"Are you?" Elisande's eyebrows twitched, as though she were mentally uprating the worth of a daughter of the King's Shadow. "Which one?"

That forced a snort of laughter from Julianne. Again it would have been a reasonable question, but for her father. "The younger. Count Heinrich's son, not his brother."

"Lucky, then."

Seen that way, she supposed she was. She'd not met her husband-to-be, but his uncle, the elder Baron Imber, had come to Marasson three summers back. She remembered a heavy, scarred man with a shaven head and a sun-bleached beard, plain clothes and a temper just as plain, a sour twist seeming permanently sewn into his mouth as he'd watched the court at play around him. At the time, she'd wondered why he stayed so long. Wise she might have been for a thirteen-year-old, but not wise enough to see what was obvious, where it touched herself. That truly was when she had been given away, for all that she hadn't learned the truth of it then. The baron had come to study and assess her, to weigh her potential as a future niece, a countess-apparent for his land; and then—once satisfied, as presumably he must have been—to negotiate with her father. Hard bargaining for sure between two unlike and difficult men, but at last there were reciprocal promises made, the terms of their trading. Dowry and bride-price in land or gold or favour, some elements to be publicly attested and some to remain private, a few more debts and guarantees stored among the many in the subtle and devious head of the King's Shadow.

And yes, it could have gone another way, had her father been another man. This Baron Imber was a widower and no doubt could have been attracted by the offer of another marriage. Not greedy for a young girl in his bed, or she thought not; neither greedy for money; but for influence, for power, for the ear of the king—yes, she thought, that self-denying man would have neither had nor sought the strength to refuse those.

But her father had had so much care for her at least, not to offer. Instead he had sold her to the uncle for the nephew's benefit, and taken two full years to tell her so; and even since the public announcement the nephew had still not come to Marasson, so that she had no independent picture of him in her mind's eye. All she could do was hope that he would not be a shadow of his uncle namesake; but she was sensible above all and always honest with herself, and it seemed all too likely that he would. The Elessan nobles she had met had been cold men all, cast from the same mould as the baron: battle-hardened, dour and devout, suspicious of comfort or compromise. Suspicious of her, she thought, for being raised in the corruption of the Empire. Presumably the advantages of her blood outweighed the taint of her upbringing. Or else they thought that taint could be cleansed soon enough, once she was chastely locked among the women in the count's high castle.

"When my father was—summoned," she said, choosing to say nothing of the manner of that summoning, "he had no time to do what he thought proper, to take me back to Tallis until Imber could come himself or send a shadow of his own to escort me. Father sent a messenger to Elessi, saying that I was gone to stay at the Roq, until I could be fetched." Like a prize animal, or a piece of looted treasure held under guard, awaiting its new owner. Not safe, her father had decreed, for her to go on to Elessi unescorted. They had been two days from the Roq, perhaps two weeks from Elessi; heat and dust and scarce forage would make for a slow journey. That her father's absence reduced her protection by no more than one man out of twenty meant nothing. His name, he had said, gave more protection than any twenty men, and that she bore the same name made her the more vulnerable without him. All of which was probably true, and none the less unwelcome.

No surprise in Elisande's nod, that they had the same immediate destination; this road led nowhere else. "We could travel together, then? If you would like that?"

"If my men can take the weight of two in the litter," Julianne amended. "You can't *walk*, Elisande. You just can't."

"Well. Perhaps not. But perhaps we needn't worry about it, perhaps neither one of us will be travelling anywhere," twisting to throw a frowning look forward, trying to see through gauze and hills both. "Maybe the road has gone, or bandits have blocked it, or—"

"There's Blaise," Julianne interrupted. "He'll know." He had ridden on himself, it seemed, to discover the obstruction; now he was cantering back with some urgency. He called something to his resting men even before he reined in, something that had them up and checking their weapons, staring down the road, visibly nervous.

And then he was beside the grounded litter and jumping down from his horse into the cloud of dust it had kicked up, coughing to clear his throat before he said, "My lady?"

"Yes, sergeant?"

"They say there is a djinni in the road. I spoke to the master of a caravan, and he says it has been there since dawn."

Her first thought was that neither her all-knowing father nor her new and insouciant friend had predicted this; her second, that she had never seen nor ever expected to see a djinni. Nor would she now, in all likelihood. Blaise would take her back, she thought, to the last village they'd passed. He'd commandeer a house for her, and they would wait until the road was clear. Wait days, if need be.

But Elisande was moving, was sitting up straight now, half reaching to draw the curtains back before she checked herself and called out through them. "Did you see it?"

"I saw a dust-devil, er, my lady. Only it was very tall, and stationary."

That fitted. Even after years of service on the desert borders of Elessi, the dour sergeant would need to have words with a cloud of dust before he would believe it to be anything more than what he saw.

Perhaps Elisande had already understood that of him. Her next question was, "Did you speak to it?"

"No."

"Has anyone?"

"I couldn't say, my lady."

"Well, did they tell you its name?"

"Its *name*, my lady? They did not."

"Oh, for the God's sake...!"

And now Elisande did draw the curtains back, in a rush of impatience; and stepped out of the litter, and paused only long enough to look back at Julianne and ask, "Are you coming?"

She didn't, couldn't possibly have more than a moment to decide. Blaise would forbid it, and she couldn't overrule him; her father's voice and his own lord's would weigh far heavier than hers. But Elisande's sudden eruption from the litter had set Blaise's horse skittering backwards, and his hands and attention both were occupied, trying to steady it. And she never had seen a djinni, and Elisande clearly meant to hold a conversation with this one.

Not running, no—*dignity, confidence, grace,* one of the lessons her father taught her early—but moving as fast as she could manage without, Julianne set her feet on the road and her heart on a new course: something that was less than total

35

obedience to her father's manipulative will, though it felt like something more. She seized Elisande's hand and tugged her almost into a trot to keep up, realising only then that she stood a good few inches taller than her new friend.

Behind them, Blaise's voice called sharply. "My lady, no! You may not...!"

Julianne didn't check, didn't so much as turn her head to acknowledge that she'd heard. All she did was stare with a cold fury at any of the men who made a move towards her. Already flustered and blushing as they were at this sight of her face unveiled, just that hint of the Marasson court's ice-maiden was enough to have them backing away, jerking their eyes aside and mumbling apologies.

And now there was only the road ahead of her, empty as far as the next bend, and she almost felt free of her cage. But there were also footsteps coming from behind, running foot-steps, and that was undoubtedly Sergeant Blaise, horseless at last and his Elessan eyes seeing nothing but his duty, ready perhaps even to handle her physically, to bundle her back through the decent shrouds of her litter.

"My lady Julianne," and his voice now was intemperate, angry, barely clinging with an effort to the outward forms of politeness, "will you please come back to the palanquin? *Now?*"

And yes, when she still paid him no heed he did lay his hands on them both, gripping her shoulder and pushing Elisande away; and then before he could turn her she turned herself, she spun around and her free hand cracked across his cheek, with the palm cupped to amplify the sound so that all his men should hear.

She didn't need to say a word. After the startlement on his face, she saw the gradual dawn of understanding, the cer-tain knowledge of how grossly he had offended, though the offence in his eyes perhaps lay more against his master than against her. If what she had been told of Elessan society was not exaggerated, she could ask Imber for his death. And have twenty male witnesses to support her.

"Your, your pardon, lady. I—I forgot myself. I was anxious..."

And he was pale now beneath his tan, except where his cheek was red; but his back was stiff and only his voice was trembling, and she thought that if she ordered him to do it, he would cut his own throat there and then.

Dignity, confidence, grace. "Yes, and rightly," she said. "I ask your pardon too, sergeant; I neglected to veil myself. It is a custom still strange to me," and as she spoke she drew her veil up and let it fall across her face. "Now, if you will accompany me, with perhaps half a dozen of your men for surety, I think we will go to see this djinni."

And she held out her hand again and Elisande took it, gripping warmly and smiling silent applause; and the two started off down the road again, Julianne urgent only with curiosity now, while the bull sergeant was still bellowing behind them.

THESE STEEP-SIDED hills threw out rocky spurs, twenty or thirty feet of sudden, sharp-edged cliff. Just where the road bent around one such outcrop, they found the tail of the queue. A mule driver with three bone-bare beasts monstrously overladen; then an ox-wagon, another, a small train of wagons; then the caravan Blaise had spoken of, a string of camels that would stretch half a mile or more when they were moving, but were hobbled in small groups at the roadside now while their drivers crouched over cooking fires in the shade. All these people, Julianne supposed, must be bound for Roq de Rançon: the trade good for them, essential for the castle. And all of it halted, for fear of a creature all the garrison of the Roq might not be able to destroy or chase away; and who knew how long the djinni would choose to dance in the road?

The caravan, Blaise indicated, was keeping a prudent but not a nervous distance from the djinni, just comfortably out of sight. They would find that around the next bend.

So they took the next bend, Blaise leading. He and the other men were visibly on edge now, touching fingers to sword-hilts or axe-hafts and muttering useless advice to each other. Even Julianne found her legs moving more slowly, her fingers sweating in Elisande's grip and her eyes with a tendency to jerk a little at every movement they caught, every sound that reached her.

Around the bend the road narrowed, to squeeze between two of those inconvenient outcroppings of rock; and just there, in the eye of the needle, was where the djinni stood.

If that was a djinni. Julianne wouldn't know a djinni from an 'ifrit from a manifestation of the God, and for a moment what she saw was what Blaise had described—only a dust-devil such as they'd seen a couple of times already on the journey, a sudden twist of wind made tangible.

But this dust-devil didn't stir, it stood rock-still between its jutting rocks; and it stood quite as high as those walls of rock, like a pillar balanced on a point; and it spun so fast that at this distance it seemed not to spin at all, but rather to be an endless coil of silver-grey rope that climbed itself and swallowed itself and began the climb again.

A few paces before the djinni stood a boy, ten or twelve years old and dressed much as Elisande was dressed, only that his burnous was torn and soaked a vivid red. He stood transfixed, staring and sobbing; and what he stared at was not the djinni, but what had been his right arm. It hung loose and dreadful from his shoulder, bare white bones barely joined now, stripped of skin and muscle.

Both girls were briefly still, as still as the djinni, as still as
the boy. Elisande it was who moved first, who pulled free
of Julianne's hold and ran forward, past Blaise's gesture of
denial. She reached the boy and took his other arm, and
turned him; and beckoned imperiously to the sergeant,
shouting, "Take him, quickly! Back to the fires, look after
him..."

Blessedly, Blaise asked no questions. This he could deal
with. He hurried to take the boy from Elisande's grasp,
picked him up and handed him to one of his men, with
quick instructions. That man ran off down the road, the
fainting boy slack in his arms. As they passed Julianne she
stirred, shook the numbness of shock from her head and
walked slowly on to join Elisande and the sergeant.

"Why...?" Her voice came out in a cracked whisper; she
swallowed dryly and tried again. "Why do you want to know
its name?"

Elisande smiled thinly. "It helps."

"So what will you do, just ask it?"

"No," fiercely. "Never ask a djinni a question, *never*. It isn't
safe. If you don't know that, just stand quiet," though her
fingers closing tightly on Julianne's sleeve said that she was
glad to have her there, if only standing quiet. For her part,
Julianne had no intention of doing anything more. This
close, she could see the roiling dust that wove the ever-turn-
ing rope of the djinni's body, that must have ripped the boy's
flesh from his arm when he stupidly, unthinkingly reached
to touch. She was frightened beyond measure; almost she
wanted Blaise to grip her again, to drag her back to the litter
and leave Elisande to face this monstrous thing alone.

Almost.

But the sergeant was rapt, stunned it seemed by this
proximity to an alien magic. He wasn't offering rescue, nor
truly did she want it. Curiosity had brought her here; a swift

loyalty would keep her at her new friend's side, despite her craven soul.

Elisande lifted her head and her voice, though both took a visible effort. "Peace be upon you, spirit."

"And upon you also."

The reply came from the heart of the spinning tower, oddly light, almost female but not in the least human. There was no body behind it, no beat of blood, no hint of mortality. Julianne shuddered, and saw Blaise stir in the corner of her eye as though he too wanted to run and could not.

"My name is Elisande."

A laugh greeted that, like the chime of cold bells; and then, a gift graciously given in return, "And mine is Shaban Ra'isse Khaldor."

"I have heard of you, Djinni Khaldor," Elisande said, with a deep bow.

Again the laugh. "And I of you."

"They speak of you in the Silent Quarter, great one, but not here."

"That is true."

"Your purposes must be momentous, to bring you so far." Her voice strained down at the end of the sentence, lower than was comfortable for her, to make it oh so plain that this was an observation only, and in no sense a question.

Once more the laugh: amusement without humour, Julianne thought. The djinni's voice dropped an octave in imitation, perhaps in mockery, as it said, "This is not far, little one. No distance is far, to the djinn."

"I have heard that. But I have heard also that the djinn are seldom interested to concern themselves with the deeds of humankind."

"That too is true."

"Well, great one," and here Elisande let go of Julianne's sleeve and sat cross-legged on the ground, even managed a smile as she tilted her head back, squinting into the hot sun, "I am notoriously slow to understand, but I see you here," with a wave of her hand at the road and the rocks, "and I see all these people unable to pass you by, and I see nothing to cause you to come from the lands where you choose to dwell, because I am sure it is not in your mind simply to cause obstruction to such little creatures as we are. Therefore I say again, your purposes must be momentous; but they are also mysterious to me."

"As they should be. But I have waited long enough." The djinni spun faster yet, and the column of its body rose like smoke into the sky; and it said, "Go back to the Sharai, Lisan of the Dead Waters. They will bring you a gift of questions."

Julianne saw Elisande's jaw drop open at that, and knew that she too was gaping. Go *back* to the Sharai? To the *Sharai*?

But then the djinni spoke again, and this time not to Elisande. "And for you, Julianne de Rance: go where you are sent, and marry where you must."

And once more this day—even here, at the foot of a tower of dust and enchantment—she felt the sting of her pride and position, and her voice was entirely ice as she replied, "And why do you suppose that I would not, or that I need a djinni to point me to my duty?"

Elisande hissed in alarm, and snatched at her skirts too late to still her.

This time, the djinni's laugh was louder. "I do not suppose either one, daughter of the Shadow. But your mind is murky now. Trust this, that your duty will come clear. The journey is necessary, and the marrying also. And trust this too, that your father's name is great but yours will be the greater, if you fail not."

And there was a thunderclap that shook slabs from the walls of rock on either side, and made the ground tremble beneath her; she closed her eyes against a great cloud of dust, and when she opened them again the djinni was gone and the road was clear for as far as she could see ahead.

ELISANDE WAS STILL sitting with her head in her hands, muttering to herself. When Julianne touched her shoulder, she glared up and said, "I told you! I *told* you, don't ask it questions!"

"I didn't mean to," defensively. "What harm, in any case?"

"What harm? It gave you answers!" And then, in response to Julianne's bewilderment, "Don't you know *anything*?"

"About the djinn, no." Nor did she care to learn, if it meant having conversations of elliptical nonsense in a constant state of fascinated terror. "It told me nothing. Though I'd like to know how it knew my name."

Elisande groaned, and pushed herself cautiously to her feet. Even through her own indignation and uncertainty, Julianne saw how drained the smaller girl seemed. She offered her arm for support and Elisande clung to it, more gratefully than either might have expected.

"It knew your name," she said carefully, "because it was waiting for you. Perhaps for me, for us both; but certainly for you. That's why it was here."

"Don't be ridiculous."

"It *said* so! 'I have waited long enough', remember? It waited, and we came. It gave us both a message; yours was a trap, and you didn't see it."

"How am I trapped?" she demanded.

"Julianne, you stand in a djinni's debt. Don't you understand? You asked, not it offered. It gave you service, which

42

must be repaid. They always claim their debts; and they choose the manner of repayment."

No, she didn't understand. What could any djinni want of her, what could she do for a spirit creature that it might think worth the doing?

She shook her head, calling up stubbornness again. Wouldn't think about it, wouldn't risk worrying it into truth.

"Have you," she said instead, "have you really been among the Sharai?"

"Yes. Once. My grandfather sent me, he said it would be good for my education."

"I suppose it would have been," Julianne said, trying to sound just as casual. "Well, it was. No one else here knew how to speak to a djinni."

Elisande made a wry face. "I've never done it before. But they tell stories, the Sharai, stories that are lessons, how to live in the world; and a lot of their stories are about the djinn. I don't know what to do, though," her voice almost breaking suddenly, now that the danger seemed past, "I don't know how to protect you. None of the stories ever offered a way to evade a debt owed to a djinni. Well, no way that worked..."

Again a shake of Julianne's head. "We'll be in the Roq by sunset tomorrow. A thousand men to protect me there, and afterwards all the strength of Elessi for the young baron's wife. And besides, I am my father's daughter. His name will do what any number of men cannot." *And the djinni said that my name would be the greater*, but she wasn't going to think about that. "It called you Lisan," she went on, remembering. "What did it mean? Lisan of the Dead Waters, it said."

"I don't know what it meant," said Elisande; but Julianne thought she was lying, at least a little.

WALKING BACK TOWARDS the litter, they passed the boy with the ruined arm, lying in dark shadow by one of the camel-drivers' fires. Though he seemed unconscious now, three men knelt beside, to keep him still.

The sergeant's man crouched grim-faced over the small hot fire, holding his dagger in the flame.

NEITHER GIRL SPOKE. Both perhaps were counting their steps, counting their breaths, waiting.

Blaise grunted something to the man, then said, "Please, ladies, will you hurry now?"

Before they reached the next turn in the road, they heard the boy at last begin his screaming.

THREE

No Daughter, No Door

THE FIRST TIME Marron and his troop came together with all their brethren at the Roq, it was at the tolling of the midnight bell and his eyes were useless to him.

Frater Susurrus the summoning bell was called, Brother Whisperer. Tonight it whispered deep in the bones of him, as a blade might whisper its own name, cutting through. Three strokes punched at his gut, the first as he slept and then two more as he jerked awake and curled protectively, uselessly against them; and three more again as he sat dizzily awake on his pallet. Stone and bone, flesh and straw and floor, everything trembled at the bell's resonance.

"Rise," Fra' Piet's voice ordered in the darkness, in the stillness after the sixth stroke. "Rise and dress, and follow."

Midnight prayers were second nature now, as normal as the sunrise and the being awake to see it, and the prayers then also. Marron's groping fingers found his habit where he had laid it to hand, pulled it over his head as he stood, and he was ready. Barefoot and obedient, as the Rule demanded. But follow who, follow how? At the abbey there had been nightlights burning at every turn, to show the way

45

to brothers new or stupid with sleep. Here the open doorway was as black as the room. Only the window afforded any light at all, framing stars that blazed surely more brightly here than they did at home. But the window was little more than a slit in an embrasure, for all that it looked onto an interior courtyard and not out over the walls; it could help the night-blind find nothing but itself. Marron's glance that way only made it worse when he turned his head again, trying to see something, anything of Aldo on the pallet next to his.

Well, if they were to go lightless, he could still listen his way to chapel. There were no voices, of course, no one stupid enough even to hiss a word on a breath, but he could hear his brothers' uncertainty and hesitation in the sounds of their dressing, of their breathing, of their waiting to obey. He could hear Aldo's feet shuffling on the chill stone floor, ready like his to go to prayer but ignorant like his of how to get there.

He listened for one thing more, the sound of Fra' Piet's footsteps. He would know that tread, he thought, in his darkest dreams; he thought perhaps it echoed there already. Fra' Piet had a slight halt in his gait, a great scar on his thigh to explain it. And yes, here it came now, that same broken rhythm which somehow underlay the screaming of an afternoon's mad slaughter, both in Marron's chaotic memory and in his equally unclear dreaming. Fra' Piet had remained mounted throughout, but it was still the whisper of his foot-falls that Marron heard through all the noises in his head. Surely the babe's wailing couldn't have had that unsteady pulse to it, neither its running blood for those few moments that it had had of running...?

There are wicked pictures to be painted in the dark-ness, true or not. Marron prayed for light, for any light to give his eyes some other thing to look at; and light came, slowly, shufflingly. There was a greying first at the doorway, enough to show its edges and Fra' Piet in silhouette between;

the greying became a flickering, a yellow light, a flame that brought sounds with it as well as seeing, the soft tread of unnumbered feet.

The flame was a torch, carried by a brother; as he passed the doorway Fra' Piet reached out an unlit torch of his own. No word was said. The brother didn't even pause in his slow marching, only dipped his brand for a moment, just for long enough to touch and share.

After that silent brother came more, many more, hooded shadows briefly glimpsed. Perhaps one in thirty had a torch.

At last the procession ended. Fra' Piet stepped out into the corridor, holding his light aloft; he made no gesture, but the troop followed him in echo of what they'd seen, going singly with their cowls flung up and their heads bowed down, watching the heels of the man ahead.

They filed through the mass of the castle by narrow and bewildering ways: like maggots in a cheese, Marron thought. Twice they stopped; he saw Aldo's sudden halt and jerked to a stand himself, glad not to have been dreaming as he walked, twice glad to be following his friend's heels and not Fra' Piet's. Stopped and waited—while other brothers streamed across their passage, Marron thought, though he couldn't have seen so far even if he'd lifted his head to look-—and then began the march again, moving as their brothers moved, unquestioning as slaves.

At last they walked a wider passage, and another file walked beside them; and so they came, two by two, strangers and brothers, through the great doorway into the great hall at the Roq.

FRA' PIET'S TORCH was a spark suddenly, an impertinent glowfly against the night, its light lost beneath a terrible weight of darkness. Torches borne by other brothers seemed already impossibly dim, impossibly far away.

Not courage, but fear that took any of the troop out into that enveloping black: fear of being left behind, of being left alone.

"Follow," they had been told, and follow they did, pressing close upon each other, some even reaching out to touch. Chill skin or neutral habit didn't matter, only contact with something other than stone underfoot and darkness all around. They breathed the darkness, and loved it not at all. One lucky man, the closest—and that was rare, to be thought lucky to be so close—followed Fra' Piet with his light, and like a chain each man behind followed the man ahead. Following Aldo in his turn, Marron lost all sense of walls on any side, or roof above. There was only the velvet pressure of the night, invading even this sacred place, destroying the natural balance that was the greatest gift of the God to His mortal dominions. That seemed heretical, blasphemous, fundamentally wrong: here if anywhere under the sky, light should be an equal brother with the dark, giving way graciously at sunset but never so crushed as this, never obliterated...

More than obedience bowed Marron's head as he shuffled in Aldo's wake. He was afraid still, and not even the presence of so many brothers all around could reassure him. He thought he was coming into the presence of something that could outweigh the purposes of the God Himself, unless perhaps it was the absence of the God that filled this hall, or left it so very empty.

FRA' PIET MADE a gesture with his torch at last, a wide swinging motion to one side: briefly they saw a line of kneeling brothers ahead of them. Slow, cautious shuffling— touching each other as they shuffled, rubbing shoulders— brought them into line behind. Marron felt more than Aldo's shoulder against his, he felt a cold hand too, and gripped it hard. They went down on their knees together, and there was as much comfort in finally being still as there was in the touch. Turning his head, hoping for a glimpse of Aldo's face beneath his hood, Marron saw instead how Fra' Piet at the end of the line turned his torch and crushed it against the stone flags, extinguishing its light. No comfort in that; he squeezed Aldo's fingers tighter.

Shadows leaped briefly, wildly, and were lost; he heard more shuffling behind, more breathing and the rustle of habits as yet more brothers came to kneel at their backs. They were welcome; he felt encompassed, though not safe. It still seemed abnormal, this tremendous darkness. A promise broken.

Then there was no more light and no movement behind them, or none that he could hear. He dared not turn his head, he thought perhaps Fra' Piet could see even in so much dark; he did stretch his back and peer forward in search of one last surviving torch but saw none, saw nothing at all.

Sinking down again, still holding Aldo's hand, he waited as they all were waiting. Soon he heard more footsteps coming from the back of the hall, coming closer. Gradually he saw light, showing him the ranks of hooded backs he knelt behind; now he dared not move at all, sure that Fra' Piet would be watching his troop for any hint of disrespectful curiosity.

Torches in pairs, borne by black-robed brothers processing up the aisle. A dozen pairs, a slow parade, and behind them came the preceptor and other masters of the Order. More torch-bearers, and then rank after rank of men in white robes with black cloaks thrown over; Marron frowned, not understanding their place here.

They marched on, and it was hard to see through all the brothers' bodies ahead, but glimpses of white helped a little. Those men spread themselves in line in front of all the kneeling brothers; beyond, the torchlight was rising, where steps must mount to the altar. Then those torches too were put out, and there was no light at all.

One long, dreadful moment of silence, when it seemed that every man there held his breath together with his brothers; and the great bell struck once more, throbbing through Marron's flesh and bone and Aldo's also, he could feel that in how his friend's fingers trembled in resonance with his own; and the voice of the preceptor cried out, "Fiat lux!"

AND THERE WAS light. Blue light, cool at first, flowing and twisting to make the doubled-loop sign of the God against the far-distant wall above the altar; then it burned more brightly, sun-bright, too fierce to look upon, though it still seemed to be running like liquid fire behind its glare. Marron's eyes watered, and he quickly turned his head away.

There was all the hall to look at now, plenty light enough for that, the holy promise holding and balance dramatically restored. But the first thing Marron saw as his eyes found focus was all his troop doing as he did, twisting and staring around; and the second thing Marron saw was the black shadow beneath Fra' Piet's hood as the confessor's head turned to watch his charges, dark eyes gleaming where no light fell.

Head snapped forward, eyes dropped; no more spying. And all he'd seen was kneeling brothers in their hundreds, and the broad shadows of great pillars at intervals ahead.

Another voice began to call the midnight office, carrying easily through this great space. Marron thought there might be magic in that also, as there was in the flaring light above the altar. But he was afraid no longer, only exultant, one believer among so many come to worship; he joined willingly, eagerly, devoutly in the responses, and the only thing he did that perhaps he should not have done was to keep a grip on Aldo's hand throughout the hour of the service.

EVEN THEIR SILENCE after seemed to echo and sing in the vast vault above their heads. Quiet and still in his soul now, fearful of nothing with the God's bright assertion before him, not even hearing the faltering beat of a baby's blood fall still, Marron didn't so much as glance upward. Obedience was a virtue as well as a duty, it was something owed which was also a pleasure to perform; there would be opportunities later, surely, to discover this place in daylight. Even with the rim of his hood hanging low across his brow and his eyes cast downward, he could still make out movement ahead of him, as brothers all along the aisle stood up and raised their arms, lifting dead torches high. Fra' Piet would be doing the same, no doubt. Marron didn't need to look; nor did he wonder why. There would be an answer.

And there was: two brilliant lines of light speared out from the glory above the altar, touching each torch in turn, bringing them to flaring life. At that signal all the brothers stood, Marron's troop just a moment behind the others. Again the masters paraded between them, torch-bearers before and between, the men in white robes behind. As he reached the doorway, the preceptor must have turned back to face the hall; Marron couldn't see him, but he could see the procession halt in the aisle. And he could hear the preceptor's voice pronounce a final benediction; and he could see how the great bright sign faded, how the flow of light slowed and died, leaving only an image of itself burning like a reminder behind his lids when he blinked. He closed his eyes to cherish it, opened them only when Aldo tugged urgently on his hand and then slipped his fingers free.

Half the hall was empty. The remaining torches burned bravely against the black, making a pale path of light into which Fra' Piet was leading his troop now. The man at his back gave Marron a shove; he stumbled to catch up with Aldo, then dropped into the steady pace of the others and walked peacefully back to the dormitory for the second period of sleep, until Brother Whisperer should call them to prayer again at the rising of the sun.

T HE HIGH-RISEN sun hung like a brazen disc in the white-hot sky, baking down on the castle's upper court-yard, where Marron sweated.

Not alone: all his troop was with him, and Fra' Piet. There had been fifty other men besides, and for an hour they had drilled together with baton-swords, round-edged and blunt-pointed wooden staves that could bruise but neither cut nor kill. *Unless used by a master,* Marron remembered his uncle saying, years before, *but in the hands of a master, an ink-pen can kill. I have seen that.*

The men Marron had faced this morning had not been masters; he barely carried a bruise. But they had not had his uncle to teach them, either. Marron carried no false pride about his swordsmanship, and no false modesty: he knew he was good because he had worked to become so, under a diligent instructor. He knew also that he could be better. He had thought to improve here in Outremer, fighting for the God and training with men who had fought for forty years. He no longer hoped for that. What need sword-skills and clever footwork for the hacking down of women and old men, unarmed boys and babies?

There was a bitterness in him this morning that the dawn service had not been able to dispel, the meal of porridge afterwards to settle nor the grim intensity of exercise to sweat out. His dreaming had not been easy, and he felt more duped than awed, more murderous than justified. Today it was difficult even to blame Fra' Piet's zeal for carrying them all into mayhem; how a thing had happened seemed not to matter, against the overmastering weight of the thing itself.

He was here, though, and he had done what he had done. He stood with Aldo among the rest of his troop, watching others disperse; and there went Fra' Piet also, leaving them alone for a rare minute as he crossed the court to greet a man with a grizzled beard and a great sword hanging from his belt, a big man not big enough to match his legend. Magister Ricard, weapons-master general, who had come to this land as a boy in the Duc's entourage and played as potent a role as any in establishing Outremer, crowning his lord as king; and Marron's hopes might be sour dust in his mouth and throat now, but still he would fight as well as ever he could under this man's eye.

Magister Ricard gripped Fra' Piet's arm and spoke to him as to an equal, which startled Marron; then the two men fell into step, walking slowly back towards the troop with their heads together. They were followed by half a dozen young men whose cloaks were black, but whose robes showed white beneath.

"Who are those men?" Marron murmured, seizing the licence of the moment.

"Knights Ransomers, of course," a voice from behind him, scornfully. "Don't you know anything?"

I know how to make you bleed. But of course he should have known this also. Knights Ransomers, sons of the nobility, not prepared to give over their lives or their property entirely to the God but making a commitment of one or two or five years to the Order. Seen as a duty in Elessi, it was more of a fashion, Marron had heard, in other states of Outremer, the black badge sported afterwards like a trophy and any young man who lacked one subtly disgraded. Or else in some families a year's service was a rite of passage, to mark the change from idle youth to adult.

Whatever brought them, they came—Marron had heard—with pages or squires in their train, they ate separately and slept separately and came to prayers or not as they chose. Apparently they dressed separately also, which Marron had not been told. There were knights and there were brothers, he had been told that, with little touch between them; he knew already which he valued the higher.

Doubly so when these half-dozen knights grouped themselves in a corner and cast aside their cloaks, gazing at the troop and speaking low, smiling with just a hint of contempt: all that such motley brothers were worth, their faces said.

Marron felt that same contempt, hoped they could see it reflected back and understand it. Beneath their cloaks they wore white, yes; they wore swords, yes—and they wore shirts of shimmering chain mail also. Mail! He'd heard that Knights Ransomers went armoured into battle like their secular kin, but he'd never credited that rumour with any truth at all. And this was only training with baton-swords, and why under the God would they need mail here? Unless it was to show how strong they were, how heedless of the heat and the weight they carried.

Around him, his brothers were whispering his own thoughts. "Mail shirts! Have they no honour? Have they no *faith*? The Rule forbids us..."

"Us," a harsh voice said behind them all, "but not such as they. They have their vows, we have ours."

Muted gasps, a sudden stillness: in their distraction, not one of them had thought to keep an eye on Fra' Piet. But for a wonder, there seemed no censure in his voice or in his gaze when they dared to meet it, for all that they'd been talking without cause or consent. Could the gulf between brothers and knights run so deep, that Fra' Piet would rank himself with his troop in this?

No matter, for now. There was no reprimand, and no suggestion of punishment to come. That was enough. Fra' Piet made a gesture, to direct their attention to Magister Ricard, four-square in the sunlight, with his shadow thrown behind him like a trailing cloak in the dust.

"Brothers," he said, and his voice was like a bell with a crack in it, loud and dissonant. "You have come as we all came once, to serve the God with your prayers, with your obedience, and with your strength. It is my task to see that the last of these is done as well as it may be. I have been watching your drills, from a window above. Some of you handle your weapons like mattocks," with a fearsome scowl that had a few of Marron's brothers shuffling their booted feet and grinning shamefaced. "I hope we will train you to do otherwise. A few obviously have been better taught. You and you, you..."

His jabbing finger picked out some six of the troop, Marron among them. Aldo not, but that was just. For all their years of practice together, under his uncle's eye or else in private, Marron had never managed to teach his friend anything more than bare competence with a sword. With a bow, the opposite was true: Aldo could take a thrush on the wing, where Marron would miss a roosting bustard.

"Step forward, and we will see just how good you are."

This, then, was why the knights had come; *six of them,* Marron thought, *against six of us.* Noblemen's sons against yeomen's, farmers', peasants'. This would be no true contest, although Magister Ricard had undoubtedly picked out the best of the troop. The nobility learned the arts of war before even they learned their letters, he had heard.

Still, he would do what he could for the troop's sake and his uncle's reputation, and for his unknown father whose name he bore, who had died in this far country for this same cause. The knights had arrayed themselves in a half-circle; the brothers walked to meet them, and Marron found himself facing a young man perhaps five years older than he, dark-haired and lean as he was but perhaps a hand's-span taller.

A longer reach he'd have, then, but the mail should slow him down. Marron lifted his baton-sword to the guard position; his opponent laughed.

"Formalities first, boy, don't be so eager. My name is Anton d'Escrivey," with a mocking bow.

"Sieur Anton." His own bow was lower and more honest than the other man's, truly formal; and thank the God he had remembered the proper form of address. "I am called Marron."

"Well then, Fra' Marron. Shall we begin?"

The knight drew his sword; and his was a true sword, no wooden training-baton, and not blunted for practice either, by the way the sun glinted on its edges. Marron couldn't mask a moment's hesitation, which had Sieur Anton laughing again.

"Don't be fearful, boy. I beg your pardon—Brother Boy. I shan't prick you—or not overmuch. Not with Ricard standing by to approve my swordplay. I shall use the flat."

If you can reach me, Marron thought grimly, coming again to the guard with his teeth set in anger but his eyes doing as they had been trained to do, watching the point and the shoulder both. He'd have watched the man's wrist also, only that a gauntlet obscured it.

Around them already were the sounds of steel on wood, hard breathing and grunts, booted feet sliding over gritty stone. Marron focused, screening out the sounds and the glimpses of movement at the edges of his sight, crouched a little lower and shuffled forward.

SIEUR ANTON CAME gracefully to meet him, sunlight running on his blade. "Never try to second-guess a swordsman," Marron's uncle used to tell him, time and again. "Watch the point, the wrist, the shoulder—react to what he does, not what you think he'll do." But—*he thinks I'm a clodpole. And he thinks I 'm afraid of his point. He'll feint a stab, just to make me jump back, and then he'll bruise my ribs for me. He thinks...*

Marron tensed on his toes, and yes, here it came—the glittering blade thrusting forward, straight at his chest, and then swinging wide to administer a stinging slap. Except that Marron was no longer there to be slapped; he'd leaped forward against the sword's stab, so nearly mistiming it that the point nicked his habit on its swing away. One brief glimpse of his opponent's widening eyes, only a foot's distance from his own; and then he brought the blunt edge of his baton-sword down hard on Sieur Anton's thumb, *there, let him drop his sword in front of his master, let him be the fool and not me.*

But Sieur Anton's sword did not fall. The young knight danced back out of reach, true, and acknowledged Marron's move with a nod of surprised respect; but, *metal links in his gauntlets*, Marron thought, chagrined. *And he's alert now, he'll not be careless again...*

Nor was he. They closed again and this time fought as equals, blow and block, feint and thrust and parry. For five hard minutes they circled and sparred, blind to all else in the court. By the end of that time Marron's eyes were stinging with sweat, his breath was laboured and his sword arm ached cruelly, and every move he made was backwards. Because they were not truly equals: Sieur Anton was the master here, and both knew it.

Marron had fought with a stronger man all his life, though. He'd never matched his uncle for size or speed or skill. Defence had always been his strength, and he called desperately on all that he knew. Block and parry, feint and retreat and block again; Sieur Anton had both hands on his sword-grip now and his face was livid with humiliation. He was using his edge too, despite his promise, striking chips from Marron's wooden blade. Would the bout end if the baton broke, would Magister Ricard call the knight to a halt? And would Sieur Anton hear or heed the call?

Marron wasn't sure, but the thought, the momentary break in his concentration was enough to drag his eyes to the side, to look for the weapons-master. And so he was the fool after all: he knew it as he did it, and snapped his gaze back, too late. Sieur Anton was already thrusting through his vagrant guard—and thrusting with intent, with a razor-sharp point and all his frustration driving the arm that drove it.

In the clarity of that moment, Marron saw the young knight's face change suddenly, even as he thrust. Marron dived and rolled—"always roll *towards* your enemy, lad, never away. Get inside his reach, knock him off his feet if you can, bite his ankles if you have to. If you roll away he'll only follow, and laugh as he kills you"—and would have died regardless, would have died spitted before he hit the ground, except that Sieur Anton flung his sword away with a great shout.

Not time enough even in that gesture to save Marron's skin, but it saved his life. The blade missed his heart, missed his chest entirely, sheared his habit and the flesh of his left arm before it skittered away across the cobbles of the yard. Marron felt the tearing chill of that touch, and a rushing heat after; but he was rolling, rolling to his opponent's feet, and he looked up at Sieur Anton's pale face and found his baton-blade still in his frantic grip.

And thrust upward, not with any strength, he had none; but with strength enough, wit enough to ignore the man's chest in its mail shirt. He stabbed the dull point at Sieur Anton's throat, and touched hard enough to leave a bruise, he thought. Hard enough to cut, if he'd had a blade with an edge to it. Cut and twist, and *a death to me, I think...*

Sieur Anton jumped back out of his sight, coughing and cursing; and then stepped forward again, one hand rubbing his throat but a thin smile on his face regardless.

"Well done. Though the first death was mine, I think," as though he'd read Marron's thoughts precisely on his face. Perhaps he had.

He reached an arm down; Marron let the baton fall, and reached up to grip it. Sieur Anton drew him easily to his feet and held him so when Marron's legs threatened to buckle, gave him a moment to catch his breath and balance; then, "Show me," with a gesture towards the other arm.

They looked together. There was a rent in Marron's sleeve, and a wide wet stain around it. Sieur Anton peeled the sleeve back, to find a long and gaping slash across the forearm.

"Not too deep. It'll scar, I fear, but not badly. Not to damage the use of it. What was your name again?"

"Marron."

"Well, Fra' Marron," teasing again, but not contemptuously this time, "have that washed and bound, and then come back here, will you?"

A nod, a slap on the shoulder, and Sieur Anton turned away, picked his sword up and examined its edge, pulled a cloth from his belt to wipe it. Marron gazed after him, dizzy suddenly and confused, feeling the pain in his arm now like a hot brand pressing deep.

Shaking his head and blinking against the giddiness, looking around, he realised at last that there was no movement else in the courtyard. The other bouts were long finished; his troop-brothers and the knights were all stood back against the walls, every eye fixed on him, or on Sieur Anton, or moving between the two of them, one to the other and back.

He staggered a little then, and Aldo came running. Stocky shoulder under his, an arm tight around his chest and whispered words stumbling over each other, "Well done, you were wonderful, you'd have had the beating of him with a proper sword in your hand, did he try to *kill* you there...?"

and Marron just stood and shook his head and watched the blood run down to drip from his fingers until Fra' Piet came to say where they should go to find bandages and water and a fresh habit. And even he had a nod of approval for Marron and a blunt congratulation, that he had fought well and not let his brothers down; but somehow the words that rang most strongly in Marron's mind were Sieur Anton's, his parting words, *come back here, will you?*

Not a question, not an invitation, almost a command; and Marron didn't know why, but he wanted to.

He would. If he were allowed.

THAT FIRST DIZZINESS passed, and at Aldo's urging Marron blotted his bleeding arm with his blood-soaked sleeve, pressing hard to stifle the flow. He could walk more or less steadily now, he found, but Aldo came with him none the less and without direct permission. *To do what you have not been ordered to do is disobedience*; they trod on the flags as on eggshells, waiting for Fra' Piet's voice to call Aldo back.

No call came, and neither one looked to see if he were watching. Better not to know, perhaps. Aldo had tacit approval or else he did not, and if not he would surely find out later. Sometimes doubt made a more comfortable companion than certainty.

They found the infirmary, by dint of asking directions twice. A brother apothecary stanched the wound with a fiery, stinging application that made Marron yelp as the wound itself had not, then bound it in linen strips and promised him a scar less than his little finger's width, if twice the length. From there to the vestry—Marron expecting to be required to wash and mend the damaged habit himself, as the rule had been at the abbey, but finding it taken from him and another given over without comment—and from the vestry necessarily back to the courtyard. Even without Sieur Anton's order, they would not have known where else to go.

All six of the young Knights Ransomers were there, duelling with each other now. Fra' Piet and the troop had gone, as had Magister Ricard.

After a minute Sieur Anton caught a glimpse of them standing in the doorway, unless he had been deliberately watching for their return. He stepped back from his bout, raising his left hand and lowering his sword; his partner nodded and stood at rest while Sieur Anton came across the court towards them.

"You," to Aldo, curtly, "your troop has gone to the armoury; you are to join them there. *That* way," pointing, against Aldo's clear hesitation. "And you," to Marron, "stand over there and watch. Oh, don't *worry*. I have begged you from your confessor, for this hour at least. Watch me."

He went back to his bout; Aldo gave Marron one doubtful glance and then took off, almost running to find the troop again.

And what of me, Marron thought, with an anxious look up at the high sun. *When the bell calls us to pray, must I walk into hall with the knights?* He couldn't envisage that; but neither could he wait outside the door. To keep the four Great Hours was the prime duty of any brother, ranking over all.

BROTHER WHISPERER WAS silent yet, though, and obedience was owed here too, or he thought so: if not from brother to knight under the Rule—that he didn't know, or couldn't remember—then at least from yeoman to lord, the habit of his life. Marron stood where he had been told to stand, and watched Sieur Anton fight.

And understood at last why these men wore mail even to drill in, and understood also quite why he'd survived his own bout so long. Until the anger of embarrassment overmastered it, some part at least of Sieur Anton's mind must have been always remembering the edge on his weapon and

Marron's lack of armour, tempering every stroke with caution. No such inhibitions now, between men equally armed, trained and protected. Marron wouldn't have survived one minute of such fierce sword-play, let alone five; nor would he have survived many or possibly any of the blows he saw skittering off the mail shirts, striking sparks.

All six of the knights were highly skilled, perhaps the best he'd seen. Sieur Anton, he thought, was the finest of the six. That man's sword was a deceiver, dancing with light, teasing and tempting and then striking true. No bout lasted long; the men changed partners often, sometimes fighting two to one, and even in those engagements Sieur Anton won more often than he lost.

Eventually they called an end to the play. They sheathed their swords, spoke briefly in soft voices; then the other five went off together, while Sieur Anton stood where he was, summoning Marron with a glance.

"How's the arm, well enough?" And at Marron's nod, "Good. Come with me."

Marron glanced at the sky, saw the sun so near to noon and wanted to ask where they were going. Whatever the answer, he wanted to say, *later, please, I have to go to prayers now*—and didn't. Said nothing, indeed, only walked silently behind the tall young knight, cradling his sore left arm in his aching right as he followed obediently through a narrow doorway and up a turning flight of stairs, along a corridor to a door that Sieur Anton opened.

These must be his private quarters: a small chamber and not luxurious by noble standards, perhaps, but to a junior brother of the Order it seemed almost shockingly easeful. The walls were hung with bright tapestries, and there were woven rugs on the floor and shutters for the window, furs on the bed. A finely carved chest stood in one corner, a bare wooden horse in another.

Sieur Anton unbuckled his sword belt and tossed it onto the bed, followed that with the battered leather-and-steel gauntlets which had saved him humiliation from Marron's baton and perhaps the loss of a finger from one of his subsequent bouts. He ran one hand through sweat-matted hair, and then under the collar of his mail shirt.

"Here, help me off with this. If you can...?"

Marron's one hand was still cupping his other elbow for support; he released it quickly and stepped forward to grip the shoulders of the mail, wondering at how fine the links were, how supple they made the shirt. Sieur Anton bent and wriggled, backed a step and slipped free. Weight dragged at Marron's hands, making him hiss at the pain rewoken in the muscles of his arm.

"Hang it there," with a gesture towards the horse.

The mail slid over the wooden frame with a rippling sound; Marron turned back to find Sieur Anton sitting on the bed, lifting one booted foot towards him.

"If you would, please."

AND SO MARRON—who had sworn to his uncle never to be any man's servant, only ever the God's—found himself on his knees before this man, hauling off his boots. And was still on his knees, still wondering what he was doing here apart from being subserviently convenient, when the shivering call of the great bell woke his bones to the hour.

He gasped, couldn't help it; and glanced urgently up at Sieur Anton with an unspoken plea on his lips, *I have to go now, though I don't know the way.* And gaped, again couldn't help it, as the knight dropped down off the bed and onto his knees beside him.

"You know the office?"

"Yes, sieur." Of course he knew the office, but—

"Good. We will say it together."

Marron waited for Sieur Anton to begin, Sieur Anton waited quietly for the seventh stroke that said the service was beginning in the great hall, and then they recited the ancient words, turn and turn about. If it was strange that a secular knight should lead while a professed brother only made the responses as any layman might, it didn't seem so to Marron.

THEY WERE QUICKER through the service, surely, than the massed congregation in the hall, and two murmuring voices were less stirring than hundreds of brothers speaking together, but Marron found it no less devout. Sieur Anton stayed on his knees for a long minute after they had finished, his lips moving in private prayer; and his glance that followed seemed so open, so inviting, that Marron ventured his first question.

"Pardon me, sieur, but do you always say service here, in your room?"

"I do, yes. I keep all the Hours, as you do—but in private." And then, with a bitter laugh against Marron's puzzlement, "What, you think I should parade my virtue with those conceited coxcombs my fellow knights, make a show of myself before your brothers and the God? Exhibit my lineage and my undoubted worth? No, I thank you. No."

He rose abruptly, and paced across to the high slit window that let in only a sombre shadow of the day. Marron stood awkwardly, an apology on his tongue though he didn't understand why he should use it, what offence he had given.

After a moment Sieur Anton turned again, to settle himself in the embrasure with a more natural smile. "No," again, "but that is not your concern, Marron. Now listen to me. We, the knights of the Order, may bring a squire or a servant with us, for the time of our service here. Alas, I have none—not through carelessness, I assure you; I didn't leave his bones

64

in a ditch—-and the preceptor has said I may choose one of you new-come brothers to make up the lack. I should like to choose you, but I am told that I may not compel it. I must ask." His speaking smile turned rueful for a moment, regretting this unaccustomed change in his status. "So, this one time, I am your supplicant, Marron. Will you act as my squire? The duties are not onerous, I am no demanding master; and I can teach you more than you have learned already, and more than you would learn in twenty years of being a garrison brother in the Roq. At sword, and at other matters also. Will you? I shan't ask twice," added as a cool warning not to prevaricate or bargain.

That was unnecessary; Marron had nothing to bargain with, could see nothing to bargain for. Only, "I, I do not wish to leave my troop, sieur." Mostly, he did not wish to leave Aldo; one friend at least he needed in this vast stern castle, this new and, yes, this vast stern life. But there was also truly a bond between all his brothers in the troop, from which he would not willingly see himself broken.

"Nor shall you. I will need no more than two or three hours of your time, most days. You will still be a brother here, with all a brother's duties; this is extra labour I would lay on you. Say yes or no, Marron, but say it quickly."

"Yes, then, sieur. And thank you."

Sieur Anton shook his head mockingly. "I cut his arm to the bone and then burden him with work, and he thanks me for the privilege. Such is the life of a lordling, Marron; we bless where we touch. Come here. No, *here*," rising to his feet and reaching, gripping Marron's shoulder and drawing him to the window, pointing out. "There, do you see?"

"That tower, sieur?"

"Yes, that tower."

The window looked out on yet another court, smaller than the last: smaller than any in the castle, Marron thought likely. There was one squat tower in the corner, with a lower wall that closed it in on two sides. The Roq proper made a square of the court, but left that tower untouched. It must be standing right on the height, on the very edge of the great upthrust of rock that was the foundation of the castle; that wall must mask a long, long drop.

"This is the oldest part of the citadel," Sieur Anton said, his hand shifting to Marron's neck and holding firm to keep him looking, "the first fortress that was raised here by the Sharai. They do not generally build, but here they built and held it until we took it from them. All else we have built ourselves, the outer *enceinte* is entirely our own. That tower, though, even the Sharai did not build; it was here before. They raised their fortress around the tower. To claim it, perhaps? To protect it? If anyone knows, they have not told me. Do you know what that tower is called?"

"No, sieur."

"If the Sharai had a name for it, I have not heard; but we call it the Tower of the King's Daughter."

"Sieur?"

"Yes, Marron."

"The king—the king has no daughter, sieur."

"I am aware. He named it himself, they tell me. He came here once, according to legend, after the fall of Ascariel but before the Conclave." Of course, before the Conclave; when else? "He looked at the tower, and instructed the Order to guard it well. They say that he laughed, as he named it."

Well he might, it was a thing to be laughed at, if anyone dared. No daughters had the King of Outremer; and no face either, that anyone had seen outside his palace these forty years. He chose to rule in absolute seclusion, without exception or explanation.

Strange though it was, the name it seemed was not the important matter here. Sieur Anton's grip did not weaken.

"*Look...*" he whispered; and that was all.

At last, "Sieur? I see no door..." No door and no windows on the two sides that were visible, only blank much-weathered stone; and the wall that framed it was surely built too close to allow a doorway that he couldn't see.

"That's right. There is no door. And that, Marron, that is how some of my confrères think that I should be: alone, isolated. No doors, and no windows. You may find that they have infected their servants also; that may be another blessing you receive from my touch. Do you know how to whet a blade?"

"Sieur?"

"Can you use a grindstone?" And his touch was gone from Marron's neck now, and himself from Marron's back; he was over by the bed when Marron glanced around to find him, hefting his sword on its belt.

"Yes, sieur." That had been the first lesson his uncle had taught him, before ever he was allowed to use a blade in practice.

"Good." Sieur Anton flung the sword, sheath and belt and all; Marron caught it awkwardly. "Her name is Josette. I nicked the edge, I think on Raffel's mail. Take her down to the stables, they will show you the stone. Bring her back when you're done—and treat her with respect, her lineage is superior to yours. Then you can go to find your troop; the service will be finished, and they will be looking for their dinner."

"Sieur?"

"Well?"

"Should I not fetch yours?" Squire or servant, whichever he was, he knew the duties of a lord's man.

Sieur Anton laughed shortly. "No. I do not take a meal in the middle of the day. Nor will that be one of your

67

obligations, morning or evening; I mess with some few of my confrères who are—you will be told—not over-particular in the company they keep. Raffel, and his kind. You saw us together at play. Their squires are enough to serve us all. But I thank you for the thought. The sword, Marron, concern yourself with the sword; you may find that I am overparticular about my weapons."

He swung his stockinged feet up onto the bed, lay back, folded his hands behind his head and closed his eyes.

Marron ran.

As he ran, he thought that there was something else he was reminded of by a tower without doors or windows, no way in. Not Sieur Anton, no—that he didn't understand—but something twitching, tickling in the back of his head.

Running, hurtling along the passages and taking corners at a twisting canter while his mind scratched vainly after a half-formed thought, of course he got lost. Probably he'd been lost before he started. Nor were there brothers of whom to ask the way; they must all still be at prayer. And the knights, and their servants too. Noon was the highest Hour, for lay folk as well as religious. Peasants would stop work in the fields when they heard the noon bell, to kneel and say a prayer; decent townspeople would flock to church; everyone in a convent would come to chapel. In a convent or a castle, seemingly, at least where that castle was held by the Order.

Everyone but Sieur Anton.

MARRON HAD TO weave his own path through the courts and the corridors, around unexpected and unwelcome corners, up inconvenient stairs when he needed to go down and there seemed no way. Every window he came to disorientated him further, showing him a view he did not expect. This must have been an extra defence, he thought, in the minds of the castle's builders, to confuse any invader who won so far. Or else it was magic, a spell laid since the builders did their work, to lead any stranger's feet astray...

I am no stranger, I am a brother here! He wanted to scream it at the obdurate walls, which allowed him no doors where he needed them, where he thought they ought to be.

No doors, no windows. That thought again—or not a thought so much as an idea, an image...

AT LAST A doorway yielded a glimpse, a moment of recognition: they had surely climbed that narrow dim-lit ramp yesterday, when Fra' Tumis led them in from sunlight to shadow, before he led them down to the Chamber of the King's Eye?

Marron sprinted down. Yes, here was the open cobbled yard and the inner moat, and here beyond were the stables, finally. And here too were the Sharai stable lads, slaves and unbelievers, unbaptised, forbidden the service. He asked for the grindstone, and one boy took him to it.

As he spun the wheel and pulled Sieur Anton's sword from its sheath, he thought, *Surayon!*

Surayon, of course, that was it. Surayon, the Folded Land: no doors and no windows, no way in or out.

He was glad the thought had not come to him fully formed at Sieur Anton's window. He might have blurted it; and just to say the name of Surayon was disobedience which brought heavy penance, and that was in the abbey at home. Here, he dared not imagine what the punishment might be.

Official punishment, at least. In Sieur Anton's room, he thought perhaps Sieur Anton's hand would have given him his penance, and that too would have been heavy. If it had seemed that Marron was making a connection between all three, the tower and the knight and the Folded Land of legend, rumour, whispered heretical horror—oh, the God's glory, he thought he might have paid for that in blood.

But his blood had been paid out already, and his arm burned to remind him. The God took his penance, it seemed, even for thoughts not spoken where they touched a thing utterly forbidden: a land declared anathema, impossible to travel to, an apostate inaccessible to justice and an enemy intangible, mysteriously gone.

Surayon, the Folded Land. No doors, no windows. And a tower the same, and a knight who claimed the same, or denied it rather, or did both. Marron was making connections despite himself, as he set Sieur Anton's blade against the spinning stone and his teeth against the aching pain of holding it just so against the kick.

He thought he heard a baby's wail in the scream of steel on stone, he thought he saw blood spatter in the sparks; he wanted to bar his doors also, to seal any windows he might own, to be a tower strong and certain, untouchable, alone.

FOUR

How High, How Far Below

AT FIRST SHE'D thought the castle was a cloud, she thought it had to be. A dark, louring, horizon-hugging thunderhead, a rainstorm out of season. What else could mass so broad and heavy against the sky?

Only as the day wore on, as the bearers brought them closer and it moved not and changed not but only loomed the larger, only at last as the sun moved around to dispel its shadows and show it in the light: only then did she believe, when she had to. When she could see that truly behind that obscuring veil of shade were man-raised walls of honeyed stone, pale as fresh-cut comb or dark as the baked crust of a honey pudding, but all cut from the same rock those high walls stood impossibly high upon.

She tried to blame the shadows for her unfaith, and then the eye-bewildering gauze of the litter's curtains. Her companion laughed at her.

"Admit it, Julianne, it's just too big, you couldn't see it."

"Well. It is big..."

71

THE DEVIL IN THE DUST

It was big. It was massive, immense, prodigious. Too big, she thought, in all honesty; and she had lived all her life in Marasson, which was by any measure easily the largest city in the East. Some splendid buildings they had there, too—the palace, the citadel, the great temple with its blue dome, the largest anywhere in the known world, she'd heard—but none that was on the same scale as Roq de Rançon.

THE ROCK THE castle stood upon—not the Roq that it was named for, she remembered, no one knew what in the world that meant or used to mean—that rock was no hill like all these other hills, scant of earth and scant of life but normal, natural, only somewhat dry and toothy at their tops. Rather it was a tremendous bare knuckle breaking up from a sudden surprising plain between the hills: a mountain peak from the World Below, her father had called it once, laughingly, from the land of the 'ifrit, a mountain that grew too large for the underworld and had to plunder space above to hold it.

And what the God had made, that remarkable naked vastness of rock, in itself a fortress, man had improved upon. He had built and levelled and built again, so that even at this distance she could see layers to the castle, just as there were layers marked out in cracks and strange dark stripes below it, aslant in the great weight of stone that held it up.

Even full in the sun's light it seemed still sombre, still shadow-draped. Threatening, she thought it. But of course: it was a fortress above all—*indeed, above all*, she thought, having to look up at it even from here, still miles and maybe leagues from the winding way that climbed it—and meant to threaten, though perhaps not to threaten her. A refuge it should seem to her, a place of safety; she was disturbed that it did not.

"How far is it?" she asked, and hated herself both for the question and for the tremulous tone in her voice as she asked it. She sounded like a child to her own ears, neither the sophisticated woman she tried so hard to seem nor the betrothed woman her father had made of her. Rot his bones, this was his fault, twice his fault for bringing her to this forsaken land and then forsaking her within it. Perhaps she could be angry, that might help.

What helped more was Elisande's practical, cheerful treatment of the question on its own terms, disregarding the nervous quaver that she must have heard. The smaller girl twisted her neck to peer through the gauze panel, then grunted in frustration and tweaked the curtain aside to see clearly. Looking at the land that lay between them and the castle, Julianne guessed, rather than at the Roq itself; its size only confused the eye, making it seem nearer than it could possibly be.

"Half a day?" Elisande said, and even she sounded uncertain for once, which was curious relief to Julianne. "If the bearers need to rest," which they must, with two to carry in the palanquin. "But we should be there by sundown."

They would need to be. Sergeant Blaise refused to travel after dark, and there was no village to be seen on the road ahead where they might break the journey.

Julianne sighed, trying to think hopefully of an end, or at least a pause in travelling. "Do you think there will be baths?"

"Cold ones. Perhaps." Elisande's face screwed comically, and her fingers twitched at the gown she wore, one of Julianne's. Blaise had demanded that at last night's halt: "She must dress decently, my lady," *and behave decently too*, unspoken but implicit. The dresses were more of a burden to her, Julianne thought, than the behaviour. Certainly, as a guest of the strict Ransomers she'd have no chance to cast them off in favour of her own rough clothing. There was a chuckling comfort there too, that this girl so deliberately obscure in her intentions should have to make such an obvious and irksome sacrifice to achieve them. Julianne still had no idea why Elisande wanted to come to the Roq; she was glad of her company, more glad with every hour and every word passed between them, but she resented the mystery of it none the less for that.

T HE LITTER SWAYED and tipped gently beneath them. It was restful, ordinarily, as well as convenient. At least, if her mind were at rest, it could be restful. Alone, she might have drowsed through the heat of the afternoon. With Elisande there, she lay back on her elbows and gazed out, watching the slow passage of the sun-gilded, dusty hills. She preferred not to look ahead. The looming castle dominated her mind too greatly. It spoke of walls, of gates barred behind her, of little air and little light; it spoke of her future, and she would not think of that.

Go where you are sent, and marry where you must. No, she would not think of that either. Of what use was magic, if all it did was underline the dreary world of expediency and intrigue where she was no more than her father's daughter, her life within his gift?

Elisande was dozing, she saw, curled like an animal among the cushions. That girl didn't share Julianne's reticence, not to sleep in the presence of a new friend. Perhaps it was a foolishness. They had after all shared a room and a bed last night, in a crude mud-walled hut above a dry ford. But Julianne was hostess here, and would not be asleep when Elisande woke.

So she watched the land go by, and longed for a little breeze to stir the curtains; and, listening in vain for the sough of wind coming down the valley, she heard an entirely different sound. Close at hand were the soft footfalls and occasional hard grunts of the litter-bearers, their voices fallen quiet in this heavy air. To the sides, to the front and behind she could hear booted feet, the men-at-arms who

guarded her; behind them the rumbling wheels of the bag-
gage-wagon, obscuring the snorts of the oxen that drew it
and the light dancing steps of her palfrey Merissa. Ranging
forward and back as ever came the thudding hoofbeats of
Blaise's horse. All that was normal, a constant. But now there
was something more besides, a distant whisper of urgency.
She sat up, frowned, wished for the thousandth time to be
rid of the muffling curtains that made a drab, disguised thing
of the world.

This much was clear, that Blaise had heard it too. He
came cantering past the palanquin, calling to his men to be
alert. His voice, sounding sharp even despite those curtains,
roused Elisande; she blinked, lifted her head and said, "What
is it?"

"I'm not sure. Listen."

They listened both, and briefly Julianne thought the other
girl would poke her unveiled face right out to hear better.
That wasn't necessary; the sound resolved itself quickly,
becoming familiar and—here at least, on this road, in this
country—threatening.

"Horses," Elisande said, sitting back on her heels, somehow finding a knife from beneath her skirt.

"Yes." Many horses, and in a hurry, it seemed. "Put that
away. The men will protect us, if there is a need." *This close
to Roq de Rançon,* she wanted to add, as though that were a
protection in itself, as it ought to be; but her tongue rebelled.
The castle still seemed as great a threat, or greater.

"And if they don't, or can't?"

"Then your little needle will do us little added good, and
likely harm," she said acidly.

"It could take one life at least, at need. Or two."

There was an invitation in that, a pact proposed. For a
moment, Julianne was tempted. Elisande knew this land,
which she did not; Elisande also, it was clear, loved her life,

which Julianne no longer did. If time came when the other girl thought fit to leave it sooner than stay, perhaps Julianne should be her guest on that journey.

But she shook her head impatiently, *don't be foolish*; and couldn't help but wonder if she might regret that brisk dismissal, and if she did, for how long the regret might last.

A single horse, catching up fast; that was Blaise, returning.

"Riders, my lady," he croaked through a mouthful of dust. Too dry to spit, he sounded.

"Yes, we know. How many?"

"A dozen, two dozen? It's impossible to tell. They ride in a cloud. But they are close."

And getting closer, and the castle was too far to help, should it even have help to offer. Even should these not be men from the castle closing in like floodwaters, dark and turbulent. "Have your men halt, sergeant. Friend or foe, we will wait for them. No sense in seeming fearful."

No sense in seeming brave, either. If the sight of her guard was not enough to deter attack, then the guard's strength was likely not enough to meet it. But she was her father's daughter, and—occasionally—glad of it; she would neither run nor be thought to be running.

Blaise hesitated, before he grunted assent. He gestured to her bearers to be still, which they were already; then he called orders to his men. Quickly there was a double ring of steel around the grounded litter: pikes to the front, swords and crossbows to the rear.

Blaise rode out alone to meet the coming horsemen, and for once Julianne didn't need Elisande's insistence. She hooked one of the curtains back with her own hand so that both girls could see clearly, and never gave a thought to veiling first. Modesty wouldn't save either their lives or their honour, if there were trouble in this.

TROUBLE THERE WAS or might be, but of a slow and insidious sort, not immediately apparent, except perhaps to a girl who saw danger where she should have seen shelter's promise.

What Julianne saw that hot afternoon, squinting through the haze and the raised dust, was a troop of twenty men well-mounted. All their horses were as black as their habits, and they rode with their cowls over their faces. She shivered and thought *castle*, thought *Roq de Rançon*, though she awarded herself no applause for the insight. The Ransomers' style was well known in Marasson.

Perhaps it was just their garb and their apparent faceless-ness, out here on an empty road with the vast rock and its castle louring at her back, but she still couldn't rid herself of that sense of threat. She wanted to cry out to Blaise, *keep away, don't go near them, don't trust.* She wouldn't have done that, though; this was his charge, and his men must see him do it. She was too late, anyway. The men in black had drawn up their mounts, in ordered ranks; one rode forward alone, and after a few words called between them Blaise doffed his steel cap, bowed his head, all but dismounted to kiss the brother's boot.

Which likely made him properly a master, Julianne thought, a senior member within the Order. And someone too whose name or rank was known to Blaise; the sergeant wouldn't accord such respect uncritically.

Now Blaise had turned his horse, to ride head to head beside the other; ranged himself with the newcomers, it seemed to Julianne, taking his stand with the castle. Well, and why not? She should have expected that. Elessans had good cause to be grateful to the Ransomers. There were outposts, small convents of the brothers all around their borders, and she knew that the Order stood high in Count Heinrich's esteem.

The two men talked briefly, and she could have told them all the content of their conversation. *The lady Julianne de Rance, yes, daughter of the King's Shadow; she's due at Elessi, meant to marry the young Baron Imber. I'm charged with bringing her to the Roq, to hold her safe until he can send for her. One other girl with her, a companion,* Blaise would be no more indiscreet than that. For his own sake, not for hers or Elisande's. In strictest terms it was a breach of his duty to have taken up a stray, an unknown and secretive passenger; senior members of the Ransomers were sure to judge such matters strictly.

Once they had spoken privily, here they came: the one to inspect the goods in transit, she thought with irritation, and approve the other's care.

She reached forward quickly, to let the curtain drop. Elisande gave her a glance, more question than protest.

"Please—do this with propriety? For our reputation?"

"Lady, I have no reputation. But for yours, of course. He will want to look at us..."

And so Elisande searched the cushions until she found the veil that Julianne had given her that morning, with the gown. She fussed it neatly into place, then reached across and did the same with Julianne's. The taller girl didn't know whether to laugh or hit her.

And then the occasion for either or both had passed, because the two men were outside the palanquin, and Blaise was speaking to her through its shrouds.

"My lady, here is Marshal Fulke of the Society of Ransom, newly appointed provincial commander of the military arm. Master Fulke, allow me to name the lady Julianne de Rance, and her companion the lady Elisande."

"Indeed. But you will forgive me, my lady; I find it hard to make my bow to fabric without a human form, however pleasant the weave." There was some humour beneath the hood, then. She still couldn't see his face for shadow but his voice was gentle enough despite the ironic crack in it, sharp as a whip. His accent was refined: homeland, she thought, and not any part of Outremer. He must be freshly come, for all his seniority.

"Alas, Master Fulke. In this land, fabric is all you will ever see of my kind. It is the habit of women to go veiled here." Was that too subtle or too barbed, a reminder of his vow of celibacy and just a hint of its opposite, the scurrilous rumours that foolish gossips liked to spread about the Order? Well, let him make of it what he would; no doubt he would shrug it off as the innocent comment of a naive girl. "But we can at least reassure you that we do have human form, though we may not show you much of it. Elisande?"

With a mischievous obeisance and an approving laugh in her eyes, Elisande drew back the curtains.

"My lady." His bow was only a stiff nod; perhaps he was not so thick-skinned after all.

Still, she didn't feel inclined to release him quite so easily. "Master Fulke, your cowl veils you as darkly as our hangings did us. There is no such custom here for men, nor is it I think the habit of your Order...?" Except in a literal sense, but Elisande was biting back a smile already, she could feel it vibrating the girl's fingers where they lay on her arm. Julianne didn't want her bursting with suppressed laughter, nor rolling with its release.

"We were advised to shield our heads from the sun's heat, my lady, at least until our skins have grown a little used to it."

But he lifted his hood back regardless, and regarded her with solemn eyes. Blue eyes, she noted, and fair brows above them, fair also the short-cropped and receding hair. Yes, he should be careful in the sun; he was not made for this country. But what struck her most, despite that deceptive hairline, was how young he seemed, to be a marshal and a provincial commander. Her father had versed her well in the government of the Order, as in so much else; she knew how much power Fulke's rank would grant him, and she knew how seldom such power was given into a young man's hands. The Ransomers were traditionally a conservative band of men.

"You were well advised," was all she said, and she made a sweet little gesture with her hand, permission to draw up his hood again. He did so meekly enough, but she warned herself not to be deceived by his complaisance.

"With your permission, my lady," *with Blaise's consent* he meant, and he undoubtedly had that already, "we will escort you these last few miles to the castle. Had we but known you were ahead of us, we should have ridden harder. This road may not be safe even here under the castle's eye, for a young woman travelling alone."

"Hardly alone, Master Fulke."

He didn't laugh, he didn't gesture; but she felt his dismissal of her men in his stillness as he said, "Even so. A mounted guard is better; and twice the number is always to be preferred."

So. Men of Elessi did not match up to Ransomer standards? She felt herself quite heated at the snub, though she was not yet an Elessan and had never wanted to be so. He had much to learn, this young marshal commander.

Blaise's men ordered themselves briskly under these new and judging eyes; the litter was picked up and the easy, swinging pace resumed.

Elisande let her veil slip around her throat and said, "Have you made a friend there, Julianne? Or an enemy?"

"I don't know." Which was poor enough, a confession she would not want her father to hear. If an enemy, then it was poor work indeed. Ransomer influence was great and would be greater, she thought, in her new home; she thought perhaps this young man had come to make it so. And she could not judge him, could not read him at all.

Not yet, her rational mind did its best to reassure her, without success. *A few brief words, what's that?*

It was time enough to form an early impression, to base a first report on; her father had had her do that often and often, in the court at Marasson. But she could not do it now. Whether this man meant her good or ill or neither one she couldn't tell, though she'd given him some chance to show her. What he might mean to the borders here or to Outremer at large, she couldn't begin to guess.

THE SUN WAS sinking, though its rays still fell full on the massive scarp when they reached its foot. They rested there, at her insistence, for the bearers' sake. Here more than anywhere, she wished she could have Merissa saddled and brought to her. If she had to enter those high forbidding walls above, she would far rather do it ahorseback, for what small gesture of independence that could afford.

It wasn't possible, though, she knew that. This break was as much assertion as she could hope for, and even this was begrudged her, granted only on sufferance. The Ransomers had not even dismounted; they walked their horses in tight, impatient circles, glancing ever upward at the road and the overhanging castle. Blaise too, she saw. His men were crouching in what bare shade they could find, but he had ridden some little distance up the slope, seemingly lost in thoughts of his own.

There was only water in her flask today, but Julianne shared that with her friend and said, "I'm afraid Sergeant Blaise and I have misled these men. They believe you to be my companion."

"Well, so I am," said Elisande, smiling. "What else? And when Julianne did not reply, "Does it distress you?"

"Not at all." She would have been grateful for such companionship all the way to Elessi and after too, though she could not ask for that.

"Besides, it gives me an entry to the castle," the other girl admitted, "which might have been difficult else."

That was true too, and Julianne had already considered it. But that raised the question again of what Elisande was seeking at Roq de Rançon; and she would not ask again, for fear of being rebuffed again. One question, though, she was not shy of asking.

"Do you think Blaise has told the marshal of the djinni?"

"You know him better than I," Elisande said consideringly. "But myself, I doubt it. Strongly."

So did Julianne. Again it was a breach of duty, to let his ward venture so far into risk; and the djinn would surely be anathema to a Ransomer, any contact something close to heresy. No, she didn't think he would talk to anyone about that. His men neither, if his discipline was as good as she believed.

In fact she and Elisande had talked little about the djinni, even last night, in the seclusion of the bed they'd shared. It was too momentous, that meeting, deeply private to each of them despite their having been together at the time. The creature's words to Julianne had left a bitter tang—what point in its speaking to her, if it only chose to reinforce her father?—and she had sensed that Elisande would not relish questions. Nor answer them, most likely.

THE BEARERS ROSE, to show that they were ready. The men took a minute or two to arrange themselves in the established order of march, and then the caravan set off on the long climb to the Roq.

Long slow climb, no one would hurry on such a path, narrow and twisting with always a wall of jagged rock on the one hand and a terrible fall on the other. How the first force from the homelands had ever taken this place, Julianne couldn't imagine; it should have been invulnerable. Twenty men could hold it, surely, against an army.

Not against an army and the God, that had to be the answer; though the Sharai had their god also, and Julianne's childhood in cosmopolitan Marasson had left her with a secret fascination for other people's beliefs, and not a few sternly unvoiced doubts about what her own priests told her was truth immutable.

The bearers were doing their best to keep the litter level for its passengers, the men at the front carrying its poles at waist-level while those behind kept them on their shoulders, but it was still a bumping, rocking passage to the top. The girls clung to each other for support, laughing as they swayed from one side to the other. Elisande seemed genuinely to be enjoying herself, but Julianne's laughter, she knew, betrayed her nervousness. She couldn't keep from thinking how there was nothing but the litter's light frame to grab at, should it tilt too far. The curtains had never seemed so gossamer-thin, especially when they swung wide at the bends to show her the awful drop beneath. And she'd been sulking down at the bottom there, she'd wanted to *ride* up here? She was a good horsewoman, but Merissa was a nervy, excitable mount, used to wide plains and fast running, likely to start and skitter on unfamiliar ground. Julianne found herself once again unexpectedly grateful for the litter. This was an uncomfortable climb, to be sure, and humiliating to her pride; better that, though, than to have Merissa shy suddenly at a falling rock and so to fall herself, to fall and fall.

THE GRUNTS AND cries of the bearers ebbed at last. They set the palanquin down for a moment, then lifted it again, laughing softly. Peering ahead, Julianne saw that they stood before the open gate of the castle. Surprisingly small the gate seemed, for so great a fastness; but that would be defence again, wide high walls and a narrow entry to defy invaders. The horsemen ahead of them were going through in single file, as if there were no room for two abreast. She wondered if there would be width enough for her wagon to follow. Surely, though, if it had climbed the road it could achieve the gate. They must be accustomed to wagons here; how else could the castle be supplied? There had been plenty, she remembered, waiting on the road where the djinni was.

The way was clear now, and her bearers went slowly forward. Once past the gatehouse they climbed a long flight of shallow steps, a chilly passage with only a slit of sky above them; and then none at all, only darkness as they entered a tunnel, it seemed, cold and dank and still sloping upward.

Too much of that. She held tightly to Elisande's hand, and all her forebodings came back to her. A broad stable yard after was nothing but relief. Here the bearers set them down once more, their sighs and murmurs suggesting that they shared her feelings; and here was Blaise, dismounted now, standing beside the litter and calling her name.

Veil pulled into place with quick, trembling fingers, she pushed the curtains back and stepped out, infinitely glad to feel solid cobbles beneath her feet. One deep breath, a self-conscious stiffening of the spine which Elisande beside her, she noticed grimly, did not need; she gazed about her and saw men standing in groups, horses being led away by white-tunic'd, wiry lads. Marshal Fulke she could not see, though almost all the horsemen had thrown their cowls back now, under this lower, kinder sun. The sky was shot with red above them.

"My lady, if you and, and the lady Elisande," and there was a mute appeal in Blaise's eyes, that she should maintain this subterfuge, "if you will come this way, the brother here will show us to guest quarters."

As she followed Blaise and the beckoning, silent brother, she caught a glimpse of her wagon's yoked oxen being coaxed out of the tunnel. And didn't turn her head to watch; she had her dignity, albeit late recovered.

THEY CLIMBED ANOTHER ramp, narrower than the last: too narrow for horses, this, let alone wagons. How did they ever bring inside anything larger than a man could carry? By rope and winch, she decided, over the parapet above the moat. That would be the only way. Here the walls almost brushed Blaise's shoulders, on either side at once. To the left, the inner side, she saw that the worked stone was older, cracked and stained and greying, the exposed mortar gone to dust. That must be the wall of the original fortress, seized by the king in a single night after a siege that had lasted all the summer. Before he was the king, of course, when he was only the Duc de Charelles and a very long way from his family estates. Julianne's father had been one of his company even then, a young squire in the service of his lord; he'd told her much about the great war they'd fought, to drive the infidel out of the Sanctuary Land and recover Ascariel for the God, but little about this battle or that night. She knew that the Society of Ransom had taken the captured fortress and made of it a citadel—this must be all their work on her right and behind her, all that she'd seen so far must be new-built since the war—but not even her other sources, her many friends at Marasson, had been able to tell her how the battle had been waged or how the fortress fell.

Beyond the ramp was a dark and narrow ward between a wall and a low tower, to which the brother led them. Stairs rising into shadow, turning, rising again into light; a lamp-lit doorway, a heavy curtain lifted back, a gesture to enter. Made to Blaise, she noted, not to her. If all the brothers were like this, mute and seemingly disparaging of her rank or person, she thought she might be too angry to feel depressed even in this gloomy place, however long she had to wait.

But no, not all could be, surely? Marshal Fulke had spoken with her. Crossed swords, indeed, and she thought he'd had the worst of it. There was a thought to cheer her.

THE ROOM BEYOND the curtain could cheer her also, if she were in a mood to allow it. There was no view over the outer walls, but at least the window was as wide as her arm was long, it let in air and light through fine-cut wooden screens in the high Catari style. And at least she could see the sky, broad and untrammelled, ever her picture of freedom. She saw a rim of darkness, purple creeping up like a bruise into the blue. That must be the east, then. Elessi over there, east and south; all her life behind her, west and north and far behind her now.

She jerked her head away from window, memory, anticipation, dread. Hangings hid the walls and a wonderful carpet the floor, a design to become lost in, so intricate, so many threads and colours. There were two beds, she saw, no need to share tonight; and water and towels laid out ready, that they might wash and refresh themselves.

"You knew we were coming?" she asked, directly of the brother. "How is that, were we seen on the road? Or did Master Fulke send a messenger ahead?"

The brother shook his head, looking both stubborn and confused; it was Blaise who answered. "My lady, they always have guest rooms prepared, in any convent of the Order. It is the Rule, to serve pilgrims and travellers."

Actually she'd known that, she'd only wanted to confront the Ransomer, to be sure that he wasn't just shy or tongue-tied or a lad of few words careful not to use up his allotment. Well, she was sure now. She nodded a curt dismissal in lieu of thanks, let him scurry almost to the doorway then called out, "Wait."

Saw him check, and turn; and turned herself, turned her back, turned back to Blaise. "Ask him," she said coldly, "if we can have baths. Here. At once."

The sergeant did glance towards the brother, but only to shake his head briefly. She felt more than heard the young man leave, a sudden touch of air as he let the heavy curtain fall.

"I *said*—"

"Lady," Blaise interrupted, tight-voiced, his big hands spreading, "it's near enough sunset now. He can't bring you a bath. No one can."

Oh. Of course. She'd forgotten the conventual Hours: it was time for evening service. All the brothers would be called to prayer.

"I'm sorry," she said, genuinely regretful, though only for the mistake. She didn't like making mistakes. "But why couldn't he tell me that himself?" *That or anything, why did he look at me as a Sharai might look at a pig?*

"He's young, my lady," Blaise said stiffly. "Young and devout, and determined. The vow is for chastity, but some brothers choose to go further. It is not encouraged, or not officially, but some confessors will witness additional vows."

"Which are?"

"Not to speak to women, begging your pardon, my lady. Sometimes not even to look at women."

Julianne laughed, with a touch of cruelty. "Women are not the problem I've heard about, with regard to Ransomer chastity."

Blaise blushed furiously. "That is not true, Lady Julianne. The brothers keep the Rule, they serve the God, they are not—debauched, in that way."

"No," she said, curious and sorry. "I beg *your* pardon, Blaise, I should not have said such a thing. Ignorant gossip, of course it's not true. But in a community of brothers, what's that young man scared of?"

"Not all serve with their brethren, lady, or in the field. Many have to do with women every day. Some brothers worry. Particularly the young. When you're young, such vows are easy to make, but may prove hard to keep."

That didn't explain why the boy had seemed so contemptuous, the couple of times she'd caught his eye. An attitude learned from his confessor, perhaps?

Never mind. She was suddenly less interested in him, more in the older man before her now. Blaise wasn't so very old, at that. He was Elessan-born, he'd told her, which made him necessarily under forty. Not too much under, though, she thought. His face was lined with more than the journey's weariness, and his eyes narrowed with more than the journey's stress. He should be relaxing, surely, here on safe ground, all his duties discharged? And yet he wasn't. He seemed more on edge than before, though he'd been edgy enough ever since her father had been called away, ever since this enforced change of plan and route. She'd thought that was only the responsibility, her life on his shoulders; now she was wondering if their new destination, this castle had been weighing on him also. *Did you take some vows yourself when you were young, Blaise? And did you maybe break them, or one of them, the one that mattered most?*

She wanted to ask, and couldn't see a way to do it. Easy in Marasson, harder in Tallis, impossible she suspected in Elessi; and the Roq was Elessi in miniature, she thought, hard men with hard secrets, not to be divulged.

A great bell tolled just as the light in the room began to fail, while she was still searching for the words, for the key, for a blade and the strength to crack him open. Again, and again; she thought her own bones were ringing in sympathy, or in response.

Blaise had stiffened further, if that were possible. He seemed pale and strained, under the day's crust of sweat and dust.

"My lady, may I leave you?"

"No," she said lightly, glancing around for Elisande and finding her watching, head cocked with curiosity.

"My *lady*, I—"

"I know," she said, interrupting him this time, but with a smile. "You want to go to service too, yes? Like the brother?"

"I have to go," he said, fists clenching and unclenching at his sides.

"Of course," and she kept her voice easy, as if this were no great matter to either one of them. "We will all go. We are their guests, after all; we should respect the habits of the house. If you will wait one minute, Blaise, while we rinse this dust away—or join us, you will want to go clean before the God—then you can show us the way to chapel. Yes?"

I'm sure you know the way hung in the air between them, unspoken but not unsaid. His nod was an entire conversation.

WHEN THEY HAD washed, Blaise led them—his own face still glistening wet as he would not use their towels, nor the curtain which Elisande had suggested, smiling wickedly—not to a chapel, but to a gallery overlooking a vast pillared hall lit by flambeaux in sconces on every face of every pillar. Shadows danced in the vaulted roof above; when she looked down, for a moment all she saw was black until her eyes adapted and she realised what lay below. The brothers were here ahead of her, kneeling in rank upon close-packed rank before the raised altar.

There was a narrow aisle between the ranks, running the length of the hall. Now a procession came walking slowly, brothers with flambeaux leading a dozen men in habits, their cowls hiding their faces from her. These must be the senior members of the Order, the preceptor and masters. They climbed the three steps to the altar and arrayed themselves in a line before it, bowing low. Behind them were men in white robes beneath black cloaks; again their hoods were raised. Knights Ransomers, she thought, remembering similar dress at services in Marasson.

The knights formed lines below the altar steps, and knelt there. At her side Blaise knelt also, hurriedly, lifting a hand to his head in a gesture of doubt; he wore his steel cap, but still felt the lack of a hood, she thought. A black hood, she was certain, and not from the cloak of a knight.

Taking her cue from him, she dropped to her knees and beckoned Elisande to do the same. The gallery's balustrade restricted her view, but not severely; not so much as the pillars must be blocking the eyeline of the brothers who knelt behind them. Still, they did not need to see. Neither did she, in all honesty, it was only that she wanted to. She straightened her back, to peer over the rail. The deep-throated bell sang one time more, its weight throbbing through her; a single clear voice began the chant. When the massed voices of the brothers replied, she felt all her skin prickle at once.

THERE WAS ALWAYS a preacher at sundown. She must have heard a hundred sermons for each year of her life, but never in a setting such as this. She was curious, eager almost; when the time came, she rose up again on her heels.

One robed master stepped forward, from the twelve on the altar's dais. She wanted to see his face, and could not— until, shockingly, he lifted his hands to his cowl and cast it back to stand bare-headed before them all. There was a shifting throughout the hall at such a gesture, here in the presence of the God, but she ignored it. A pale head, blond and balding...

Marshal Fulke looked deliberately about him, left and right; and looked up too, looked at the gallery, looked directly at her. Then he bent forward, cleared his throat and spat loudly onto the altar steps.

That brought more than a discontented shuffling from the kneeling brothers, it brought a great hissing, hundreds of men catching their breath at once, as she did.

He spread his arms to settle them and said, "Yes, I will meet my penance for that, and for uncovering at the altar during prayers. But this, this contempt for the God and His church—this is nothing. I say it is *nothing*, to you it is nothing, you mock yourselves and me to pretend otherwise. It matters not a tittle, not a whit. I could lift my habit, bare myself like a babe or an impudent boy and defecate on the altar here; and you, you Ransomers, you soldiers of the God would have no cause and no right to protest it. Neither would the God condemn it. Not in this house.

"You are false, my brothers. You are hypocrites, you deceive the world. You cry the God, you make great show of your virtue and your swords, you stand at all the borders of Outremer and pull faces at the desert to frighten the Sharai, and at your backs the heart of the kingdom is rank and rotten, and that black heart will poison the whole body, and so Outremer will die and our souls will die with it. And you *know* this, my brothers, and yet you do nothing. You stand with your backs to the most foul corruption that ever touched this land, and you pretend. You pretend that *it is not there...!*

"What is my spittle on the altar steps, against the great heresy that is the Folded Land, that place we do not name? Spittle can be washed away, it will not harm the stone, and he who spits can be forgiven. Heresy is more malign, it eats at virtue as a canker eats at good flesh; it needs steel and fire to expunge it. Heretics should seek forgiveness in the flames, for they will find it nowhere else.

"But you, my brothers, you who stand and let this canker grow—how are you to be forgiven? You deny the God, by denying your duty to Him. You betray the God, by betraying your duty to His people. You dishonour the God, by dishonouring your duty to this His land.

"You say you cannot find this enemy, this heretic state? I say look within yourselves, find how you have blinded your own eyes, gagged your own voices against telling truth. You will not even *name* the foe? Then how can you hope to find him out?

"I say let us speak of him—yes, even here, before the altar of the God he so traduces. Surayon! I say Surayon is the enemy, the great betrayer, the canker that will kill us if it is not cut out. Surayon and all its people, from Princip to peasant. How can we face the Sharai when we cannot face what lies within us, our own dark heart...?"

IT WAS ONLY as she rose at the close of service that Julianne realised there was another in the gallery besides herself and her companions, one who must have come in silently behind them, some time after the processional entry of the masters. She would surely have noticed, before.

He was a young man, tall and dark and intense: his eyes on the altar still, his hand on his sword, his hair uncropped and wild.

His hair uncovered, though the black cloak that he wore over his white dress had a hood to it.

And Blaise, she saw suddenly—Blaise beside her had taken off his cap and was turning it and turning it between his big hands, looking uncomfortable, looking determined, looking away.

And glancing over the balcony, she could see bared heads among the brothers also as they waited their turn to leave: hoods thrown back and eyes fierce as falcons' gazing about them, seeking out others of their kind and mind.

No bold soul stepped out of his line to walk forward, to go to the altar steps and spit; but she guessed, no, she was sure that some had thought of it.

Not a gesture of disrespect, she thought, nor discontent; not a momentary swaying by a passionate speaker, though passionate he had been and almost had she been swayed herself. Not a rebellion, even. This was a revolution, or the first seeds of it.

She wished she had a way to tell her father.

B LAISE SAW THEM quickly back to their room, and then excused himself: off to the refectory, she thought, not in pursuit of a meal so much as company, like minds talking together, encouraging each other. Boys, working each other up to face a challenge.

"The brothers will bring you food, my lady," were the words he left her with, for fear she should think herself neglected. When next there were footsteps beyond the curtain, though, and a voice calling through, it was not food that was brought to them.

It was a tub and towels, a box of soap, and water.

Hot water...

« ¤ »

T WENTY DAYS THEIR trail measured, at their backs. It was a long shadow over the sands, the salt-pans, the lava plain. The grazing had been bad, the wells bitter and brackish; they had left the bones of ten camels behind them, and two men unburied who would be bones as soon as the foxes found them. *Or the Kauram,* Jazra had whispered that night, *they'll be slipping back now, with their cooking pots...*

Much snorting laughter muffled wetly under blankets, not to disturb those who were sleeping. But there was a truth hidden in the laughter, which was maybe why they'd laughed so hard, and why they'd tried so hard to smother it. Not that the Kauram truly ate men, of other tribes or their own: that was an old joke and only the children believed it, although it was undoubtedly true that the Kauram were a sly and dirty people with no sense of honour, who kept water-secrets hidden to themselves. How else could they live so long with their herds in the *mul'abarta*, the great white sands, if they didn't know of wells they never spoke about, and good grazing that they never shared?

Unless of course they did eat men as the stories said, drink their blood and the liquid in their bellies. No grown man would believe that—though it might of course be true regardless, who could say?—but every man said it, and every man sneered at the Kauram for it, true or not. That was the tradition. The Kauram were cannibals, the Ashti were cowards, the Beni Rus loved only gold and silver, the Saren loved only boys and needed men of other tribes to make their children for them.

He was Saren himself, he and Jazra both, and they were bloodsworn to each other and would never marry; but he would still kill any man he heard to spread that lie. Even here, even under all the oaths that he and every man besides had taken, to ride peaceably together and fight only with the infidel. That was the real truth, he'd thought: that even Hasan could not truly unite the tribes.

That was why the two men had died. There was bad blood between their peoples anyway, and a blood debt long outstanding between their families, a history of raids and deaths

94

and stolen camels told and retold through the generations. And there had been an argument on the march, an argument of nothing, of whose grandfather had been the greater warrior. No one had heeded them; any Sharai could and would argue about anything on a journey, it passed the time and mattered not at all.

But when they couched their camels and rested under the sun's most heat, the argument had gone on. Suddenly it was a case of knives, as perhaps had been intended all along, these men had so much hatred for each other. Steel flashed in the light, steel grated on steel and then a thud and a gasp, and one was down and dying and the red sands drank his blood.

The other had died within the hour, on Hasan's order. The two were left lying by the trail, their weapons taken from them and their flesh open to any dishonour. That night young men might snigger together beneath their blankets—those who had blankets—but there was a doom, he'd thought, written in their laughter. He'd thought perhaps the infidel would win at last, because Sharai knives could not in the end be kept from Sharai throats.

BUT THERE HAD been no killings in this party since, although three hundred men of a dozen warring tribes rode side by side. Hasan's discipline was holding, where the imam's oaths perhaps were not. Now they were come to Bhitry well, where men of the Rubel were waiting for them as had been promised. There were no more sands to cross. Here they must trade their camels for horses and go on into strange country, guided by strangers.

Bhitry water was sweet and plentiful. The camels had drunk their fill and the men also, for the first time since Rhabat, and still there was enough to wash with before they prayed. And then there was fat and meat to roast over their many fires; the sheikhs of the Rubel had sent fifty goats to welcome them who had eaten nothing but desert bread for days.

With so much meat there seemed no point in dividing it and drawing lots, to say which share was whose; so he and Jazra fought as they always did, "You should take more; here, I have too much, this must be yours," until the older men at their fire intervened.

As they ate, his eyes turned to the dark shadows on the horizon, north and west, the hills they must skirt tonight. There would be water and meat there also. Hunger and thirst were no more a worry, a camel's dying no longer meant danger or death to a man; now his thoughts were free to run forward, to the great killing they had come for.

FIVE

These Things Happen

AFTER THAT WHIPPING sermon, meant to do more than sting, Marshal Fulke raised no more welts; or none with his tongue, though he had not yet done with talking. To the brothers he talked of obedience largely, telling them of the charter he bore from the Grand Chapter of the Order, that commissioned him to use all means within his power to purify and sustain the kingdom. In obedience, he could do no other than to lead them in holy war against the God-defying apostates of Surayon; in obedience, they could do no other than to follow him.

To the knights, it seemed, he talked of other things: of duty and honour, of courage and the great adventure that lay before them, of the long-delayed completion of what their fathers and grandfathers had begun forty years before.

Marron heard none of that directly, but his day had already assumed a pattern very different from that of his brothers in the troop. By Brother Apothecary's order, he was excused strenuous duty until the gash in his arm had healed. By Sieur Anton's order, he passed the hours this gained him in doing a squire's service, waiting on his knight.

In practice, it meant that he spent much of each day with his hands more idle than they were used to, and his mind more preoccupied. Sieur Anton seemed to have unusual, even unlikely ideas of the proper duties of a squire; Marron saw little of the other knights' attendants.

In the mornings he was required to stand and watch Sieur Anton at exercise with sword and shield. "I may need you," Sieur Anton had said, "to fetch and carry for me. Perhaps to carry me to the infirmary, as your friend did you," with a twisted smile that said *little enough danger of that.* The smile spoke true; his knight outclassed the others, Marron thought, beyond argument or challenge.

At noon each day they went as before to Sieur Anton's small chamber, and said the office together when Brother Whisperer struck. Marron could join his brothers in the pillared hall instead, Sieur Anton made that clear; but he found a curious satisfaction in this quiet murmuring of potent words, a new revelation to set against the massed celebrations of the other Great Hours.

Then he was dismissed to eat with his troop while Sieur Anton fasted. After the meal, though, the troop had chores assigned now, kitchen duties that Marron was forbidden. Fra' Piet would send him off with a sneer, and a comment to the others as to how carelessness could sometimes be rewarded; and Marron would run back to the knight's chamber, to ask how he could be used.

Every day brought a different answer. There were broken links in Sieur Anton's mail; it must be taken to the armoury for repair, waited for and then oiled and cleaned with a soft cloth against the dangers of rust and the unacceptability of dirt. Or the knight's fine linens were in need of washing, and again must be watched over in the laundry and on the drying-racks, because those local women were heavy-handed in their work but light-fingered afterward.

Or—once—Marron arrived at the chamber door and scratched on it lightly, and then went in to find Sieur Anton standing by the window with his drawn sword in his hand, frowning as he tipped the blade this way and that in a fugitive beam of sunlight. He didn't so much as glance up to acknowledge Marron's entrance.

"Sieur? Is the sword notched again?"

"What? Oh. No, the edge is good. It wants work, though. I think Sister Josette is thirsty, Brother Marron. Fetch me your sword."

"Sieur?"

"Your sword, Marron. You do have a sword, other than that cow-beater you thrashed at me?"

"Yes, sieur." He had a sword, racked in the dormitory with every brother's else until the troop was judged competent to use them in training. Given the choice, he would delay that day until the sword had rotted. He thought it tainted past use, he thought the memory of blood would etch its steel to rags and rust.

"Then fetch it."

Marron fetched his sword, at a canter. Sieur Anton took it, drew it from its worn leather sheath, gazed at it a moment in that same solid-seeming bar of light and tossed it dismissively onto the bed.

"Adequate for practice. Adequate for a peasant, perhaps—or a yeoman?" shrewdly, watching Marron's face. "Your father's?"

"My uncle's." His father's sword had been lost with his father. Never before had he been glad of that, nor ever imagined that he would or could be, but he'd been glad for days and days now.

"Well. It suited him, no doubt. Or he it. Though he has trained you well enough," touching a finger to his throat,

99

where a faint yellow streak of bruise still showed. "To begin with, at least. I think we will look a little higher for you now. Here." He opened the chest in the corner, and lifted out what was lying ready there on a bed of folded clothes, what certainly had not been there when Marron had folded and stowed those same clothes yesterday.

It was a sword, in a finely tooled scabbard of white leather reinforced with silver edging. The grip was bound with the same leather; the pommel and hilt were chased steel, much like Sieur Anton's own Josette, expensive work but not gaudy, not ornate. No jewels, such as he had seen on some of the other knights' weapons.

"Take it. Draw it out."

"Sieur..."

"Marron, obedience is the first duty of an esquire, as well as a brother Ransomer. Take the sword."

Marron took the sword. It nestled into his hand like a warm and living thing, slid from its scabbard as though it very much wanted to. For the length of his forearm the blade also was chased, on both faces, with a fine tracery that finished in a crest of some sort; the room was dim, he couldn't see well enough to make it out without moving to that vagrant beam of sunlight, too close to Sieur Anton.

The sword was a little shorter, he thought, and noticeably lighter than Josette; and oh, it felt sweet and easy in his grip. He touched the edge and drew blood just from the touch, feather-light and fleeting; and sucked his finger to the sound of laughter, and moved his body and the blade rapidly through the five major and seven minor positions, which a moment before he had been determined not to do; and sheathed it with a flourish, released the hilt with a pang, held his bleeding finger carefully away from the unblemished white of the scabbard as he said, "Sieur, this is too, too—"

"Too fine a weapon for a cloth-headed, muck-handed oaf like you? Quite so. But you may improve. No, you *shall* improve; I will see to that. I have hopes of you, Marron. The positions again."

Sword whispered from scabbard, almost before Marron had consciously registered the sharp command. And then it whispered again, whispered differently in the air as he took first position—*elbows so, feet thus and the hand high,* his uncle's voice, as ever in his head when he performed this drill—and slashed the sword sharply down into second, stabbed forward to reach third...

"No."

Sieur Anton's voice checked him, stilled him as he was, in a semi-crouch with the sword thrust out before him; and he expected to feel Sieur Anton's hands on him as his uncle's had been so often, pulling and pressing, only that he couldn't guess what was wrong with his line. So far as he could tell it was perfect, all the way from his back foot to the far-thrust tip of this beautiful sword.

"Stand up."

Marron straightened slowly. Sieur Anton had Josette in his hand now, and gestured with it—with *her*—to send him back against the wall.

"Your line is good, but you jerk in your movements, you use too much energy. You should flow from one position to the next. Don't force the blade so, let it rather lead your hand. Learn to trust your sword. Like this."

He demonstrated, and yes, his movements were precise but liquid, like a dancer's. Marron tried to imitate and was stopped, corrected; tried again, and was corrected again. And tried again, and again.

THERE WAS SWEAT on his skin and his lungs were labouring when he finally came from first major to seventh minor position without an interruption. He glanced at Sieur Anton, and saw him smiling.

"Good. Not quite such an oaf after all, are you, Fra' Marron? There is a deal more work to do, but you may yet not disgrace the blade, when you find yourself in battle."

Hot though he was, a sudden memory chilled him. He had been in battle already, and disgraced himself and his blade both.

"Sieur Anton, I would—forgive me, but I would prefer not..." The sword dropped in his hand; he reached blindly for the scabbard.

"Why so?"

The baby's scream was deafening. He shook his head wildly against it, wanted to dissemble, couldn't do it. "The work they give us is not worthy," he said bluntly, and the bitterness in his voice all but stained the air.

"The work...? Well. Put the sword up, Marron, and rest. That's right, lay it on the chest and come, sit." Sieur Anton sat himself, on the furs that covered the bed, and patted the space beside him. "Here."

Reluctantly, Marron did as he was bid. He pushed his hands through sweat-damp hair and hid his eyes against his palms, pressing hard to deny the visions in his head.

"Now. Tell me. What work have they had you do?"

SIEUR ANTON WAITED out Marron's silence, and then listened without comment to the tale of the heretic village, Fra' Piet's exhortations, madness and slaughter in the sun. Marron spared himself nothing, from the first use of his uncle's sword—an old woman running stumblingly, and the steel sliding into her back—to the last use of his blood-washed hands, snatching the babe from its dead father and swinging it through the air like a father's game with too cruel an ending. And then he told awkwardly how the memory haunted him waking and sleeping; how he saw the taint still on his uncle's sword, how he heard the baby's wail in wind and stillness, in sweet singing and raucous cries, even sometimes behind the chanting of the brothers at prayer.

Sieur Anton was quiet for a measure after, and Marron thought it was disgust that had caught his tongue, and no wonder at that.

But the knight put a hand on his shoulder and gripped hard, touching now where he had not throughout the long lesson that had gone before; and he said, "Have you told your confessor?"

Had he not been listening, had he not heard? "He was *there*," and he was the cause of it all.

"I meant—But no. Of course. It was a stupid question, how could you? Listen to me, then, Marron. Things happen, and you cannot prevent them; sometimes you cannot prevent your own part in them, sometimes they happen to you and through you. Here in Outremer, especially. We walk more closely under the God's eye, and that is not always a blessing. His anger can touch us, as well as His peace; that can make us mad, for a time."

A pause, a slow breath that was nearly a sigh, and then, "When I was fourteen, my father had a family hanged. They were Catari, villagers on our estate, infidels who wouldn't convert. There are hundreds such, of course, on every large estate. The amnesty declared at the Conclave protects them, but not their holy places. There was a shrine in the village that my grandfather had let stand, he said it kept them passive; but he died, and my father is a more devout man. He had the shrine destroyed.

"This was an old and honourable family, if there be any honour in poverty; but one of their sons came up to the demesne that night and fired our chapel. For revenge, I suppose, or for justice. He stood in the light of the fire, and cursed us all. One of the guards shot him; Father was angry over that, I think he'd wanted a slower death for the lad, the better to appease the God. But he had the body thrown into the flames, and then in the morning he took us down to the village, my brother and I and a dozen men in case of trouble; and the whole family was hanged. Nine of them, from grandfather to suckling."

His hand still lay on Marron's shoulder, though its grip was looser now. Marron stirred slightly against that touch, and said, "Forgive me, sieur, but it is not the same. Your father made you watch; but we, I, I *did* these things..."

"Marron, I said he *had* them hanged. By me, by us, my brother and myself, while he watched. There was one tree, and one rope; I put the rope around their necks, one by one, and my brother helped me haul them up. The lightest of them took an age to die, the old man and the children. And I decided the order of their deaths; my father granted me that privilege. I was fourteen, after all. My brother was only twelve. So it was by my choice that the mother was last to die, that she saw all her children dead before her. Neither did I have your excuse, the heat and fury of the moment. I have known battle-rage, and it does blind a man to reason or mercy; but everything I did that day was done coldly and clearly. My father ordered it, but I was not bound to obey. These things happen here, that is all we can say. That they happen to us, that we regret them later—that is the way of our world, or the will of the God, or however we choose to name it."

This time it was Marron who let the silence lie between them. He felt comforted, and grateful, but could find no words to say so.

"The blade was my brother's," Sieur Anton said, stirring, standing abruptly. "It is named Dard. I had best keep it here for you, I think, to save your brothers the sin of envy; you can practise with the other."

"Yes, sieur." Reluctance and relief mixed within him. His uncle's sword would never feel the same in his hand now that he had held one so much better, and already he felt the thrill of owning something so fine, so perfectly balanced, so perfect; but he quailed at the thought of having to explain the gift of it to Fra' Piet, or to Aldo.

"Be patient." Sieur Anton was smiling again, Marron could hear it though he could not see his face; the knight was standing at his window, gazing out. "The time will come when you can wear it openly and use it in the service of the God. His true service, with honour. Did you hear Marshal Fulke in the hall, when he spoke of Surayon?"

"Yes, of course. But—were you there, sieur?"

"I was there. In the guests' gallery, not among my con-frères. I had heard that he would speak, and that the matter was important. He has also talked to us since."

WHICH WAS HOW Marron learned what had been said to the knights, so different from what had been said to the brothers. He resented that, a little: it was not only obedi-ence that sent the brothers to battle. They fought for honour also, the honour of the God alone, untainted by knights' dreams of personal glory.

Not that Sieur Anton wanted glory for himself. That much was clear; also that he was fired as so many of the brothers were, by the marshal's call to arms. Marron's mind was still clouded. When Marshal Fulke or anyone spoke of heretics, he saw only slaughtered innocents, and his own hands dripping red.

"Sieur? Have you seen Surayon?" The Folded Land he still wanted to call it, as he had been trained to; but after the sermon in the hall and Sieur Anton's own casual naming of the place, he assumed permission. Though he still flinched, anticipating a bruise.

No blow, no bruise; only a laugh, short and harsh. "Seen it? Of course not. No one has seen Surayon for thirty years."

"No, but—I mean, have you been there? I mean..."

"To where it was, or is, or will be? Hard to speak of, is it not? But yes, I have been there. Once. It is—strange. You ride the road that led there, and where the border was you see a twist in the landscape, in the air itself, a shimmer like the desert heat although that land is green. Through that you see the wrong country, the land beyond Surayon, as though twenty miles of mountain and valley were simply gone. And the shadows fall wrongly on the other side, or seem to, because the road you ride runs north but the road you ride towards runs north-west and the place where it turns is missing, so that what you see is impossible, a straight road lit by two separate suns, it seems.

"And you ride into that shimmer that lies across your way, and for a moment you see nothing at all and feel nothing outside yourself, only a great twisting, as though your skin were turned to the inside and all your bones were free.

"But your eyes clear, and—well, I found myself clinging to a frantic horse that galloped wildly off the road and into some thorn-bushes. Luckily, those stopped him; I had to dismount very quickly, to throw my breakfast at their roots. I believe that is quite a common reaction. When I had recovered myself and my horse, I found that we were on that other road, twenty miles from where I had been a minute before. Surayon is—closed; it is not there."

"But how...?"

"How is that possible, or how will we find it? I cannot answer either question, Marron. Maybe Marshal Fulke can, but I am not in his confidence. Yet."

There was a determination to that last, that quite convinced Marron. Sieur Anton had an aim, an intent, and would not see it denied.

SIEUR ANTON ALSO, it seemed, had private business now, and would not need his squire. "Take your sword— your uncle's sword—back to where you keep it, and seek out your troop. You need not tell them what we have spoken of today," added as a warning, quite unnecessary.

"Sieur, I never do!"

"No? Not even your little friend, Alden was his name?"

"Aldo. And no, sieur, not even him." Just as he would not tell Aldo's smallest secrets to the knight.

"Well. My thanks for that. I value my privacy, and your discretion." Then, as Marron lingered in the doorway, his eyes straying one more time to the white sheath shining in the gloom of the corner, "Yes? Something more?"

"Sieur, a question. If I may?"

"In view of that valued discretion, you may." Did he mean as a reward, or simply because he could be sure of Marron's silence? Both, perhaps. Sieur Anton's words were sometimes subtle beyond Marron's ability to weigh them.

"Sieur, you said it was your brother's sword..."

"Yes. Made to his measure. He was a year younger than you, perhaps, but much of your height; and I think you will grow no further upward. A little more flesh we might look for, though not on a brother's diet... Yes, it was my brother's sword," when Marron still hesitated. "What of it?"

"Sieur, did he outgrow it, then? Or buy a better?" *Why does he not wear it yet?* was the true question, and *how do you have it in your gift?* was another, and he couldn't ask either one plain.

The answer he was given, though, was plain enough, and dealt with both together.

"No, he did not outgrow it; and no, he did not buy a better. He could not, there is none better. He was using that blade, or trying to use it, when I killed him. I took it from his hand. I will see you in the morning, Brother Marron."

107

THE DEVIL IN THE DUST

A *FRATRICIDE*?

No, it wasn't possible. It wasn't *possible!* Sieur Anton played games with words, he liked to talk himself darker than he was and he loved to shock Marron. This must be that same black habit, dyed blacker still. No more than that, it could not possibly be true...

And yet, and yet. Sieur Anton did not lie, not ever; or never had, at least, in Marron's short acquaintance. He had and kept his secrets, that was sure, and he could be deliberately mysterious at times, but not deceitful. And this, why would he lie about such a thing as this?

So it wasn't possible, and yet it had to be. Walking slowly back to the dormitory, his uncle's sword clutched between his hands, Marron tried desperately to marry those two thoughts. Not fratricide, not murder—*these things happen* whispered in his head, in Sieur Anton's voice, but he would not hear it—so there must have been some legitimate cause for brother to kill brother. If one had been grievously hurt, perhaps, hurt past recovery in an accident or a duel, the other might use his misericorde in grief and pity, to send his brother on to the God. Or, wait, there was a simpler story: a bout, a trial of strength between the two of them, *let's test that sword of yours*; and by cruel chance or a moment's madness, the mock battle produced a true death. Marron himself had nearly died, after all, spitted on Sieur Anton's furious, frustrated blade. Perhaps that had been the second time. Perhaps his interest in Marron stemmed from that, perhaps Marron was a new brother-elect given him by guilt, and so the sword.

But Sieur Anton should not have the sword. By all custom and honour, a knight was always buried with his arms. If the brother's death had been an honest affair, Sieur Anton should have laid the sword on the body's breast himself, and folded the cold hands over the hilt, and prayed for the God's kinder grace on his brother's soul. Something surely was wrong, that he had taken it and kept it and now sought to give it away.

Perhaps the brother had disgraced himself and the family, lost the name of knight and the sword with it? Perhaps the blade needed to be purified in Sieur Anton's eyes, and hence his gift of it to one who would use it in the God's service and none other?

Perhaps. But perhaps not. Marron felt somewhat reconciled to his uncle's sword: less fine by far and less grand also, having no pretensions to a name, but so much less complicated with it. Marked, damaged, dishonoured only by his own dark acts that he might eventually redeem, at least it carried no questions in its simple lineage, no doubts, no hint of things done that were darker yet, that would paint the midnight black.

HIS WOUND WAS aching—no, more than that, his wound was in pain, aflame. Thinking back, Marron could remember a throbbing that began during that difficult, challenging exercise, which he somehow hadn't noticed at the time. Now the throbbing was a burning iron laid across his arm, and when he rolled his sleeve back he found fresh wet stains creeping through the linen bandages.

If he took it to the infirmary in this state, there would be questions asked, perhaps by Master Infirmarer himself; and no more than Sieur Anton—he believed—was Marron a liar. Besides, his skin was sticky and his hair was stiff, he could say, *No, master, I have done nothing against Brother Apothecary's order,* and his own body would deny his words.

He was not a coward; but this had been a war between duty and duty, obedience to the apothecary against obedience to the knight. He surely didn't merit punishment for choosing the one and not the other, nor for trying so hard to please the one he chose. Perhaps if he simply washed the wound and bound it up again, bound it tightly, perhaps it would heal without Brother Apothecary's potions. And if the scar were a little thicker as a result, if it drew his skin a little tight across the arm and restricted his use of it a touch—well, no doubt that would serve well as a reminder, not to find himself caught again between two masters.

NO BLUNDERING THROUGH the castle now, mazed by its many heights and angles; running Sieur Anton's errands had taught him quickly to find his way around. The knight was not patient with delay. Marron took the sword to his dormitory first and racked it with the others, then hurried down through the lower courts towards the stables.

Sunlight dazzled him as he came out of the ramp's shadow into the open yard before the moat. Squinting, his eyes found a bucket beside the stone trough where they watered the horses. He filled that, squatted down in the trough's shade and set to work on the bandages with fingers and teeth.

He was still struggling to loosen Brother Apothecary's ties when a hand touched his shoulder. Startled, he glanced around and saw bare feet, a white woollen tunic, a curious smile, dark eyes and cropped black hair: one of the Sharai boys, a captive slipped away from his labour, come to see what a Ransomer brother did down here, alone and private.

Blinking against the sun, Marron thought that he knew the face behind the smile. *Soap*, he remembered, after a moment's searching of his memory. This was the lad who had brought the soap to his troop in their first hour at the Roq.

The smile faded; the boy was stooping over him, concerned, saying, "You have a hurt?"

"Yes." And then, with a breath of surrender, "Can you help me? These knots are tight."

And his one hand was tired and clumsy, but the boy's two not; nimble fingers nudged his aside and picked briefly at the ties that were not only tight but also wet with spittle now where his teeth had tried them.

Then, "No," the boy said softly, "these must be cut. You wait, I will bring."

He trotted away. Marron sat back, felt the stone of the trough cool against his shoulders, and made a conscious effort not to hunch his head down low, out of sight. He wasn't hiding here, no, of course not; simply resting a little while, to be the stronger later.

THE BOY CAME back, and brought no trouble with him: only a knife and a cloth, and a big clay pot with a lid on it.

The knots yielded to the blade, and Marron yielded to the boy's tending, after a half-hearted gesture of protest. The bandages were peeled away as carefully as might be, but still pulled cruelly at the last, making him gasp and his eyes water. Beneath, the long gash was gaping wide and darkly wet again, leaking blood.

The boy hissed softly between his teeth, and murmured something in his own tongue to himself or possibly to Marron, who couldn't understand it either way. Then he moistened the cloth and dabbed the wound clean, holding the arm tight against Marron's flinching; even the lightest touch stung savagely. He looked again, shook his head a little, and reached for the pot.

The lid came off, and Marron saw a greasy salve gleaming in the light. "What is that?"

The boy was smiling again. "*Haresh*, it is called. We make it for the horses, when they have a hurt."

He scooped out a fingerful, but Marron jerked his arm away. "No! I am not a horse!"

111

"It is good for men too," the boy assured him, suddenly solemn. His eyes were fixed on Marron's; his unsalved hand closed gently around the wounded arm and drew it back towards him. "Oil and grasses, good for any hurt. And this," with a nod down at the slow-welling gash, "this is not good. It must be—"

A gesture with his greasy fingers finished the sentence. He didn't have the words, but his intent was clear. *It must be treated,* he meant; and *you have not gone to the proper place, so you must take my treatment,* perhaps he meant that also.

At any rate, Marron argued no more. The salve was soothing on the open wound, where Brother Apothecary's preparation had been caustic. The bandages were wrapped firmly in place again, and the cut ends tied off; then the kneeling boy sat back on his heels, smiling brightly. "You must not use it now."

"I know," Marron sighed, "I know." *Put me in a stable stall, and chain me to my manger.* He wondered how it would heal this time—if Sieur Anton gave it a chance to heal this time—and then thought he was being ungrateful; the boy had done more to help its healing than Marron could have managed alone, however dubious his medicine.

"What's your name?" he asked.

For a moment, the boy seemed taken aback. Then, "Mustar. Mustar ib' Sahir."

"Thank you, Mustar. My name is Marron."

Their eyes held, in the yard's silence; then the boy made a quick sign with expressive hands, *I must go, before I'm missed.* He rose swiftly and was gone indeed, no more farewell than that. Marron sat where he was for a minute longer, before pushing himself up and turning back towards the shadows that hid the castle's narrow entrance.

« ¤ »

WHEN HE FOUND his troop, they were on their way down to the stables. By the God's grace, he'd been just a few minutes ahead of looking up to find not Mustar but Fra' Piet at his shoulder. With what awful consequences, he dared not wonder.

His confessor sent the troop on ahead, to await a camel train reported on the road; then he turned to Marron.

"I am told," he said, "that you have been fetching and carrying for Sieur Anton. A servant's work."

"Yes, Brother Confessor. In obedience," added hastily, and in doubt.

"And yet, in obedience, you cannot share the duties of your troop? Well. If you can serve a knight, you can serve your brothers also. Even those who have placed themselves beyond merit of your serving. Go to the kitchenmaster, and say you are to take the penitents bread. He will tell you where."

THE WAY TO the penitentiary cells led down from behind the great ovens, a low doorway and a narrow spiral stair. Even fumbling his way in the dark with a basket under his good arm, he could tell that this was old stone down here, the buried heart of the castle. The steps were worn and uneven beneath his feet, making him wish more than once for a light, though he'd have no way to carry it. What did a brother need to do, to be incarcerated here below? Marron didn't know; he hadn't taken the measure yet of this place, so much harsher than where he had come from.

At the foot of the stairs was a small chamber, not built but hollowed from the rock. Here there was light, an oil-lamp burning yellow in a niche; and a barrel and two buckets, one larger than the other; and two brothers with staves in their hands, standing either side of a passageway that ran away into darkness.

One grunted at Marron's arrival, laid his stave aside and moved to lift the lamp from its niche. He walked a few paces into the passage, glanced back impatiently and said, "Come, then."

THE PASSAGE WAS chill and damp; the warm smell of baking had followed him down the stair, but did not penetrate this far. Instead the air had an acrid tang that took Marron back again to his first hour in the castle, this time to the wonder and terror of the King's Eye, the touch of magic on his soul.

There was no magic here. Only dark wooden doors thrown back against the walls of rock, and a small rough cell behind each open door; inside the first was a man on his knees and wincing from the sudden light, a brother in a penitent's white shift. A brother and a bucket, Marron saw, and a wooden goblet also.

At the warder's gesture, Marron took a loaf from his basket and handed it in. The man took it in silence, and the warder moved on with Marron at his heels.

And so from cell to cell, and only once was it different. That one the warder moved past with just a brief glance inside; when Marron hesitated, seeing the cell not empty, he was told, "No. Not him. He is for the steps tonight; if he eats, he may defile the stones."

Marron understood none of that, only that the man's face lifted blindly and there was despair written there, and all his flesh was shuddering with something more than cold.

THERE WAS STILL bread left in the basket and there was still more to the passage, the light hadn't found its end yet, neither an end to its doors; but those further cells were closed and empty. It was a cold touch, Marron thought, not to lock in the penitents, to lay such weight on their obedience.

The brother with the lamp led him back to the chamber, but his duties were not finished yet. "Fill the bucket, that one," the smaller, "and give them all one dip of water. No more."

The water was in the barrel, under a green scum. Marron scooped that aside to the warder's snicker, plunged the bucket in, lifted it out with his good arm; looking around as the shadows shifted he saw the lamp being held out towards him, and understood that this time he would have no guide to lead the way.

He took the light in his bad hand, praying not to drop it, and made his way along the passage. In each cell, the penitent brother dipped his goblet wordlessly into the bucket; some gave Marron a nod of thanks, some kept their faces turned away.

When he came to the one who had been forbidden bread, Marron was unsure. He took a step into the cell, but the man there shook his head, his eyes wild in the lamplight. Marron whispered a blessing in lieu of water, and passed on.

BACK TO THE chamber once more, and still one further task. This time, Marron had anticipated it; some of the cells smelled of more than rock and bad water.

A glance from him, a nod from the warder; he took the larger bucket down the passage, and collected each man's wastes. And hauled the sloshing, stinking weight carefully up the steps and through the kitchen, along to the latrines; emptied it into a barrel there, rinsed the bucket out and hurried it back to the chamber.

And was done at last, the warder's passive silence told him so. Once more up the stair, then, the basket of bread returned where he had found it, and he went in search of his troop.

THEY HAD SWEATED, Aldo told him, under heavy sacks of grain, and a long and winding way to carry them; but that was finished now, and it was time to bathe. For them and for a hundred brothers more, several troops at a time; they ferried water in a long line from the moat—and here at least Marron could take his part, passing full buckets with his good arm, returning empty ones with the other, seize and swing in rhythm, forward and back—and splashed briefly in the bath-house tubs, in and out and make way for the next man, only those who'd had the dirtiest or the hardest labour looking for soap.

Marron stripped, splashed, gasped at the chill of water drawn from deep in the moat where even a day's sun hadn't reached it, jumped out and pulled his habit on over shivering wet skin—and still was not quick enough to deny Aldo's sharp eye. His friend's hand caught at his wrist, drew the sleeve back, and, "That's blood!"

"Yes."

Aldo's fingers picked at wet linen, that darkened too slowly to hide what was darker.

"It's been rebound," he said slowly, tracing the broken pattern of stains, "but they should have given you a clean bandage."

"I didn't go to the infirmary."

"How did it happen?" And when Marron didn't reply, "What have you been *doing*?"

There was an easy answer to that, *carrying bread and water to the penitents*; but he couldn't lie to Aldo. He said nothing.

"You've been with him," a statement and an accusation both.

"Yes, of course. But only in his room, Aldo. We talked..."

"Talking did not do this," with a hiss and a tight gesture.

"No." His friend's anger was too much for Marron; and it was only the talk that had been in confidence, so, "He had me drill for him, with a, with a sword." No need to say more about the sword.

"Left-handed?"

"No. But the positions, again and again, and the cut opened..."

Aldo scowled, turned his back, kicked off his sandals and pulled his habit over his head.

"Aldo..."

But Aldo had jumped into a bath and plunged his head beneath the water. Marron groaned with frustration; and then he was jostled, elbowed aside, other men pushed forward and he lost sight of Aldo in the crush.

WHEN THE TROOP gathered together outside the bath-house, wet and cool and fresh, they were under Fra' Piet's critical eye and there could be no more talking. Marron found Aldo and squeezed into line beside him, trying to talk with his eyes; Aldo cast his hood up to deny him.

Brother Whisperer began to strike, and they marched in silence to the great hall. Head held piously low, Marron watched Aldo's heels rise and fall, kicking up the hem of his habit; even that told of his temper.

So did his tense and upright body, kneeling beside Marron's in the hall. Slowly, though, the service seemed to relax him, familiar words and massed sonorous voices; his anger ebbed as surely it must before the peace of the God. By the hour's close he was sitting easily back on his heels, and it was the edge of Marron's habit and not his own around which his fingers had closed.

Marron sighed softly and sat more easily himself, leaning slightly forward to glance past Aldo to the end of the line. He was watching for Fra' Piet's rising, the signal for them all to rise and go to supper.

But Fra' Piet knelt quite still in his place, as did all the confessors, and thus all the other brothers also. The preceptor had left with the masters and the knights behind him as always; now, though, here came two of the masters back again. Magister Rolf and Magister Sewart, the Masters Confessors, responsible for the morals and obedience, the faith and discipline of all the brethren at the Roq. And in their train two massive brothers, bulking like bulls beneath their habits; and between those two a man in a flimsy white shift, bareheaded, downcast and shuffling, the penitent who had been given neither bread nor water this afternoon and was not allowed even to cover his head tonight, brought in shame before the God.

He is for the steps, the warder had said; and he was led all the way to the front of the hall, to the steps leading up to the altar. He knelt before them, lowering his head to the stone while his guards remained standing on either side. The masters had mounted the steps, and bowed to the altar; now they turned to face the congregation, and spoke turn and turn about.

"Brothers Ransomers, you are all sworn to this Society, and its three redeeming oaths of chastity, poverty and obedience."

"Here is one of your number, Fra' Collen he is called, who has paid money to lie privately with a woman in the place below this castle. In doing this he has broken each of the three oaths: he has been unchaste in his body and in his mind; he has kept secret amounts of money to his own use, and enriched his thoughts with privities; he has been disobedient to his oaths, this Order and the God."

"The God is merciful. Fra' Collen will not be denied the habit, and sent forth naked and without brethren, as he came to us. His penance is less than that; but it must be made before you all, that you may see his sorrow."

NO MORE TALKING. The penitent had been condemned and sentenced; the two masters folded their hands in their sleeves and stood motionless.

It was the other two, the big men who lifted Fra' Collen to his feet, holding as much as helping him up, as it seemed. They ripped the shift from him and cast it aside; then they laid the naked man spread-eagled across the steps.

Each of them unwrapped a strap from around his waist, wide dark leather of a short man's length perhaps, though these men were not short. The straps glinted strangely in the torchlight; Marron twisted his head and squinted, heard Aldo gasp beside him—always the quicker, Aldo, especially to see pain or danger—and finally understood, as his own eyes found the answer.

Those straps were studded with iron barbs.

THERE WAS NO count, or none that Marron could hear; neither had any tariff been declared, so many strokes for such an offence. Brothers might be counting in their heads, from either dread or righteousness, but Marron thought that most would lose the count quite quickly. He hoped so. For himself, he could hold nothing in his head except the moment, the bright image that made this altarpiece: the whirl of one long strap through the air, above the heads of all, easy to see; the soft and distant sound that was the strap biting at the penitent's body; the high wailing sound that came after, cut short only by the hissing drone of the other strap as the man heard it coming and tensed, Marron was sure, clenched his fists and held his breath, had nothing left to scream with. And so the moment began again, in sound and motion, and Marron thought he never would be free of it.

Until a hand nudged against his, and that was Aldo asking for help here, asking for comfort, just a touch, fingers linked to draw each other through the moment and beyond.

Marron's reaction was instinctive, appalled. He snatched his hand away, *not here, not now, by the God's good grace don't be such a fool! Do you want that to be us up there tomorrow? Each man must come before the God alone. And Fra' Piet is sure to be watching. They'll charge us with breaking all the oaths and heresy on top, they'll flog us till our bones show...*

Would they? Perhaps not. But Fra' Piet would beat for such an offence, nothing more certain, and he had a heavy stick for it and a heavy hand. Marron tried to say that to Aldo also, with a nudge and a nod and a prayer that his friend should hear his mind's whisper; but the nudge missed its mark, a tip of the elbow was as much as he dared and Aldo had moved away. Not far, only a thumb's-length of shuffle across the floor, and that must have brought him hard up against the brother on his further side; but it was enough. Marron could hear this message, at least: *you fail me, you betray me, I turn to you and find no one where I used to find my friend.*

And that made another moment to be trapped and held by, and now he had two. One was vivid triptych, blood and pain and humiliation, and the other was an alcove of shadow and regret. Both were born of stupidity, nothing new in the ways of man; both sucked at him, and he thought they would tear him from himself. He turned this way and came back, turned that way and came back, blood and shadow, pain and regret. It was the God, he thought, it was always only the God and how could he hope or expect anything else but that looping road, here in the God's place, before His altar?

NO COUNT THAT he could hear even after the screams had died to nothing, no signal that he could see—though he wasn't looking nor trying to look, not now, he only wished he dared to look away—but at last the penance was ended, for them all. All who had paid it, at least. Fra' Piet showed nothing but satisfaction as he led them not to the back of the hall but forward, to the altar steps themselves, where they might the better see how their brother had paid.

In full, Marron thought he had paid; there was no movement in that sprawled red scarecrow figure, no sign of breath or life. The head was covered now with the torn linen shift, to show that his sins were expiated and he could again offer his respect to the God. The rest of him, though—from shoulders to calves he was ripped meat on those marble steps, meat fit only for the dogs and it seemed that they'd been at it already.

THEY LEFT THE hall by a different door; and in the ward outside Marron threw back his hood and stared directly at Fra' Piet, crushed down the voice inside his skull that whispered, *stupid, stupid!* and asked the question directly.

"Will he live?"

"Perhaps." It seemed this was a legitimate thing to ask: not curiosity—which was disobedience disguised—but necessary to their understanding of the Order and their own place within it. "If the God wills. Sometimes they live."

"And if not?"

"Why, then he dies shriven and goes to the God. A happy man. I have seen men cast out, denied the habit; they go broken. He will be new-made, however the God chooses for him."

Marron thought personally he'd have chosen the other, he'd have been cast out before he'd have been so brutalised. That sounded not so bad: naked in this heat was no penance, and the women in the village below would have clothing to spare even for a white-skinned beggar. And alone sounded not so bad either, if it meant having no brothers who would strip you to the bone, likely to the death.

He wondered if that were heresy; and on the thought he turned to find Aldo in the group behind him, and found him just to see him turn away; and thought perhaps he had been cast out, naked and alone he felt suddenly, and liked it not so much after all.

SIX

Heights of Folly

HUMILIATED WAS HOW Julianne felt, largely. And angry, and childish, and stupid, when she should have been laughing and free; but humiliated largely.

And it had seemed such a neat plan, so perfectly manipulative. One for her father to be proud of, on a small scale: and he'd worked on a small scale all her life, as well as on the great canvas that was Outremer. Manipulation was his definition of fatherhood.

These days in the castle—and mostly in her room, satisfying Blaise's notions of propriety while Elisande came and went and nosed around with total licence—had made her not simply restless, they had made her wild. She had wanted to scream and throw things. Instead, she had quietly suggested to Blaise that her palfrey Merissa would be suffering, losing condition in a stable stall, much in need of a canter on the plain below.

"That's true, my lady. My horse, too. I will tell the stablemaster; I'm sure he can find men to give them exercise."

"No," she said immediately, "Merissa is a difficult beast; she will allow no one but me on her back. We'd best see to it ourselves. Ask him to have them both saddled and ready after the midday meal."

Blaise frowned, as she'd known he would; and then—as she'd known he would—he said, "I'm sorry, my lady, I can't permit you to ride a mettlesome creature down that road. It would be too dangerous."

"Blaise, that's ridiculous! Do you think I can't control my own horse? I was riding before I could walk." *Well, almost.*

"Nevertheless, my lady..."

"Then we will lead the horses down. Or you can ride and lead Merissa, and I will walk behind."

"Not behind, my lady. Not in my dust. Ahead, where I can see you safe."

VERY PLEASED WITH herself, she'd been. She wanted nothing in the world more than she wanted an hour's hard riding outside these prisoning walls, but she was frankly scared of the long drop that lay between her and that ride. Only she hadn't felt able to admit it; so she'd let Blaise's fears for her, his anxious responsibility take on that difficult task on her behalf. Perfect. She would walk—and enjoy that also, her feet were as fretful as her mind—and then at the bottom of the climb she could have speed and wind and freedom for a while.

But Elisande had been listening, and she'd wanted to come too.

"You have no horse. My lady." He always seemed to have difficulty with the honorific, as though he trusted Elisande not at all, and no blame to him for that.

"No matter. I would enjoy the walk; and I can sit on a rock and watch you, while you ride."

THE AFTERNOON WAS hot as always, though a haze of thin cloud hid the sun that day. Julianne had begged a lump of sugar from the stablemaster, to pamper Merissa with; then Blaise had mounted, hitched the palfrey's reins to his saddlebow and followed the strolling girls down the covered ramp and the steps that followed, to the gate and the road beyond.

In places, the road was steep even for feet. Julianne had found hers wanting to scurry, to carry her down at a run. She'd gripped Elisande's arm to restrain them, and discovered that to be no help at all. The shorter girl was skipping beneath her skirts, and beaming broadly.

"This is better! Even the air broods, behind those walls. And no one laughs, have you noticed? Even the knights don't laugh. Not around us, at any rate, and the brothers can't find a smile. No wonder they wear black, their souls are in mourning. It makes my bones ache, living in that shadow."

You were the one of us who actually chose to come here, Julianne had thought but not said.

Down to the first corner then, Julianne taking care to stay on the rock side, on the wall side, not to be near the fall. Behind them the steady clopping of Blaise's horse, the lighter skitter of Merissa's hooves—and then a whicker, and the sergeant's voice cursing loudly, heedless of his company.

They'd both turned to see him fighting, tugging at Merissa's reins while she reared and danced at his back, pulling so hard she might overbalance all three. Julianne had gasped; Elisande had gasped and then run.

Had run back, squeezing between the rock wall and Blaise's unhappy, snorting mount; had run to Merissa and seized hold of her saddle. Had pulled herself up awkwardly, hampered by her skirts and the palfrey's shying; then had lunged forward to grab the ornate bridle, hugged herself to the horse's sweating neck and murmured urgently into the nearest ear, all the time tugging the tossing head downward, turning it away from the drop.

It had seemed to take only a moment, though it must have been longer. Soon, though, Merissa had stood quietly under Elisande's hands and voice.

"Loose the reins, sergeant," Julianne had heard that clear voice call. "She needs someone on her back, that's all, she's nervous without."

Blaise had huffed to himself, looked back, glanced forward at Julianne like a man betrayed—*she will allow no one but me on her back,* she remembered, and blushed for the lie exposed—and then had deliberately undone the reins and let Elisande draw them into her hands.

A ND SO THEY had gone on down the road, Julianne walking alone and bitterly humiliated, with one hand brushing the rock for surety and extra shame while her sergeant and her friend rode behind.

At the foot of the climb Elisande had slipped down without a word, holding Merissa's head for Julianne to mount from a convenient boulder and then, smiling up with no sign of smugness, had perched herself on that same boulder: a gesture, *go on, ride, don't worry about me.*

J ULIANNE WAS RIDING still, cantering hard across the dry and dusty plain, aware of Blaise behind her but not looking back, never wanting to see his face again. Nor Elisande's. She was playing the child, she knew; but there was no stomach in her to resist it, unless and until the wind of her passage should blow this sulky resentment out of her head.

She closed her eyes against the dust and sting, trusting her horse to bear her safely—and nearly she lost all trust, all faith and her seat also, all dignity and maybe even her life as well.

Merissa didn't falter, she didn't check or turn or shy aside; she stopped. Stopped suddenly, stopped dead in her tracks. Her hindquarters dropped as she dug her hooves into the ground; Julianne slammed forward against the arched neck, toppled and slid, lost her stirrup, snatched frantically at the long mane and only just caught herself in time. She struggled back into the saddle, trembling; found Merissa trembling also beneath her, and looked past the tossing head to see a whirl of dust and sand hanging in the air before them, and just beyond it a gulf opened up in the plain, only a pace, a running horse's stride ahead.

NO, NOT A gulf, and not newly opened. She looked again, and it was a river bed baked dry under the summer's sun, a fall of perhaps twice her own height before she would have hit the cracked mud and stones at the bottom. Not a gulf, but enough, perhaps. Enough to have broken bones for sure, and possibly every bone they had between them, herself and Merissa both.

A whirl of dust and sand—her eyes jerked back from the drop and saw only a sift of dust and sand falling. She barely had time to think, to wonder *djinni?* before there was another horse drawing up beside her; she stared neutrally ahead, not to see Blaise's anger.

She felt him reach over to Merissa's bridle, felt him seize the reins and draw them from her slack fingers.

"My lady..." His voice was tight with fury, and rightly so; like a child, she awaited her scolding. But, "My lady, we will return to the castle now," was all he said, perhaps all that he could trust himself to say.

She nodded a mute acquiescence; he tugged Merissa's head around and led back the way they had come, at a slow walk. Humiliation again, but Julianne deserved this. And Merissa needed it. There was still a constant shake beneath her skin, she needed calm and cooling to settle her, to help her forget that moment's terror. Terror of the fall or terror of the djinni, either one.

With nothing to do but sit the horse and feel the shame, Julianne turned her head away from the sergeant's stiff back and gazed around her, as she had not before. The land was brown and barren, growing only thorns. Thorns and dust—she saw a dust-devil and her heart skittered against her ribs, once more she thought *djinni* for a moment before she blinked and stared and saw a shadow within the dust, a horseman coming fast.

Blaise had seen him too. He reined in, gestured to her to be still; his hand went to his sword.

One good thing, he wouldn't want another horse tied to his, if it should come to fighting. He let Merissa's reins drop; Julianne reached forward to retrieve them. She could flee if she had to, if there was cause. If not—and likely not, surely, this close below the castle—at least she could meet this urgent newcomer with her own horse under her own command.

He was slowing now, the man who rode towards them, kicking up less dust: a young man, she saw, on a massive destrier. He wore white, though a black cloak flowed behind him. One of the knights from the Roq; she released a breath she hadn't realised she was holding.

Blaise had relaxed too, at least to the point of taking his hand away from his weapon.

"Hullo!" the knight called. "Is all well with you? I saw the lady riding hard, with someone in pursuit, it seemed; and I knew of the river, and thought perhaps she did not?"

"I thank you for your care, sieur," Julianne said briskly, taking control of more than Merissa. She was pleased to find her voice quite steady. "We were exercising the horses, that is all. Merissa likes to run." But that was not quite all; he cocked an eyebrow, and she felt herself obliged to confess. "You are right, though, I did not know about the river. It's quite hidden, in this drab ground. Luckily, Merissa's eyes are sharp." *Mine were closed,* but she was not going to confess that.

"Indeed. I've never seen a horse halt so suddenly. She's taken no hurt, I hope?"

"None, I thank you, sieur." Except to her nerve, perhaps, but this was not the time to test it. Neither Julianne's.

"That's good. Are you riding back to the castle now?"

"We are, sieur," Blaise, grimly.

"You'll permit me to accompany you, I hope."

"Please." She'd be grateful for his company.

"Thank you. Ah, your veil has come adrift, my lady..."

He was laughing at her, she thought, this young knight. She scowled, swallowed her tongue in preference to thrusting it at him—*not childish, not again*—and reached to draw her dusty and disarrayed veil across her face.

"Too late for discretion, I fear," she said, as lightly as she could manage.

"My lady, I shall breathe not a word." He bowed low in the saddle, and yes, he was definitely mocking her now. "But as I know so much of you already—I know your beauty, and your horse's name, and that you like to ride faster than caution would decree—may I not know your name also?"

"I am called Julianne de Rance. And you, sieur?"

"Anton d'Escrivey. A sworn knight of the Society of Ransom. But I have heard the name of your father, I think, my lady de Rance?"

"And I yours, perhaps." The Earl d'Escrivey was vassal to the Duke of Ascariel, and held a large estate within that dukedom. So far as she knew, he was childless; the heir-presumptive was a brother. This might be a nephew or a young cousin, though, or else an acknowledged bastard.

"Indeed?" His face was neutral suddenly, a mask; very likely the bastard then, she thought. Sent away to the Ransomers, perhaps, for discretion's sake, with no more than the name to look for from his father. "Well. If we ride a little to the west, I left my other horse there, and my, ah, my squire. But here they come now, I think..."

There was another, lesser cloud of dust approaching, that resolved itself soon into a horse and its rider. Julianne's eyebrows twitched; the horse was another great destrier, but that was no squire on its back. It was a young brother of the Order, barely more than a boy by the look of him, and he was in serious difficulty.

"One moment, my lady, if you will forgive me."

D'Escrivey turned his horse and went to meet the lad. His voice carried back to Julianne's straining ears, with a bubble of cool amusement in it. "Marron, the art of couching a lance for battle is very different from the art of conveying a lance home. And no one, no one at all has ever successfully couched two at once, however great an advantage there might be for the knight who first achieved it. Take them further under the arm and grip them so, here, where they will balance. Good. Now follow; and as I told you, be firm with Alembert. He will be wilful, if he thinks you weak."

The lesson learned to the knight's satisfaction, he trotted back to Julianne's side.

"You have an original esquire, Sieur Anton."

"He is unique," said solemnly. "I came close to killing him a few days since, and now he dotes on me."

Julianne wasn't sure that she believed either part of that; but the young brother was close enough to overhear any challenge, so she held her tongue.

S HE FELT SOMEWHAT surprised to find Elisande exactly where they had left her. Now, though, the other girl was standing on the boulder, staring up the slope. There was a party on the climb ahead, above, perhaps halfway to the summit: mounted men Julianne could see, and some on foot also, with what seemed to be a small wagon in their midst.

Elisande turned at their arrival and made a vague bow towards the strangers in the company, then remembered her skirts and made a worse curtsey. It was obvious, though, that her interest was elsewhere. Her eyes were already shifting back to find the group on the hill.

Behind Julianne's shoulder, d'Escrivey laughed lightly. "The wind does play havoc with a lady's veil today, does it not?"

Elisande grunted, and wrenched her veil somewhat across her face.

"Who are those people?" Julianne asked, forgoing the introduction that she should properly have made. She didn't want the insinuating Anton d'Escrivey wondering if perhaps he knew Elisande's father also.

"A baron from the south, with his retinue. They have— they *say* they have a man with them, a prisoner. In a barrel." Her face twisted, and Julianne thought there was something more, that she was not saying. "They certainly have a barrel. A wine-tun by its size, sealed and roped to a wheeled platform. Which they have dragged twenty miles, up and down, along this road."

"To what end?" d'Escrivey demanded, smiling once more.

"To bring their prisoner before the king's justice, they said."

"The king is in Ascariel."

"But the King's Eye is here, they said."

Behind her, Julianne just caught an insuck of breath from the brother-squire boy, Marron.

"The King's Eye is everywhere," d'Escrivey observed blandly, "and it is the duty of any noble, even a petty baron, to dispense his justice. In his, ah, absence. Who is the prisoner?"

"They gave me no name," Elisande said slowly. "Only, they told me he was, was Surayonish."

"Surayonnaise, for preference." But that was a murmur, and the last for now of his wit. D'Escrivey stared bleakly up the scarp at the distant figures, marked more by their sharp black shadows than themselves. "I hope it's true."

"Why so?"

She was answered with a shrug. "He will be tortured in any case; the accusation is enough. The more he denies it, the less he will be believed. At the last, I daresay he will be executed. Why suffer and die for a falsehood, what martyrdom in that?"

It sounded reasonable, for so cool a soul; but once more Julianne did not believe, and this time she had a reason. She had recognised him now, finally. He was the man from the gallery, from her first evening in the castle: the man who had listened so avidly to Marshal Fulke that he had uncovered his own head in the God's presence, as a gesture of an oath unspoken, a bond, a commitment. She thought that he really did hope to open that barrel and find a Surayonnaise within.

MERISSA SHIFTED BENEATH her, bringing her mind back to a more immediate shadow in her life. Elisande made a sign to her that said, *get down, if you like, I'll ride her up.* Julianne was tempted; but pride could override fear, that was an early lesson from her father, and oh, she was too proud to confess such a weakness in this company.

"Can your—squire take Elisande on his mount?" she asked d'Escrivey instead.

132

"If he's not too fearful of woman's flesh." The knight seemed quickly to have recovered his biting humour. "And if he doesn't lose hold of those lances. Marron?"

"Yes, sieur. I can manage."

"Then do so."

D'Escrivey gestured Blaise to ride on and followed immediately after, not bothering to watch. Julianne was less insouciant or more curious; she saw Elisande's slightly graceless scramble up the big horse's flank, Marron's blush as they tried to adjust two slender bodies to one heavy saddle, Elisande's grab that only just saved the lances from clattering to earth. But the knight was getting too far ahead, and Julianne wanted that man's company; she kicked Merissa on at a trot.

The road was already steepening beneath them. D'Escrivey courteously made room for her on the inside, between himself and the rock; she'd been depending on that. Iron manners, the lords of Outremer had, and hammered them into their children.

Iron manners and a wicked tongue in this one. "Does your horse dislike the drop, my lady?"

He must have seen the relief on her own face and not Merissa's as they came into the somewhat shelter of his body, the greater shelter of his horse. "She does," and that was nothing but true, that was how this afternoon's humiliation had begun. "I think yours will reassure her, though. And having me on her back, that too."

AND SO IT seemed; Merissa at least was calm enough as the road climbed and turned, climbed and turned again.

It was Julianne who was anxious, who felt a chill sweat on her skin at every corner, where try as she might she couldn't help but see the ground so far below them and nothing to clutch at, only the endless fall just a step, a breath, a moment away.

At last her nervousness seemed to reach down and touch her horse; Merissa snorted, sidled, balked suddenly at an outcrop jutting from the rock.

"Lady Julianne," and d'Escrivey's voice was soft and serious, entirely bereft of humour at her expense or any, "I think perhaps Merissa would be more settled if I took the reins and led her, by your consent? She would still have you on her back, for reassurance." The pure diplomat Julianne thought him, just for a moment; until he added, "If you were to close your eyes, she wouldn't know."

And neither would Blaise ahead of them, a turn ahead; neither Elisande, mounted with the clumsy brother at least a turn behind.

S O FOR THE second time that day, Julianne agreed to have her horse led beneath her; and for the second time she rode with her eyes screwed shut.

A murmured word from d'Escrivey warned her of the approaching gate. She took back the reins, and rode collectedly through and on up to the stables. There she gave Merissa over to a boy's care, and stood with d'Escrivey and Blaise as the two laggards of their party came into the yard. Marron, she saw, was blushing still.

Once they'd dismounted, the lad glanced at d'Escrivey, she thought for permission to leave; the knight delayed him, with a casual gesture of his fingers.

"Marron, can you attend me after supper? If I ask it?"

"Yes, sieur." And there was almost a pleading in his voice, she thought, some reason he'd be glad to.

"Good. Then make it so. My lady Julianne, will you permit me to call on you this evening, in your chamber? Between

your companion and my holy squire, I think we have chap-
erones enough."

"Sieur Anton, thank you. I should be delighted." The
evenings hung heaviest; it was a long time, often, between
nightfall and sleep.

"Excellent. Marron shall bring me to you, then, after the
supper hour. Until then, Lady Julianne, Lady Elisande."

A flourish and he was gone, with Marron following a
little flustered, a little uncertain, glancing back to make an
ungainly farewell himself.

Elisande chuckled, but Julianne was quiet and thoughtful
all the way back to their room in the guests' tower.

WHY A BARREL?
That was the question that occupied them most
through the hour before evening prayers and the hour afterwards, when they ate quietly together in their room. There
was something laughable and sinister both, about a man in
a barrel. They did laugh, but uncomfortably; and Julianne
didn't need d'Escrivey's prediction of torture and inevitable
death to sober her.

"The boys in Marasson," she said slowly, "they have a
game where they will take a dog from the streets, and put it
in a barrel. Then they roll the barrel through the city. When
they get tired, they put it in the river, and gamble on how far
it will float through the falls. They call this game Shaming
the Emperor's Brother."

"Do they?"

"Historically, brothers are notorious. The Imperial throne
is no safe place to sit, if you have a brother. The current
Emperor had three, when he ascended the throne; now he
has one."

"Are the rest in his cellar, then, does he keep them in barrels?"

"One was poisoned and one died making war, though he was probably not killed by the enemy. But the children's game is older. It is said when the Emperor's great-great-uncle sat the throne, *he* used to have his family put into barrels and rolled through the streets of the city, to keep them submissive. It is also said that his favourite method of execution was to put a man in a barrel and send him down the river to the falls. With all his family floating in line behind him, like as not. I never spoke to anyone old enough to remember if it was true."

"The children remember," Elisande said, "in their games. Believe it. But there's no river here, or none with water in it. Do you think they'll just roll him off the walls?"

"No, I'm being foolish. Of course they'll take him out of the barrel, they must have done it as soon as he arrived. But why put him in it, then? Why not just put chains on the man and let him walk at your horse's heels?"

"I think because it's like a dungeon they can move. It's safe, they have him penned, he can't escape; and also it's dark, it's cramped, I'm sorry but it must stink in there by now. That's punishment, Julianne, as much as the baron dares. He brings the man to face the king's justice, to be sure; but he administers a little of his own along the way, he makes him suffer. Just because he can."

"Yes. Perhaps. Could the man stand up, in the barrel?"

"Not if he's as tall as I am," said Elisande, who was not tall at all.

"How do you suppose they gave him food and water?"

"Through the bunghole, if at all. But a journey of twenty miles? I don't suppose they did. Even if they took two days over it. He's from Surayon, Julianne. Or they think he is."

136

Heretic, blasphemer—of course they wouldn't feed him. He might have been in the barrel a week before they took to the road, and they might not have fed him at all. Twenty slow miles in a barrel under an unrelenting sun, and no food, no water—and she'd been laughing? No longer. Julianne had more than one reason to be grateful when there were footsteps and voices, no, one voice rising on the stairway outside, and then the soft sound of a finger scratching at the curtain that overhung their doorway.

She made a hasty sign to Elisande, and they fumbled with their hated veils. Then, "Yes, come."

There was a moment's hesitation beyond the curtain, sounds of shuffling and confusion; then a short barking laugh that held more impatience than humour in it, and his voice again, "No, Marron, *you* take the curtain, and you hold it back for *me*. You see?"

"Yes, sieur."

The hanging was pulled back and the knight came in, ducking beneath the lintel. Behind him, Marron had a blazing flambeau in one hand, the curtain gathered in the other; Julianne could see him twisting his head almost frantically from side to side, but couldn't see why until he shrugged and stooped to grind his brand out in the angle between floor and wall, with a shower of sparks.

The curtain slipped from his grip and fell down to mask his antics. Julianne perforce turned her eyes to his master, but still kept an ear cocked towards the doorway. Whatever they used here in the Roq to give a head to their flambeaux, it was potent but obviously friable; some of those sparks had been live coals, not dying cinders. She could hear scuffing sounds, and pictured Marron stamping urgently on the glows in rope-soled sandals; she heard a yelp, and grinned pitilessly.

The veil should hide the grin, but alas, she hadn't heard a word of the florid greeting with which d'Escrivey had been gracing her. And alas, the veil had not hidden that from him. With a malicious smile of his own, he called out, "Marron, leave that heathen dancing and come inside."

The curtain twitched, and Marron sidled through. Blushing again, she saw. He hesitated at the carpet's edge, and shuffled his feet oddly; when he stepped forward, his sandals remained behind.

D'Escrivey made a soft sound of amusement in his throat, and gazed around at the room's furnishings. "It wants a little elegance, perhaps, compared with what you must be used to, my lady. I hope you feel comfortable here?"

"Perfectly, thank you." She sat down on her bed to prove it, and gestured him towards the settle opposite. He ignored that, choosing to stroll over to the window, and talking all the way.

"Good, good. The Order is careful of its guests. We knights must supply our own poor comforts, while the brothers are actively forbidden any comfort—is that not so, Marron?"

"Yes, sieur."

"Yes. I took the liberty, my lady, of fetching a little wine with me, for fear that the Order's care did not run quite so far."

It was Marron, of course, who had actually carried the wine. He slipped a scrip awkwardly from his shoulder and delved inside, producing a flask and goblets that gleamed silver in the candlelight. He broke the seal on the wine and poured, brought a goblet to her and blushed once more as their fingers touched. At least his eyes had met hers directly, though, just for a moment. He wasn't one of those who held females in contempt, she thought, only a boy on the threshold of manhood who had probably had little to do with women since he left his mother's teats. They ordered these things differently—better, she thought—in Marasson.

Marron served Elisande, and d'Escrivey; then he returned to the cold hearth where he had left his scrip. He knelt there and folded his hands passively in his lap.

"And the fourth, Marron," d'Escrivey said quietly.

The young brother lifted his eyes, gazed at the knight and said, "Sieur, I think wine is a comfort."

"You are not required to think, lad. That's why you take the vow of obedience, to keep you from the need of it. Pour yourself some wine, and drink it. Oh, and I absolutely forbid you to mention it to your confessor, do you understand me?"

"Yes, sieur."

D'Escrivey nodded and turned back to the window, folding back a leaf of the screen to see out more clearly.

"Won't you sit down, Sieur Anton?" Julianne insisted.

"In a moment, my lady. I just wanted to see—Ah, yes. There it is."

Almost, she stood up to go and see what so intrigued him; it was an effort to stay where she was, but she made it determinedly. He was teasing again, and she refused to satisfy him.

Elisande, it seemed, had no such inhibitions. "There is what, Sieur Anton?"

"A fire, in the stable yard. I had heard, but I wanted to be sure." Anything, it seemed, might amuse this man, but this time his voice was cold, and the smile she heard could be nothing but contemptuous.

"What are they burning?" Elisande asked.

"The barrel you saw on the road, my lady. The cautious baron has ordered its destruction, for fear of its being contaminated. I thought perhaps they might keep it to fuel a later fire, assuming that the prisoner burns, but the baron wanted this done in haste. The stablemaster may have felt the same; I imagine it cannot have smelled too sweetly."

"Sieur Anton—why a barrel? It seems so, so foolish a way to transport a man."

"The baron is a cautious man," he said again, showing her that smile now, that had no hint of generosity in it. "And a man from Surayon is necessarily a sorcerer. He feared spell-casting on the road, I suppose, a summoning of demons to rescue their benighted brother; so he had the man sealed in a barrel to deny him light and air and earth and fire, which, as is well known, are all essential to the making of a spell."

"That is... ridiculous."

"Indeed. You have had the pleasure not to meet the baron; I was less lucky. He is a ridiculous man."

"What is more ridiculous," Elisande said, from where she sat decorously on her own bed, "is the accusation that this prisoner comes from Surayon at all. That land has been closed for thirty years; why would a man leave it now? And how can they tell his country, in any case? Is it branded on his skin?"

"There have always been rumours that some men come and go from Surayon. Inevitably, therefore, there have always been an unlucky few wanderers accused and questioned, and I never heard that any were found to be innocent. Confession and death must seem easier in the end, I suppose. When the question is unrelenting."

Julianne shivered. She had seen exotic deaths in Marasson, they were almost a commonplace in that exotic city; and of course she had always known of the Emperor's inquisitors and their work, invisible but not secret, spoken of in speculative whispers. Indeed she had met some of those men at court, had touched their hands in politeness and been amazed that their skin was not chilled by their duties, that they carried no reek of the dungeons on them.

D'Escrivey noticed her shudder, and smiled. He had been merciful on the hill, but not here, not in company. "My answers upset you, my lady. I'm sorry."

"No. You tell the truth, and I am grateful for it. It's the thought of innocents suffering that upsets me."

"It is always the innocents who suffer," he replied bleakly. His expression turned inward for a moment; then he shook his head and offered her a brighter smile. "How long do you expect to remain with us, Lady Julianne?"

"I can't say. My father sent a messenger to Elessi; no doubt an escort will be on its way shortly, if it has not set out already."

"No doubt. If the messenger arrived safely. There is dangerous ground between here and Elessi."

That she knew. Sometimes she caught herself hoping that the message had miscarried, if only to grant her a few days' more grace, even in this dull castle. She was not eager to meet her future husband. But, "The preceptor has also sent messages, by a man and a bird, for surety." The preceptor had called on them here, their first morning in the Roq. A kindly man he seemed, with gentle manners and a beautiful voice; she had had to remind herself forcefully that he was master of this stony place and all its men, and that no man given guard and command of the kingdom's northern border could truly be so sweet-natured as she had thought him.

"That is as well, I think. But even so, a bird might meet a hawk and a good man on a good horse will take some days from here; a squad would take longer to return. We have you for a while at least, my lady. Has anyone given thought to your entertainment?"

"Oh, I need none," said lightly, against her stifled heart. "I have Elisande for company, and all the castle to explore," though that was a lie pure and simple. Elisande might explore, and did; Julianne felt the weight of her reputation, and stayed within. She wanted no taint of gossip for Blaise or his men to carry back to their country, that must be hers also. "So long as I can ride sometimes, and meet congenial company occasionally," with a little bow in his direction, a feather's-weight of mockery to set against his, though actually she meant it, "I shall be quite content. Certainly you and your confrères must not trouble about me, you must have burdens enough."

"My lady Julianne, you are no burden." *Not even when you gallop near to destruction on the plain, or tremble with terror on the climb home,* his eyes taunted, outscoring her a hundredfold, a thousand. "I would take you hawking or hunting to ease the time, but alas, it is not only the brothers who take grievous oaths. Such sports are forbidden us, so long as we wear the black. Marron, I think the ladies' goblets are empty; I know mine is."

"Your pardon, sieur. My lady, ladies..."

He hurried around with the flask, not staying to see her sympathetic smile. She thanked the back of his head regardless, and sipped. It was good wine, red and warm and spicy; certainly a reason to cultivate d'Escrivey if he had given her no other, so long as he had access to more of this.

"And yours also, Marron."

The briefest of pauses, then, "Yes, sieur," and the sounds of pouring. Julianne didn't turn her head. His face would flush to match the wine, if he felt her gaze on him.

"Sieur Anton," Elisande demanded, "are you truthfully telling us that the Knights Ransomers do not *hunt*?"

"No, my lady. I am truthfully telling you that we are forbidden to do so. Many of my confrères hunt regardless; I choose not to imitate them."

Yes. He was a man who would take his vows seriously. Julianne wondered for how long he had sworn his sword to the Order; and then—*sorry, Father*—forwent all her training, and asked him directly.

"For the period of my life, lady," he replied just as directly, and his face was set and bitter for a moment. "Or until my superiors dismiss me, or my king summon me. For no less cause will I leave the Order."

At her back she could hear Marron choke as he swallowed down a question, and then choke again as he chased it with a gulp of wine. All right, he didn't dare to ask, but she did. Her mood was fey suddenly, or d'Escrivey's honesty provoked her own, or else his mystery her curiosity. "Then, if your commitment is so great, why do you not take the habit and serve as a brother, be truly a part of the Order?" *And rise as you surely would, be a master, a preceptor, marshal, Grand Master at last?*

He laughed, briefly. "My lady, I am a trained knight of the kingdom. My father set me on horseback before I could walk; I have had a mail shirt made to my measure since I was old enough to carry the weight of it; all my swords have had a noble lineage and a name. Saving your presence, Marron, the brothers are a peasant army, farmers and artisans. I will willingly fight with them, but I cannot fight as one of them."

He was trying to make himself out a proud man, disdain-ful, protective of his family's honour. Once again, she did not believe him.

To her surprise and visibly to his, the voice that chal-lenged him came from behind her. "We are the God's soldiers, sieur. Not noble-born, no, though some of us too have families that deserve your respect. But we are the finest soldiers in the kingdom, because we fight for the God alone."

"And you think that I do not?" The question—if it was a question—snapped back, cold and furious. This time Julianne did turn her head, in time to see Marron flinch. But d'Escrivey crushed his temper in a moment; his voice was

143

soft and teasing and familiar as he went on, "The Brothers Ransomers are the most feared army in Outremer, it's true. But you fight in your habits, Marron, because the God protects you. I prefer mail for protection, I am so much weaker in faith."

"No, sieur." Another surprise, that flat contradiction; Julianne wanted to read the expressions on both their faces, and so saw neither properly.

"Well. Let us not fight about it. It's demeaning, to argue with one's squire. Remind me to beat you later, for contradicting me in front of these ladies."

"Yes, sieur," but Marron said it smiling. Julianne thought that probably the reminder would be given, but the beating surely not. Oh, he was complex, this d'Escrivey, his moods and his mind were quicksilver; and his brother-squire Marron was only one aspect of his complexity, one small thread in the tangle that she was finding so hard to unravel.

ENOUGH OF TRYING, at least for tonight. Here was a girl with wit and charm and mystery, in Elisande; in d'Escrivey here was a man with wit and charm and mystery and wine, and what more could she need or want?

The wine, she thought, might be having some small effect on her mood. It was very good wine, they were drinking it unwatered, and a second flask had followed the first out of Marron's scrip. Even so, she hadn't taken anywhere near enough to make her foolish or muzzy-headed. Any girl growing up even on the fringes of the Imperial court learned early to hold her alcohol well, or else to abstain from it.

She didn't know where Elisande had grown up, but that girl also showed no signs of flagging. As for d'Escrivey—well, it was his wine, after all. And it had always been considered a young nobleman's duty to drink his peers into unconsciousness if he possibly could; it was an art they practised much.

D'Escrivey, she thought, could go on like this all night and still be smiling in the morning. Laughing, indeed. Elisande had said that even the knights didn't laugh; here was one who disproved her. Julianne even thought that once or twice this evening she'd heard him laugh from pure merriment, with no other message in it.

What she had forgotten was that they were not the three of them alone. She was so used to being waited on, to having servants watch her every move against a summons—*though not on this journey*, a slightly bitter memory, a problem not resolved—she'd forgotten that d'Escrivey had made Marron more than a servant tonight. And sitting where she was, with her back to the hearth, she saw him only when he came around to replenish her drink and the others'; and if she thought about him at all, what with the wine and the talk and the laughter, she thought that was all that he did, that he watched and served and waited to serve again.

Until she heard him snoring.

Startled, she betrayed him completely, twisting her head to gape. He was still on his knees but slumped now, head and shoulder resting against the wall and his mouth hanging a little open. It hadn't been a loud snore, exactly, but here was another; and if the other two hadn't heard the first, they certainly heard the second.

Elisande snorted. Just for a moment d'Escrivey looked abashed, embarrassed either by his squire's gaucherie or else by his own, for having attached such a gauche boy to his service.

He recovered quickly, though, rising and making a bow so low and decorated that his sleeve was in danger of brushing the carpet.

"Ladies, my regrets. My squire reminds me, I have stayed too long."

"Not at all, Sieur Anton. He has no head for wine, that's all."

"Ah, but I was using him as my timekeeper, his snores my signal. I am inclined to overrun at the mouth, when the company is congenial; I had hopes that he might prove convenient in this way. If you will excuse me," as Marron snored again, "I believe he is getting louder. I will remove him."

He tried a boot, a gentle nudge to the ribs. Marron only stirred, muttered and subsided, snored again. D'Escrivey sighed, stooped and slipped an arm around the boy's shoulders, another beneath his knees. And rose, lifting him smoothly and easily, where Julianne had expected no more than a sharper kick or two.

Marron stirred a little against d'Escrivey's chest, and the left sleeve of his habit fell back to his elbow. Julianne frowned. "What's that? On his arm?"

D'Escrivey glanced down. "Oh. That's where I nearly killed him. He was lucky to come away with so little harm. Fast, and fast-thinking, but lucky also." Then he frowned slightly. "It seems to have been bleeding again."

"That dressing is overdue a change," Elisande said, reaching to pick at a crusted stain on the bandages. She bent closer to sniff, and an odd expression passed across her face before she added, "There's no corruption, though. I think it's healing clean."

"Even so," Julianne said, pitching her voice low as Marron was astonishingly still sleeping, and he really couldn't have a head for wine, "someone should look at that wound, Sieur Anton."

"Someone will, my lady, I assure you. But not I think tonight, and certainly not you, if you were thinking of it. He would die of shame."

Of blushing, perhaps, if that were fatal.

146

"Better us than a horse-doctor," Elisande suggested, quite forcefully.

"Perhaps; but better Master Infirmarer than either one, I think. I will send him in the morning." He turned towards the curtained doorway then, but checked, glanced back at Julianne and said, "I have been wanting to ask this all evening, but could not find a way to frame it without seeming offensive to your father's care of you. This gives me an opportunity. I might perhaps have handed Marron to your women tonight to be washed and bandaged afresh, if there had seemed an urgent need; but I am told you have no women to attend you?"

"No." Except for Elisande, who didn't count.

"May I ask why? It seems curious, that a high-born lady should travel to her wedding with only men to serve her."

"Sieur Anton, in Marasson I had companions to attend me who were also my friends; I had servants; I had slaves. I could not ask my friends to come to a country such as Elessi. I would not order my slaves to come; and when I asked my servants, none of them chose to do so." Nor could she blame them for it. She'd been relieved, mostly, not to have that guilt to bear atop her other burdens.

"Ah. Yes, I see. That is—admirable, Lady Julianne, though I have hopes that you will find Elessi less of a cage than you fear. May I suggest, however, that you not say that to others, or not quite so bluntly? The Elessans are a more sensitive people than they may appear."

"And they expect their women to be silent but grateful? Thank you, Sieur Anton, I am aware of that. You I can trust, I think, but I have been more careful elsewhere."

D'Escrivey nodded, bade them both goodnight and turned again towards the doorway. Elisande drew the curtain aside, and peered a little uncertainly down the stairs.

"Sieur Anton, I could carry a candle for you, if you wished it. The brothers leave few lights burning after dark."

"Lady, the brothers leave no lights burning, except outside your door. But there is no need for you to stir yourself. I have the eyes of a hawk."

Elisande's eyebrows twitched, but she said no more. Julianne joined her in the doorway, to watch while d'Escrivey felt his way cautiously down and out of sight. They both heard his sudden curse a few moments later, and both guessed its cause; there was a raised step from the tower into the court outside, which his eyes had clearly missed.

"Sieur Anton," Elisande called down, soft and mischievous, "hawks cannot see in the dark."

His voice came back to them, echoing oddly in the stairwell. "Thank you, I *know* that..."

STILL CHUCKLING, ELISANDE let the curtain fall and walked over to the hearth.

"He left the wine, Julianne." She stooped to pick up the flask, and shook it gently; there was a suggestive gurgle.

Julianne nodded. No doubt they should go to bed, but there couldn't be much left. Pity to let it spoil.

With her goblet replenished, she returned to sit on her bed. Elisande drifted to the window, twisting her neck to gaze upward at the stars."I wish I could come with you, when you leave," she said slowly.

"No." There might have been an opportunity there to ask why it was impossible, to try once more to learn why Elisande had come to the Roq; but Julianne would not prevaricate. Not in this. "I will not take a friend into that seclusion. You would hate it, Elisande, more than I will."

"Yes, but I should be there none the less. You will need me."

"For what?"

"For when the djinni comes. You know nothing of them."

Julianne sighed, sipped, said, "Elisande, the djinni will not come. Why should it? How can I serve a creature such as that? Even if I acknowledged the debt, which I find ridiculous?"

Elisande had no answer, only, "It will come." And, again, "You know nothing."

« ¤ »

JEMEL HAD BLOOD on his robes and grease on his fingers, meat in his belly and a guest at his fire; and not only Jazra's eyes to see what honour was paid to him this night, though Jazra's were of course the only eyes that counted. Still, from where he sat he could see the soft red glows of other fires, the shadows of men moving around them; and every one of those men he knew could see who else had come to eat of his kill, to speak with him and with Jazra.

THE BLOOD WAS a boy's, a child's. Hunting in the last of the light, hunting hares for their own fire before the night's march, they'd surprised a flock of half a dozen goats, strayed too far in search of grazing. Easy work for their ready bows; they'd made a game of it—and Jemel had been winning, three to two—when the boy had come stumbling from behind a rock, rubbing sleep from his eyes and staring, sobbing.

Staring, sobbing and then running, but not back behind his sheltering rock, neither towards his fallen charges. Running towards their slaughterers he'd come, and pulling a clumsy knife from his belt as he ran.

There could have been an arrow for him too, and Jemel the victor in the game. That knife was brave, though, and deserved a better answer. He'd dropped his bow and pulled his own knife, leaving the last of the goats to Jazra. He'd slipped past the boy's wavering blade, gripped the tear-wet chin and drawn his edge swiftly across the exposed throat; and only then had he seen the thong around the child's neck, the blue bead that hung from it, bespeaking his faith and his allegiance.

Well, too late, and it could have made no difference in any case. The boy had seen them, might have seen others, would certainly have carried the tale back to his village. His death had been needful, and as swift as Jemel could have made it.

Even so, they had taken time to build a rough cairn above his body to keep the foxes off, and had said the *khalat* for his spirit's sake; then they'd carried a goat each back to where their tribe was camped, and told them where to find the rest.

THEY HAD NOT meant to share that meat with others. Each tribe foraged for itself now, and rode apart, not to leave too obvious a sign of many men's passing. But a guest at the fire must be fed, welcome or otherwise; and where Hasan rode, where he walked, where he sat he was always welcome. If he chose to sit this night at Jemel's fire, to eat of his kill, he was more than welcome. He shed honour as a flame sheds light, and all men marked him.

He leaned forward to cut at the blistered, blackened meat, and his face was lit by the fire's glow. Shaven cheeks, a sharp hooked nose above a neat beard, white teeth and glittering, hooded eyes: Jemel wondered what it was about this man, what power he carried in his voice that could make so many listen and believe, and ride together to follow him against all custom.

Hasan chewed and swallowed, asked what was proper of Jazra's family and Jemel's, spoke of Rhabat and of the desert; and at last he tossed a bone through the dull cloak of ashes to send up a shower of sparks from the fire's heart and said, "I need men. A few men, a small party to lead the attack and open the way for the rest. I do not wish to favour one tribe above the others; will you two come with me, for the Saren?"

Jemel caught his breath; it was Jazra who said, "You do us too much honour, Hasan. There are older men at every fire here, wiser in their thoughts and with their swords."

"There are; but I do not need age, or wisdom. I need men not afraid to climb in the dark. I have spoken with your elders, and they say you two are goats with owls' eyes, vicious as foxes. Will you come?"

It was true, they had been children in caves on a high cliff's face, scorning the long slow paths where hands and bare feet could scramble directly, up or down in sun or star-light.

"Oh, yes," Jemel said softly. "Yes, Hasan, we will come."

SEVEN

What They Carried

A HARD HAND gripping his shoulder, a dizzy exhaustion in his head: Marron struggled against both, mumbled something unclear even to himself around a tongue too thick to shape words, gave it up willingly and rolled back towards the insistent suck of sleep—

—and hit his nose sharply on stone. Stinging pain jerked his eyes open; he found himself trying to outstare a wall. What wall, he couldn't think.

The hand was back on his shoulder, shaking him vigorously. There was a voice too, a voice he knew. "Marron, wake. Wake *now*, it's midnight. Can't you hear the bell?"

Hear it, no. He could hear the voice, hard by his ear, and he could hear his own thudding heartbeat, and a groaning that he thought was coming from his own dry throat; he couldn't hear Frater Susurrus. Him he could feel, though, thudding into his bones.

He twisted himself away from the wall, fell onto his back and lay staring up at Sieur Anton. The knight was wearing a simple white sleeping-robe, and holding a candle.

"Sieur...? Where—?"

"You're in my room, Marron. Never mind why. Up you get now, it's time for prayers."

Midnight prayers. And his brothers, his troop half the castle's width away, perhaps filing out of the dormitory already behind Fra' Piet's torch; and him not there, which Fra' Piet was sure to notice, he noticed everything.

Marron struggled to his feet under an overmastering feeling of doom, of calamity. The last he remembered was drinking wine with the Order's lady guests, and arguing with Sieur Anton. He'd been promised a beating for doing so, he remembered that also; but it hadn't seemed to matter then, and really didn't matter now.

"Sieur, I must, I must go..."

His feet felt the unfamiliar textures of Sieur Anton's rugs, his toes curled around a rumple; he was barefoot. He cast about for his sandals, and couldn't see them among the furs that had made his bed. Never mind. A pair of sandals lost would no doubt bring its own penance, but that was nothing, *nothing*...

"No." Sieur Anton's hand was on his shoulder again, holding him fast. "It's too late for you to join your brothers. We will say the prayers together, here. Tell your confessor that I kept you late; the fault is mine, not yours. Forget that now. Our duty is to the God."

Perhaps so, but it was not the God's anger that Marron must face in the morning.

Still, he had neither strength nor wit to argue, with Brother Whisperer tolling his final stroke. In the hall, the preceptor would be calling light from darkness, his nightly miracle; here there was only that solitary candle to speak of balance, of two paths and one promise.

They knelt by the bed as they did each noon, and said the words together; but Marron's tongue stumbled and he couldn't concentrate his thoughts. They kept turning from midnight to dawn, from Sieur Anton's shadowed face to Fra' Piet's hooded eyes and his cold, disfigured hands. Rumour said that Fra' Piet had been a prisoner of the Sharai, that they'd broken all his fingers and tattooed their own god's name across his knuckles before they traded him back to whichever lord he'd followed then. That was when he'd come to the Ransomers, rumour said, to take the black habit and the vows. The vow of chastity was not necessary, rumour sniggered, because it wasn't only his fingers that the Sharai had broken.

Marron knew only that there were faded blue lines etched into each of Fra' Piet's knuckles, and that his fingers were twisted out of true. But he could still swing a sword or an axe, or a stick with wicked effect; and he had other uses for his hands that could make a defaulting brother feel worse, far worse than any simple beating.

At last they finished the prayers, though Marron took no good from them. He stayed still, his head sunk into his hands where they rested on furs still warm from Sieur Anton's sleeping. The knight's hand touched his neck lightly, and Marron came close to sobbing.

"You had best stay for what remains of the night, I think. Here..."

Marron heard Sieur Anton stand and move around the room, heard a flask uncorked, lifted his head and stammered, "Sieur, I—I want no more wine."

"I agree. Drink. This is water."

And it was, cool and instantly welcome to a parched, greedy throat. He drained the goblet and held it out, mutely asking for more; Sieur Anton chuckled and refilled it.

"Sip this time, it'll do you the more good. Then back into your corner, boy. And this time see if you can wake me at dawn bell, as a squire ought."

"Yes, sieur..."

H E THOUGHT THAT was a test, and he was determined not to fail. He'd stay awake the rest of the night, rather than have Sieur Anton rouse him again. But the knight blew the candle out and the darkness drew Marron down into itself, and thence into sluggish, difficult dreams that held him in confusion until a deep thrumming sound shook him free.

This time he knew exactly where he was. Where and when, because that was Frater Susurrus calling again; which meant that the sun was creeping up over the horizon, and there was no time for him to creep for all that his body yearned to.

He threw off the furs that covered him so warmly, such rare comfort; *the brothers are actively forbidden any comfort*, he remembered, and wondered if he would have to confess this too. No time for panic either, though. Not now, not yet. He rolled to his feet and scurried the width of the chamber, three quick paces to Sieur Anton's bedside.

The knight's eyes were open and clear; he was wide awake. Marron felt a stab of guilt, of failure, but Sieur Anton only smiled, and said, "Yes, boy?"

"Sieur, the bell, the dawn bell..."

"Ah. Thank you," for all the world as though he hadn't heard or felt it himself. He rose gracefully from his bed, knelt and gestured for Marron to join him. "This time, try to keep your thoughts on what we do, boy."

"Yes, sieur."

And he did, he managed that more or less, despite his fears for the day. Sieur Anton's soft voice was a guide this morning, drawing his attention back to the God each time it threatened to wander.

WHEN THEY ROSE, he thought he would be dismissed straight away to the morning meal. And to Fra' Piet, to confession and awkward attempts at explanation, to stammering half-truths and disbelief and a hard penance thereafter. But Sieur Anton had not done with him, it seemed. He gestured towards Marron's hidden arm and said, "Tell me about that."

"Sieur?"

"The wound has bled since it was bandaged, Marron. By the look, it's been unwrapped and bandaged again. But not, I think, by any brother apothecary. Am I right?"

"Er, yes, sieur."

"Why so?"

Confession, awkward attempts at explanation that were ruthlessly cut short. "You're saying that it was my fault, for overworking you?"

"No, sieur. Not your fault. It, it happened, that's all..." *These things happen.*

"Well. Perhaps; but I should have been more careful. I did know of the wound," with a flickering smile like the flicker of light on his blade that morning, when it happened. "Who treated it for you?"

"Sieur, one of the boys in the stables."

"One of the *Sharai*?"

"Yes, sieur."

"Why?"

"I was washing it, sieur, washing off the blood, and he saw. He fetched me something to put on it."

"Oh? And what was that?"

"An ointment. He said, he said they used it on the horses, but it was good for people too, he said, sieur."

"Horse-liniment?"

"He said so, sieur."

For a moment, an odd, thoughtful expression touched the knight's face, as though a curious memory had touched him, or a question been answered only to raise another question in its stead. But then his eyebrow quirked, and he said, "No doubt it'll do you no harm. But tell your confessor after the meal, and ask him to excuse you to the infirmary. That's an order, Marron."

"Yes, sieur."

"Go on, then. And after Brother Apothecary, come to me as usual."

MARRON WENT. AS he went, he anticipated. He would join his troop-brothers at table in the refectory. No one would speak to him as they broke and shared bread, because that was the Rule, that meals were taken in silence. Afterwards, he thought, still no one would speak to him. They would all know his dereliction, they would stand in awe of Fra' Piet's anger, none would dare stand with him for fear of the taint. None except Aldo; and Aldo would not stand with him or speak for him, because Aldo had not willingly done either now for days.

He would be one alone among his brothers, as he always was these days, these bitter days; and Fra' Piet would set the others to their daily tasks, but Marron he would beckon, lead aside. He would trace the God's sign on the floor in some quiet, shadowed, stony place. Marron would kneel there, raising his habit so that it was bare skin that settled on the stones; and then Fra' Piet would close his hands around Marron's head, gripping hard. They would gaze into each other's eyes—no shifting, no dissembling: they spoke to each other but they spoke before the God, and nothing could be hidden or secret there—and Marron would confess.

IN FACT, HE turned out to be wrong from the start, the very beginning of his tale of woe. Fra' Piet met him at the door to the refectory, standing like an avenging angel, dark and ominous.

"Marron. The dog seeks his dinner, I see. Had you not, the dogs of the castle should have been seeking you within the hour. Come with me."

He led and Marron followed, much like a cringing dog. Through the castle they went, along ways that were no longer strange but dim and threatening none the less, woven with shadow. At last they passed through a doorway and into the small chapel where the troop had been brought on their first evening in the Roq, though never since. A lamp burned on the altar; Fra' Piet genuflected deeply towards it, and Marron imitated. Then a gesture had him scurrying again at his confessor's heels, over to where the sign of the God was set in brass on the stone flags between two pillars.

This was worse than he had anticipated, that he should make his confession here and hungry. He drew up his habit and knelt, shivering from more than that chill touch. Fra' Piet laid his fingertips on Marron's cheeks, and there was a touch that was more than chill.

"Now. Here, brother, before the God: you have absented yourself from your troop without permission, and you have missed holy service twice. You will tell me where you have been, and why."

"Brother, Sieur Anton, the knight I must serve..."

"Yes?"

It was hard, so hard, with Fra' Piet's eyes boring into him and the God listening, the God who knew already. Marron thought of wine and drowsiness, of dozing off to the sounds of laughter, of waking to muddle and headache and the warmth of furs; he struggled to tell truth but not that truth,

CHAZ BRENCHLEY

to deceive with honesty. Better the anger of the God than Fra' Piet's, he thought.

"He did not dismiss me, brother. When we heard the summoning-bell at midnight, there was no time for me to join the troop. We said the service together in his room, as we do at noon; and then he said I should sleep there until the dawn, and again we spoke the prayers together..."

Those hard, distorted, icy fingers clamped harder around Marron's skull. "You passed the night in his *room*? In *Sieur Anton's* room?"

"Yes, Brother Confessor." Here was an opportunity to lie by omission again, to distract with a small confession. "I should have slept on the bare floor, I know, but he gave me furs from his bed, and I did use them..."

"What more?"

"Brother?"

"We do not sleep softly, Brother Marron. That is the Rule and you have been tempted from it. Very well. What more have you done, that you ought not?"

"I—" His bare feet were cold against his buttocks; he snatched at that. "I forgot my sandals," *and pray he does not ask where.*

"You forgot your sandals. What more?"

"Brother, I do not know how else I have offended." Those were ritual words, the end of confession, and a lie direct. The wine burned acid in his stomach, Fra' Piet's nostrils flared, and he thought his confessor could smell it on him.

But, "I cannot fault your absence, as you owe obedience to the knight. It is not my place to fault him for keeping you. But for the furs you slept on, you will not eat this day, brother. Going hungry to your bed will be a restitution. For discarding the sandals which the Rule prescribes, you will go barefoot about your duties until I say otherwise."

"Yes, brother." That should have been all, and he felt so lucky with it, and so besmirched. He hadn't lied in confession since he was a child, and he half thought the God would disown him with thunderbolts. But there was still one thing more, and that was a penance in itself. *After the meal* had been Sieur Anton's command, only there was to be no meal, not for Marron. Better now, then, do it all at once...

"Fra' Piet, may I have your consent to attend Brother Apothecary?"

"Why, are you ill?"

"No, brother, but my wound has bled again."

"Show me."

Reluctantly, Marron bared his arm. Fra' Piet looked at the stained bandage and said, "This has been opened and rebound. By you?"

"Yes, brother."

Fra' Piet's fingers gripped his forearm, and probed through the bandage. Marron winced, though there was little pain. Those twisted fingers worked silently against the knots, and peeled back the bandages.

The scar was red and raw still, but the cut was healing. Mustar's salve had left a stain, though, yellow on his skin. Fra' Piet rubbed at it, lifted his finger to his nose and sniffed.

"What did you put on this, boy?"

"A liniment, brother." And then, still on his knees, still confessing, "From the stables..."

"Horse-liniment?"

"Yes, brother."

Incredibly, Fra' Piet laughed: a single, hoarse cough of a laugh. His hands gripped Marron's head again, and yes, this was still confession. He said, "Who gave it you?"

The fault was his own; he couldn't name Mustar. He lied again. "No one, I took it myself. I had... overused the arm, in exercise," he couldn't name or blame Sieur Anton either, not in this, "against instructions..."

"And so you were afraid, and sought to hide it. To do what you are not ordered to do is disobedience, brother. To treat yourself for an injury is rank disobedience; if you had done it poorly, if the arm had been poisoned through your stupidity, your service would have been lost to the God. This body is not yours now, to do with as you will; it is pledged to Him."

"Yes, brother."

"You may not go to the infirmary," Fra' Piet said slowly. "There is no need for it. Since you have treated yourself as a beast, so will we treat you. The troop will be riding horses on the plain this morning, but one beast does not bear another. Instead you will bear burdens, as a packhorse does. Go to the stablemaster, say that I sent you, and tell him you are to be used so."

"Yes, brother. Uh—"

"Well, what?"

"The bandages, brother...?"

"You managed before," Fra' Piet said. "You can manage again."

Left alone, he could and did, with one hand and his teeth; though he managed badly, and the linen would surely work loose again before his long day was done.

MARRON WAS SWEATING already by the time his troop came filing down into the stable yard in Fra' Piet's wake. Defaulting brothers sent to the stablemaster for penitent labour clearly had no more status than a slave. There was a duty he would not set a horse to, he'd said, that might yet be fit work for such a brother; and so Marron had been sent to the far corner of the yard, where the dungpile was. Marron knew the rich smell of horse manure and rotting straw, but the stench from this massive heap spoke of something more. A thin liquid trickled from it, running warm and foul under his bare feet; flies swarmed around his head. This must be where the brothers' latrines were emptied, and the chamber pots used by the knights and masters. Emptying Sieur Anton's pot was one of his daily tasks, but he'd always taken that to the latrines. And still would, he thought, breathing shallowly through his mouth against the miasma rising from the slurry.

Magister Raul was watching him, from a little distance. Marron hefted the wooden spade he'd been given and began to shovel the stinking mass as he'd been told to, into a handcart that stood beside the heap.

It was heavy work, but he was used to that. And the courtyard was still in blessed shadow, the sun hadn't climbed above the walls yet to bake the sweat from his skin and leave him panting for water. Only the foetid air made this vile, so that he poisoned himself with every snatched gasp of breath.

Another shovel drove into the pile close beside his, making him startle. One quick glance showed him a dark head, a white tunic; the boy even spared him a smile, white teeth flashing against nut-brown skin, before he bent again to the work.

They filled the cart, mounding the dung high. Dribbling liquor oozed out between the planks, to spatter on the cobbles below. At last the boy gestured, *enough,* and tossed his shovel up into the cart. Marron copied him, then said, "What do we do now?"

"Now we pull," the boy said slowly, frowning over the words. "Down," with a wave of his arm towards the sloping tunnel that led to the castle gate.

A pole ran out from the front of the cart, ending in a crossbar. When the boy trotted over, gripped the bar and lifted, looked back and gave a summoning jerk of his head, Marron understood. This oozing refuse might be nothing but waste up here; on the plain below it would feed the parched and greedy soil, and be welcome.

He took his place at the pole, put both hands on the crossbar and leaned all his weight against it. Bare feet slipped on slimy cobbles, and for a moment the cart felt impossibly heavy; but Marron heaved, glancing across to time his effort with the boy's, and the wheels jerked forward.

Once the cart was moving, it was easier. They'd only gone a few paces, though, when a voice called, soft and liquid, and another Sharai lad came running over. Marron stopped pulling, necessarily, because his partner had. He looked up, and saw that the newcomer was Mustar.

The two boys had a brief conversation, then the other stepped away from the bar and Mustar took his place.

"We will do this," he said, smiling across.

Marron glanced around anxiously. No sign of Magister Raul. Even so, he was uncertain; no brother would swap a duty so, after he'd been ordered to it. Mustar seemed to have no doubts, though. He just set his slim weight against the bar and pushed with a will. Nothing Marron could do, then, but match him step for step.

They hauled the cart across the cobbles to the head of the ramp. Mustar checked there and said, "Now we turn, yes?"

Marron didn't understand until he saw the boy hauling at the pole, dragging it around. Marron ducked under and joined him; they turned the cart until the pole was at the rear, then they gripped the bar again and pushed. As soon as the wheels met the smooth slope of the ramp, the cart began to roll. Marron felt the tug of it and leaned back as Mustar did, pulling against the dragging weight.

After the darkness of the tunnel came the steps in their dim-lit canyon of stone. The cart jolted down from one to

163

the next, veering wildly so that they had to fight to keep it straight. Then the gatehouse, the gate and a little level ground, where they had to push again; and then they were out on the road and hauling back, rough rock biting at bare soles as they struggled to steady the cart.

The road had never seemed so long, nor so steep. The cart dragged them into a constant, scurrying trot; at every corner it tried to plunge straight on, over the edge; Marron's weight and Mustar's were barely enough to hold it, to bump the wheels around. Halfway down, though, he saw Mustar grinning. Another desperate turn that had their heels flying out over emptiness as they teetered on the very edge, only pulled back to the road by the cart's own rolling weight, and he heard Mustar laugh.

No, it had to have been a sob of fear, surely? But a glance across showed the boy visibly enjoying this hectic progress. He beamed at Marron, and shouted above the noise of the wheels. "It is like riding a horse, yes? A young horse, not trained yet..."

Marron forced a smile in return, thinking his companion mad. But a second thought followed hard on that, and denied it. Not mad, no. Only young himself and enslaved, taken from his people—and, yes, his horses—to be forced into drudgery. Mustar's life must be an endless round of work and sleep and waking to work again. Small wonder if he snatched at any thrill that offered.

Thinking that way, thinking for the first time about the thrill and not the danger, Marron felt his own spirits ease. He was short on simple excitement himself, and young himself, he remembered; and there was a curious pleasure in running the risk and defying it, another in using his body's strength. Another too in being free for a short time, unwatched by censorious eyes...

He heard himself laugh abruptly, and forgot that this was meant to be a penance. Where the road ran straight for a while and Mustar began to run also, he didn't hold back; he just let the cart pull him on in great leaping bounds. Never mind the shock of it as his bare feet slammed to ground, and never mind their shared panic and the crazy skid that barely carried them around the bend that came up all too quickly, this was still the closest he'd ever felt to flying.

The road levelled out too soon now, the rock beneath his aching, stinging feet turned to dust and pounded earth and the cart was suddenly heavy again, needing to be forced along. They stopped to turn it, to pull instead of push; and having stopped they did neither, just grinned at each other with sweat-matted hair and glittering eyes, pounding hearts and labouring chests.

Marron's legs decided not to hold him suddenly, his knees turned treacherous; he had to grab hold of something or else sit down, and there was only Mustar to grab hold of. Mustar or the cart, and that reeked, so he grabbed at the boy. Hung onto his shoulders, wheezing with laughter, and felt thin arms circle his waist and a hot wet snorting head settle against his neck.

"WHERE NOW?" EVENTUALLY, penance and duty resurgent. "With the cart?"

Mustar pointed to where a rough track left the road, to wind around the base of the great scarp. That would be hard and weary going, and no trace of pleasure to be found in it. Marron sighed, huffed once, then stepped deliberately back to the pole. Mustar shadowed him; they bent to their work, dug their toes through dust to find the baked earth beneath, and heaved the cart away.

The track led them around the southernmost point of the scarp, to a village of mud huts and narrow alleys. These people were believers, or they were said to be, though they had their own rites and prayed in their own tongue. It was their women who came up to the castle each day to wash and cook for the knights, a laughing, jabbering counterpoint to the brothers' grim silence.

No women in the village now, or none visible. Only old men crouching in their doorways, smoking their *khola*-pipes and spitting, watching the cart's progress with sunken eyes shadowed by heavy white turbans. Marron couldn't even see any children, nor hear them. *Perhaps the brothers came,* he thought savagely, *perhaps Fra' Piet led his last troop here and beat their brains out for saying the wrong prayers.*

No, he was being ridiculous. These were no heretics. There was their temple, the largest building in the village, and the God's sign raised on the wall above the door, eyes properly open. Marron bowed his head as he passed under their implacable gaze. Almost he asked forgiveness for the baby, though that surely would be heresy. *These things happen*, he reminded himself bleakly.

Through the village they went, unhindered, unapproached; and came to fields on the far side, or the best this dry country could supply in the way of cultivated ground. All the land between the village and the river had been broken into rough plots, where millet and maize struggled to grow. There was no water to be had from the river, though; only a well where an old blind camel walked an endless circle, harnessed to a beam that turned a wheel that raised a leaking leather bucket from the depths. And here were the children: one leading the camel and another driving it from behind with a long switch, one emptying the bucket into a trough and perhaps a dozen more filling gourds from there and running to water the crops. Some seemed no older than five or six. This must be their life, their childhood.

They came running now, to meet the cart. Boys and girls were almost indistinguishable to Marron's eyes, with their dusty brown curls and pinched faces, big eyes and pale pocked scars. They were thinner even than Mustar and his fellow slaves, bone and skin and nothing more under their ragged robes. And they were shy or wary, talking to each other in hissing whispers but not to Marron, though they clustered on his side of the cart, purely it seemed to keep that much distance between them and Mustar. The Sharai must be devils to them, murdering devils, even here under the great castle. Even a young boy captured and shamed was a creature to be feared, seemingly.

Mustar clambered up into the cart, gesturing to Marron to follow. He did, reluctantly, his feet sinking to the ankles in the stinking load. This was true penance, pitching the dung out onto the track as fast as possible while the stench rose around him like smoke in the heat and the flies swarmed from nowhere, thick as smoke. After a short time his head was swimming, as though he breathed khola smoke like those old men in the village.

Quickly though they worked, the children were quicker. They snatched up this precious filth in their hands and ran off, laying it carefully above the roots of each thin pale stalk before hurrying back for more.

At last Marron leaned on his spade, breathing hard through his mouth, watching Mustar scrape up the last shovelful from the planks of the cart.

"Now we go back," Mustar said, smiling at his weariness, "and then we come again."

Marron groaned. But at least the empty cart would be a lighter burden for the climb, no danger and no thrill. He'd have breath enough to talk with.

"MUSTAR, HOW DO they live, these people? Those plants will never feed so many."

Mustar shook his head. "This is second food," he said; and scowled, and tried again. "Second time of growing, yes?"

"Their second crop? Second this year?"

"Yes. Now is hot and dry, and bad crop; but in spring the river is full, and all the hills are flowers, and they grow good crop then. This is extra."

But that extra was obviously needful, or they wouldn't work so hard for such poor results. Likely a second crop made the difference between having just enough and going hungry, starvation-hungry.

Then, "We must hurry," Mustar went on. "The master watches for us; if we are slow, we are beaten." And Marron no different from Mustar in Magister Raul's eyes, not today, just as liable for a beating.

They hurried. Indeed, they ran at Mustar's urging, at least while the road was flat; and took the hill at a trot for as long as they were able, and so much for having breath to talk with. Marron was gasping and sweating again long before they came into the stable yard.

When they did, they found it full of horses. Three or four troops were there, all saddling up at once, taking horses out for exercise and training; and Marron's troop was among them, and as he and Mustar edged their cart between the moat and the sidling mass of horses and men he saw first Fra' Piet, and then Aldo.

Fra' Piet gazed at him, at his companion, at what they drew behind them; and he nodded, satisfied.

This was appropriate, obviously, this was what Marron deserved.

Aldo gazed, assessed as their confessor had; and his face moved no more than Fra' Piet's, in the short time before his head turned the other way.

MARRON DIDNT UNDERSTAND Aldo. All their lives they'd been friends, close as brothers; everything that had ever seemed worth doing, they'd done together. Even

Marron's decision to join the Order had only been possible because Aldo came too. It was what he'd wanted all his life, but he couldn't have done it alone. "We'll both go," Aldo had said. "You join for your father's sake, and I'll join for your sake, and we'll both be famous warriors for the God's sake. There's nothing for me here anyway. My brother will have the land when our father dies, and I don't want to be beholden to him. I'd rather be with you."

So they'd taken their public oaths together, and trained together; they'd taken ship together under Fra' Piet, helped each other in times of trouble and sworn private oaths to outmatch the public; and now, in the space of a few dreadful days, that lifetime of love and trust had all turned sour and unkind.

It was jealousy that had come between them, Marron at least understood that much. What he couldn't understand was why. His service to Sieur Anton brought him many extra duties, and few rewards. There was the sword called Dard, he supposed, but that was a secret gift and one that only a part of him wanted to accept, for all its craftsmanship and beauty. It was properly a knight's weapon, not a brother's, and its dark history disturbed him greatly. As everything about Sieur Anton's interest disturbed him. Aldo wouldn't let him explain, though, he wouldn't listen; so Marron had taken to avoiding Aldo's company whenever he could, seizing every opportunity to serve Sieur Anton instead, though he knew that each of those occasions only inflamed Aldo's jealousy more.

THE CART FULL again, down they went again. This time they met a camel train coming up and had to go slow and careful all the way, fighting against the cart's weight rather than swinging with it, squeezing past each high-laden beast with the outer wheel running on the very edge of the road because the beasts preferred to hug the wall.

Down at last, and on the rough track that led to the village, they walked in fierce light now. Mustar glanced at the sky, and reached across to touch Marron's arm.

"The sun is highest," he said.

Marron squinted up, guarding his eyes with his fingers. The boy was right, it was noon or near enough. "So?" No noon meal for Marron today, and none he thought for the Sharai either; what did they have to stop for?

"You will want to pray," the boy said simply, "and here is better."

Of course he would want to pray; only that he had forgotten, and it had needed an infidel to remind him. Marron couldn't believe it, that a lifelong habit could slip his mind so. Hungry and thirsty though he was, sweating and weary and disturbed, his mind on other men rather than his duty to the God—he still couldn't believe it.

The heavy tones of Frater Susurrus rolled down the hill, a minute too late for Marron. The tinny clanging that echoed them must be coming from the village, the priest there calling the children in from the fields and the old men from their doorways, calling anyone else within earshot to come and worship. Marron could answer that summons, he supposed, even Fra' Piet couldn't fault him for it; but he didn't know the order or the language of their service, and he preferred not to be dumb and stupid before the God. He'd pray alone here, as Sieur Anton would be praying alone up above.

Praying alone, but not expecting to: expecting Marron, he remembered suddenly. *After Brother Apothecary, come to me as usual*—and Marron had done neither the one thing nor the other, had gone neither to the infirmary nor to the knight. Not his fault, but another trouble for him all the same. No doubt Sieur Anton would devise his own penance suitable to the occasion.

Well. Nothing he could do about it now, except perhaps to compose an apology and an explanation, though he doubted Sieur Anton would have the patience to listen to either. Brother Whisperer was making the air throb about his ears; it was time to clear his mind, and get down on his knees.

Mustar was ahead of him, gone a few paces off the road and kneeling himself. Picking up stones and making a little heap of them, Marron saw, like a cairn. He watched for a minute, once more forgetful of his own obligations. Mustar laid a flat shear of rock across the pile like an altar-slab in miniature, then reached inside his tunic and produced three small slate-blue pebbles, which he placed in a careful triangle atop his construction.

"What is that, Mustar?" Marron asked, seeing that the work was finished and he still didn't understand it.

Mustar glanced back at him, solemn and scowling. "You pray when the sun is high. So do we, when we are allowed to. Will you stop me?"

"Oh. No, of course not. I'm sorry, I didn't realise..." And he was backing away, he realised, nervous before the challenge of a slave and a heathen. Fra' Piet, Sieur Anton, Aldo—any-one else would have stepped forward, kicked the pile of stones apart, cuffed Mustar and promised him a master's beating later. This was blasphemy, after all, right before his eye. Praying to the Sharai's devil-god might be tolerated elsewhere in Outremer—all the native population was Catari, half of them were infidel even now, and most landowners would endure the offence of their beliefs in exchange for peace and labour—but never here under the shadow of the Roq, and never from a boy who belonged to the Order.

Never until now. Let Mustar pray; Marron wouldn't disturb him. Neither interrogate him, what those three blue pebbles meant. Even slaves were allowed their secrets, or should be; every religion had its mysteries.

Certainly Marron's religion was becoming a mystery to him. He'd thought his God a kindly one, once; he'd thought magic the work of devils. Then there had come the heretic village, the King's Eye, every night the miracle of light in the great hall, light from nowhere at the preceptor's word. He was no longer sure of who or what he prayed to. He'd thought to be closer to the God, here in His own country; instead he felt himself further and further distant.

But he prayed none the less, from habit and obedience and yearning. He wanted to rediscover the easy faith of his childhood, though he was starting to doubt if he ever could do it in this troubling and difficult land. He moved a little way away from Mustar, dropped to his knees, and barely remembered to pull his sleeves down and his hood up before he began his prayers.

SAYING THE WORDS alone, without even Sieur Anton's firm voice to hold him to a rhythm, he mumbled his way through the office more quickly than due respect demanded. All the time a part of his mind was listening curiously to hear Mustar's prayers, and hearing nothing but himself. Soon he was not mumbling but whispering, and still his was the only sound he could catch. Puzzled and embarrassed both, he tried to force himself to a proper concentration and couldn't do it; instead he hastened, concluding in a hissing gabble that could give no satisfaction to him or to the God.

Then he looked around, to find Mustar still on his knees before the makeshift altar but paying no heed now, watching him. Marron wanted to ask questions—*do you pray in silence, then, is that what your god and your priests demand?*—but he was too shy or too cautious of giving offence. He stood up and walked over to the cart, Mustar followed him, and they heaved it slowly on along the track.

THIS TIME THERE were no men to be seen in the streets of the village, no children in the fields to meet them. They must still be at prayer. *As I should be also*, he thought, with a spasm of guilt for that poor devotion.

When Mustar moved to climb into the cart, Marron stopped him. "No, look, it'll be quicker," and less vile, "if we just tip it. Like this..."

He bent his back beneath the cart's side, and heaved upward. Felt it lift a little and then drop back, too heavy for him alone. Mustar joined him; they strained together, and the cart tilted, toppled, fell with a crash. Marron winced at the noise it made, hoping that nothing had broken.

Half the manure slithered into a heap beside the track; they picked their spades out of the mess and began to shovel at what remained. Mustar was laughing, throwing it high and far to scatter across the crops; soon Marron was doing the same, they were vying to outdo each other, and again it seemed like no penance at all.

Still he sweated, though, his muscles ached and his throat was so dry his laughter scratched at it. When the cart was clear they righted it with a heave; Marron checked the wheels anxiously, decided they had taken no hurt, and then glanced longingly across to the well, where the old camel stood patiently nosing at a pile of dry forage. Even fasting brothers were allowed water, and surely labouring slaves the same...?

There was no one to ask, but equally no one to see. He said, "I want a drink," and set off determinedly. Behind him he heard a soft scurry of feet, and then Mustar was at his elbow, smiling and panting like a dog to show his thirst.

There was a thumb's depth of water in the trough, enough. He made a cup of his hands, filled it and drank, gulped rather, and then sucked at his wet fingers. Beside him Mustar dropped down and thrust his head into the trough, slurping at the water and splashing it over his hair.

173

Splashing Marron, too. Warm though it was, it felt cool on hot skin. He threw his hood back and his head down, and splashed enough to feel the wet trickle down his neck when he straightened. He shook his head hard, spraying water like a dog, spraying Mustar. Who scooped a handful of water at him in return, so Marron scooped a double handful back; Mustar ducked and the water hit the camel, which lifted its head and roared.

Marron lost his grin and stared anxiously from the camel to the distant village, for fear someone should come running. There was no movement in the streets, though, and after another bad-tempered roar and a questing turn of its head that seemed to fix its milky, sightless eyes right on him, the camel belched loudly and stood quite still. Marron gazed in fascination as a lump the size of his doubled fists rose slowly up the beast's neck and into its mouth. It belched again, and then began to chew thoughtfully.

It was too much for Marron. He slid slowly down the trough, laughing so much that his ribs hurt and his eyes watered, so that he had to close them against the spangling sunlight.

After a moment he heard Mustar's shrill laughter join with his, and felt the boy's shaking shoulder settle against his side.

"MUSTAR?"
    "Yes?"

"There's a tower in the castle, very old, that has no doors or windows. We call it the Tower of the King's Daughter. Do you know it?"

"Yes," but the boy's voice was very quiet now, and had no echo of laughter left in it.

"Do you Sharai have a name for it, do you know what it is?"

174

"Yes," again, in a whisper. "It is, it is called the Tower of the Ghost Walker. But please, I did not tell you this?"

"A secret, between us. I swear it. What is the Ghost Walker, what does that mean?"

But Mustar only muttered, "It is *teref*, it is forbidden. I cannot say."

Nor would he, though Marron pressed him hard, repeated his oath not to tell, pleaded and almost begged.

Mustar tightened his lips and shook his head hard, looking more scared than stubborn.

At last, "All right, then. We'd better get back."

"Yes," and Mustar scrambled to his feet, eager to be off. "We must bring the cart down one time more, and the master will be watching for us."

Marron groaned, as he followed the boy back to the cart. His body was stiffening already after that brief rest, but his itch of curiosity was redoubled now, and he knew no one else to ask.

U P THE HILL at a trot again, back once more to the dungheap, stink and shovel and sweat. Through the buzzing that he thought was only flies, Marron heard voices, hooves, the scream of a hawk; and then suddenly one voice, cold and cutting.

"Marron. There you are. I believe I gave orders that you were to wait on me? I am not accustomed to come searching for my squire; nor to find him preferring, ah, agricultural pursuits in curious company."

Marron dropped his shovel, turned reluctantly, stepped forward out of the constant run-off from the heap and saw the knight step an equal distance back.

"Sieur, I—"

"Did you have your arm treated?"

"No, sieur, but..."

Sieur Anton's nostrils flared slightly, against his impassive face; Marron flinched inwardly. But then a wonder, Magister Raul appeared at the knight's shoulder and it was the first time Marron could remember ever being truly pleased to find a master watching him.

"Is there a difficulty, Sieur Anton?"

"Only that this brother has been assigned to do duty as my squire, Master, and he seems to have chosen other tasks without my authority."

Magister Raul was not a laughing man, but his lips twitched into some semblance of a smile. "Not of his own choice, I think. This is a penance, set him by his confessor. For what offence, I have not asked."

Neither did Sieur Anton. His eyes found Marron's again for a moment, and he gave a brief nod of excusal, even a touchy smile of his own. Then, "Too late today, and I'd be glad if you could spare a boy to saddle one of my horses for me; but perhaps we need to discuss this, Master Raul, to be certain whose orders take precedence where they conflict in the same body."

Tell that to Fra' Piet, Marron thought sourly as the two men walked away; then, *please?* he added, picturing the scene. They were both stubborn, both demanding, both intolerant of neglect; only that Sieur Anton had humour too and all the confidence of his birth and position, where Fra' Piet had the grim certainties of doctrine and the Rule. Marron would like to witness that confrontation, just so long as he was not caught in its midst.

Behind him Mustar whistled, barely more than a hiss of breath between his teeth. Marron nodded, turned, picked up his spade again but had to lean on it for a moment against a sudden wash of weakness. The flies' buzz was louder now, dizzying, biting at his mind; his skin prickled with a cold sweat even under the brutal weight of sunlight.

CART FULL AND spades loaded, he bent his back to the bar and pulled across the cobbles, feeling himself truly fallen to a beast's mentality now, unable to think. He followed Mustar's lead without words, turning the cart at the ramp and using his body as a brake, down through the castle gate and onto the road. No caravan's obstruction this time, they could fly again; his body only mirrored his mind, which was flying already.

Down and down, with a hectic swing at every bend. He was distantly aware of Mustar's laughter at his side, but couldn't share it; his heart pounded in his chest, each gasping breath brought less air than he needed, his sore feet stumbled even on the straight and his head swam sickeningly.

Almost to the bottom now, where the God grant him rest; but they took another corner, nearly the last, and disaster met them. There was a man in the road, right ahead. At least Marron guessed it to be a man; his dim eyes showed him nothing but a blur of red and yellow. He heard Mustar's shriek, though, and knew at least that it wasn't a phantasm.

They threw themselves against the bar, yanking the cart aside. It veered sharply, and by the God's grace just missed the leaping man; Marron had a close glimpse of him, brown hair and beard framing a startled face as they hurtled by. Too fast and the cart too heavy, they couldn't recover. A wheel slipped over the edge, the cart tilted and plunged, the bar jerked and leaped skyward against their frantic grip. Marron felt something tear deep inside his arm, and screamed with the wrenching pain of it as he was dragged off the road.

HE LOST HIS grip, and fell. Hit and rolled, sprawled and slid into the cruel spines of a thorn-bush, and only lay there helpless while his mind went on rolling and spinning, lurching and tumbling far beyond hope of his control.

FAINT VOICES, CALLING; and then closer, perhaps the same voices speaking a name he thought might be his, only that he forgot it again the moment after.

Hands then, tugging hands under his arms and the drag of rock against his back. Everything glimmered and hazed; he closed his eyes.

Now he was lying flat and hard fingers were probing his head, his ribs, lifting his arm and turning it. There was nothing that didn't hurt, but that hurt worst; he grunted and tried to pull free, drawing a grunt also from the man who held it.

"Don't panic, boy," he heard, and this time understood the words and clung to them in his mind, something to root him to the dizzying world. "He's all right, or he will be. Lack of a little blood won't kill him, he'll be lighter for it." Then the hands resumed their rough passage, feeling for the bones inside him, tracing the lines of his legs. He slipped away.

AND CAME BACK to the sound of a horse's hooves, a muttered oath, a voice he knew. "What has happened here?"

His eyes opened instantly, his mouth tried to shape a word but there was no breath to sound it; he felt not physical but hollow, eggshell. Broken eggshell.

"An accident. My fault, I should have heard them coming and made way." It was a stranger's voice that spoke, but the other, the newcomer slid with a jingle of harness from his horse and loomed overhead, blotting out the sky. He knew that silhouette as he knew the voice it came with.

"You mean they were coming down too fast. Is the boy badly hurt?"

"I think not, except that he's opened a wound in his arm here. A sword's cut by the look of it, half-healed before."

"I know, I made it. What, then, has he knocked himself silly?"

"Again, I think not. He went over the side, but his skull is whole and his other bones too, so far as I can find. A Ransomer doing a slave's work, though, barefoot, this must have been a penance; which if I know the Order means that he has had no food today and too much work, under too much sun."

"Heat-mazed, is he? Well, that we can attend to."

The shadow stooped closer, and he felt the rush of cool liquid over his hair. Dribbles ran down his face, and he tried to lick them; then the mouth of a flask was there, water touched his lips and he swallowed greedily.

"Not too much at once."

"I know."

The flask was taken away, before he'd had half enough.

But the dust had been washed from his throat and his voice was there again, or a whisper of it. "Sieur..."

"Marron. You are becoming much more trouble than you are worth."

Fingers touched his wet hair, far less stern than the voice; he smiled pure gratitude, for the gift of his name returned. With the name came pain, pain and soreness all over and a burning pain in his arm, but no matter for that. The name was worth it.

"What of the cart?"

"Oh, it's lodged in the bushes there, the boy and I can salvage it. It may have to lose the rest of its load, but no worse than that. This lad needs more than a sip of water, though."

"And shall have it. I'll take him to the infirmary now. If I mount, can you pass him up to me?"

"He may spew on you, when I lift him."

"I'll chance that."

Marron clenched his jaws, his throat and his stomach. Sieur Anton might be prepared to take the chance, but not he.

H E WAS LIFTED in one pair of capable arms, and passed to another. His stomach did lurch a little against the lurching of his body, but a couple of hard swallows settled it. He closed his eyes again and cradled his bad arm against his chest, feeling blood trickle down to his elbow; then before the great horse began its slow swaying walk uphill, he heard: "I am Anton d'Escrivey, a knight of the Order. And you, sir?"

"My name is Rudel. A jongleur."

Sieur Anton laughed shortly. "A jongleur, come to Roq de Rançon? To entertain the brothers, is it?"

"I had thought perhaps there might be guests, who would not be averse to a little music. And I have heard that the brothers' hospitality extends even to my kind, however they find their own entertainments."

"Well. As it happens, there are guests in the castle. There are also knights, whose pleasures are a little less circumscribed than the brothers'. You will be welcome, Rudel, if you sing as efficiently as you rescue fallen brethren."

"My voice has likely been ruined by the dust of the road, Sieur Anton," in a voice deliberately mellifluent, "but if there be a little wine to soothe it..."

"Oh, there is wine. Good, then. We shall hope to hear you tonight."

EIGHT

The Hidden and the Lost

JULIANNE WAS NOT made to be alone.

That was a decision she came to, quite forcefully, after a deal of pacing and gazing out and working her fingers through the wooden screens of the window like a child or a prisoner, like both. There were some, she knew, who thrived on solitude. Hermits, and the like. Similarly, there were those who needed society; she counted herself emphatically among their number, and never more so than now. She wanted laughter and conversation, she wanted bright wit and challenge; above all she wanted someone to talk to, however mysterious that person or evasive that talk might be.

Specifically—because she was practical above all, a girl of her thrice-damned father's making, and there was no point wishing for the unattainable, her old life back again—*specifically* she wanted Elisande, and Elisande was not there. Nor had she been for hours, for the best part of the day.

Unfettered by concerns of tact or diplomacy or the need to preserve a future husband's honour, unworried by the brothers' patent distrust of womanhood, Elisande had made herself far more free of the castle than Julianne dared. Every

181

day she'd go exploring, nosing out its secrets and its hidden corners; but every day she'd return within an hour or so, to talk of fine views or dark damp passages. It had been quietly understood between them that all of this was shadow and deception, though Julianne never was deceived. The wandering and the searching had a purpose, but that purpose was not to be spoken of, or not yet.

Today, though, Elisande had slipped away shortly after breakfast, and she hadn't returned by noon. Julianne had made her way alone to the great hall's gallery for prayers, and had returned alone also; had eaten her midday meal alone; and was alone still and snarling at it. She felt unkindly abandoned and worse, she felt her generosity abused. Elisande knew herself as much Julianne's guest as the Order's, had said as much and meant it.

She knew herself a friend too, though, and usually took no more than a friend's liberties in her comings and goings. Today was more than unusual, it was unprecedented; and quite unlike Elisande, or so her friend thought. She with her darkling hints about the djinni, she who had an element of watchfulness about her always: she would surely not go off like this, without warning and for so long? Julianne was genuinely anxious beneath her anger, although the anger was genuine also.

Whether it was the anxiety or the anger that drove her, at last she stormed across the floor and through the curtain, down the steps and out into the courtyard below before she could think better of it.

She knew the way from here to the great hall unguided, but that was no use to her. She could find the stables too, though, which perhaps held out better prospects. So down the long narrow ramp, dark with shadow; down to where sunlight glinted on water, and the air smelled of horseflesh and dung. There she discovered the stablemaster, and interrogated him. He was hardly forthcoming, but did at least deign to speak to her, albeit with his head twisted awry and his eyes askance, never meeting hers. No, he had not seen her ladyship's companion this day. No, she had not gone out on horseback, not on anyone's horse. She might have left the castle afoot; he was not aware of it, but he had no time to watch all who came and went through the courtyard, he was a busy man. If her ladyship cared to ask the guards at the gate, they might know more than he...

The guards had been on duty only since the noon meal. They had seen no lady leaving, on foot or otherwise; nor had their predecessors reported any such. They were sorry, they said, not to be of any help to her; almost she believed that they were. They couldn't see past her veil, but she put as much of a smile as she could manage into her voice as she thanked them, and hoped it had reached her eyes also.

Back up at the stable yard; she thought about questioning the Sharai boys, but the master's eye was on her—some time he seemed to have found, to watch at least one who came and went through his dominion—and she was reluctant to feed his animosity further.

Where now? Elisande hadn't eaten, or not with her, and must have grown hungry before this; the refectory, then, and the kitchens. Where they lay, Julianne had no notion. But she had a tongue, and the will to use it; she waylaid a brother on an errand.

This was a blushing youngster: nothing more than his age, she decided, that made him duck his head and stammer. Nothing more than a willingness to help that had him scurrying on ahead of her, and pausing awkwardly to wait at every junction. Puppy-enthusiastic and puppy-trained, he was, and she'd always liked puppies. She thought perhaps she'd keep him for a while, to be her guide all through this labyrinth.

Which thought implied that she knew already that this particular trail would be cold at best, dead more likely, time wasted either way. Somehow she just couldn't see Elisande sitting down to break bread with the brothers, nor the brothers allowing her to do it. Begging a crust from the kitchens was more likely, perhaps; but what guest would be allowed to eat so poorly of the Order's charity, and what woman would not be conducted gently but firmly back to her quarters and her proper meal?

So no, Julianne didn't really expect to find Elisande in the one place or the other. The refectory didn't disappoint; there was no one there but a few brothers scrubbing tables and benches and floor. She had her escort speak to them, to save embarrassment from whatever cause, but none had seen her friend that day.

She spoke herself to the kitchenmaster, and that was tactics too: however he felt about women in his bailiwick, he'd take questioning better from a guest than from a junior brother. So she asked, expecting once more the answer no; and was told yes instead, was told that the lady's companion had indeed been to the kitchens this morning. Soon after breakfast it was, and he wasn't in honesty sure what she had wanted there, she hadn't been at all clear about it. Idle curiosity, he suspected, with a sniff that said Julianne should keep a closer watch over her inferior, keep her hands busy with a needle or other woman's work, not let her roam the castle to interfere with men about their business.

How long had she stayed? A while; and only left after the questioners had gone down to the cells—with a nod towards a dark corner, an unremarkable doorway—and the filthy heretic they had imprisoned there had started up with his cries. Not fit hearing for a lady, that, and so she had found it. No, he didn't know where she had gone from here; no, nor would any of his labouring brothers, there was no point in asking them. Not their duty, to keep track of a wandering guest.

Nor his to criticise, so never mind that she'd taken a pair of apples with her without asking, which in a brother would be greed and theft and disobedience all three.

Julianne apologised graciously for the shortcomings of her woman, sketched a diplomatic curtsey and left the kitchens. As she'd hoped, her young guide followed her unquestioningly, assuming himself attached until dismissed."What's your name, brother?"

"Estien, my lady," he muttered, watching his fingers as they picked dry skin off a raw red knuckle. She suppressed a smile, seeing how he wanted to bite it, and barely knew enough not to do that in front of her.

"Well, Estien, this castle of yours is too big to go straying about at random, we could chase each other all day and never catch up." *And I'm only a girl and a stranger here,* her voice was saying, *I need a young man like you, I'm depending on you.* "We'll have to try to guess where she might have gone; but my guesses have come to nothing, so..."

She expected little use from his guesses either. If Elisande was a mystery to her, how much more to a callow boy like this, how could he hope to guess better? But she did need an escort who knew the castle. Once get him feeling involved, make it his hunt as well as hers, and he'd be far more use to her.

He thought, scowlingly; his hand did stray up to his mouth, where his unconscious teeth nibbled on that flaking skin; at last he said, "There's the infirmary, my lady, she might have gone there."

Indeed she might: might have gone, might have been taken. Estien clearly had no idea in his head beyond memories of his mother carrying herb tisanes to a poorly neighbour, *women visit the sick.* Julianne had another altogether, *she's been gone all day, she's curious and heedless and a stranger here, anything could have happened...*

She'd been hoping to keep her thoughts away from the infirmary, at least for a little longer. Too late now.

"So she might," she said brightly. "Can you show me the way, Estien?"

HE COULD; HE did. There was a room of benches and bottles and stone jars, barrels and mortars, herbs in hanging bunches and a shelf of books. A dispensary: no one there, but she could hear quiet voices coming from a doorway at the end of the passage. Soft though it was, one voice she thought she knew. Estien's face twitched uncertainly; she gave him a smile against her own doubts and took the lead, walking through into the long chamber lined with cots.

Only one of the cots was occupied, and not by Elisande. That much she took in at a glance, and felt her worst anxieties leave her, on a breath of relief. The next breath fought hard to be a giggle; she had to clamp her throat tight to contain it.

He was little more than a boy who lay pale and still on the mattress, and he was quite naked. Two brothers knelt beside him; one had been sponging his face and chest, while the other swabbed at a bleeding wound on his arm. Both were now staring at her in deep shock, giving rise to that treacherous giggle.

There were two men more, standing at the foot of the cot. The elder she thought must be Master Infirmarer; the other was Sieur Anton d'Escrivey. It was his voice she'd heard and recognised in the passage. It was also he who recovered his wits fastest, stooping to pick up a stained and stinking habit which he tossed neatly over the boy on the cot. The movement carried her eyes with it; his presence made her focus on the boy's face. Yes, that was Marron, the young brother who was also his unusual, his most unusual squire.

"My lady Julianne." The voice as ever held a sardonic twist, as though nothing in this bitter world were worth more than a derisive laugh; the hands wiped themselves fastidiously on a damp cloth. "Are you in need of Master Scobius' good offices?"

"Not I. I was seeking my companion, but I see she is not here. If your squire needs attention, I beg you, don't let me delay it. I'll withdraw."

And she did; but d'Escrivey came with her. Estien effaced himself, she noticed, scuttling back down the passage and out of sight.

"It's nothing to be concerned about. Too much sun, and a little foolishness that has opened his arm again. Master Infirmarer will sew the wound; a fresh dressing, an afternoon's rest in the cool and he'll be well enough. Though I really ought to beat him, for giving me so much trouble."

"You ought to," she said, this time letting the chuckle come, "but you won't." He wasn't the only one who could be amused by the idiocies of life, and allow it to show.

"No. Likely I won't. The boy has charms, which appear to prevent me. And he will be sore enough, I fancy, for the next few days. You have, ah, mislaid the lady Elisande?"

"I suppose I have," but the frustration of that was all gone suddenly; she could laugh at it now, and at herself. Company, someone to talk to: she sought no more, now that she was reassured. "She'll be spying out some dark corner of the castle, I imagine, making herself unwelcome among the brothers. She finds our chamber... unentrancing."

"As do you, my lady." Not even a question, that; he gave her no opportunity to deny it. "The brothers are endlessly hospitable, but not entertaining. Well, I can at least offer a little respite against your tedium. There is a jongleur come to the Roq. I met him on the road, tending my fool of a boy there; I hope that he will sing and play for us tonight. Will you come and hear him?"

Her heart yearned to—if she'd found Elisande by then, if the setting sun hadn't given her new cause to worry about the wretched girl's disappearance—but, "Only if I may do so without giving the brothers offence."

His turn to laugh aloud. "My lady, the very presence of a jongleur gives the brothers offence. It offends them greatly, that their Rule forbids their turning him away. If he will sing he sings for us, for the knights; for knights and guests, if you will come. Only recover your chaperone, for decency's sake, and you will be welcome."

"In that case, Sieur Anton, we will come, and gratefully." *If Elisande had returned by then.*

D'Escrivey bowed. "I shall send my squire to fetch you, and light your way."

"Your...? Oh no, not Marron, he needs—"

"He needs," severely, "to learn that duty overrides weakness. He will come for you, after you have eaten tonight."

D'Escrivey led her out into the sunlight, saying, "May I see you back to your quarters, my lady?"

Estien was waiting for her in the court, but it would be too ridiculous to go on searching fruitlessly, through all this vast castle. She smiled a grateful dismissal to the brother, and said, "Thank you, that would be kind," to the knight. And then, "Tell me of this jongleur, Sieur Anton, who is he? Is he known?" These wandering minstrels seldom wandered so far as Marasson, but she'd heard that some were celebrated throughout Outremer.

"Not to me," d'Escrivey murmured. "His name is Rudel, and all I can say else is that he showed a charitable concern for both my squire and the welfare of a dung-cart. We can hope that he will have washed, I think, before tonight. More than that, we must discover together."

"Indeed?" There was a story there, obviously, but it was equally obvious that he was disinclined to tell it. Julianne forbore to question further, having already met the man's infuriating talent for evasion. They walked on in silence, and he left her with a bow and a promise, "We will meet later, my lady, for songs and tales, washed down with a little wine. Though none, I think, for Marron. I'm not sure I could tolerate his excitement."

JULIANNE HAD GIVEN her travelling-dresses over to the village women to be washed. Having seen the results, she was glad to have one chest of gowns still untouched. She felt no great need to impress an unknown jongleur, but the affianced bride of an Elessan baron—the count's heir-apparent, no less—should not go into even this poor shadow of society in a stained robe.

With no servants to attend her, she tackled the chest herself, and was busy with the unaccustomed and not-so-easy task of shaking out creases and the intrusive dust of the road when she heard soft footsteps mounting the stair outside. She glanced around, the curtain stirred, and Elisande slipped into the room.

All Julianne's earlier irritation had returned, under the effort of her labour; when she gritted her teeth, she felt and tasted dust and resentment in equal measure.

"Where have you been?"

"Everywhere." There was a ewer of water on the window-shelf; Elisande poured herself a goblet and drained it in one long swallow. The light falling through the traceries made patterns of lace on her skin that did not disguise her pallor and weariness, nor the streaks of damp and mould on her dress.

On *Julianne's* dress, that the ineffective washing here would certainly not shift.

"What have you been *doing*?" with a flat-handed slap at the gown she held, that was meant only to emphasise the question but raised a cloud of acrid dust which had her hacking blindly, like an emphasis to her mood.

"Looking for a way out. Why, was I meant to be dancing attendance on you? Brushing out your hair, maybe, after I'd sponged your gown?"

Did it need sponging? She was momentarily uncertain, and had to make a deliberate snatch at her anger before she lost hold of it again. "You must do as you please, of course. But: *if* you are here as my companion—and it was my name that brought you through the gates, Elisande—then it would not have been inappropriate for you to have helped me with my dresses. If you are here as my friend, you should not be all day away from me without a word, because you should know that I would worry. And if you are neither my companion nor my friend, if as it seems you are nothing of mine, then it is very much my business to learn what you are and what you are doing here, because I may have brought an enemy into the castle under my shadow."

"Actually," Elisande said heavily, "I think you have." She dropped onto the settle, brushed at her skirts with a vehemence that would only work the stain in deeper, and then asked abruptly, "Have you ever heard a man screaming? I mean, *really* screaming?"

Julianne didn't answer the question, nor she thought did Elisande expect her to. She said only, "Was it very bad?"

And then, when the other girl offered her no more than a bleak gaze in response, "I looked for you. In the kitchens, as well as otherwise. The master said that you left when the cries started... You've not made a friend there, by the way. He was most aggrieved about his apples."

"Oh." Elisande fumbled inside her bodice, and produced two small yellow fruits. "I took them, didn't I? I forgot. I thought I'd be hungry, I think."

"And so you must be, if you've not eaten since breakfast." That was an instruction thinly disguised, deliberately so, to be easily recognised; but perhaps her voice had lost its snap since Marasson. Elisande smiled, shook her head and laid the apples aside.

Very well. She wouldn't eat, and she wouldn't talk of what she'd heard. "Where did you go, then?" No accusation in the question now, only concern and true curiosity. She'd left the kitchen and snatched apples on the way, thinking she might be hungry later; wherever she'd been in the castle, she'd gone so far in her head that she'd lost or forgotten her appetite; she'd come back with her dress filthy and her hands too, now that Julianne was sitting beside her and taking those hands in her own, seeing and feeling and smelling the dirt on her, and the green mould caked beneath her nails.

"Down," Elisande said, with a twist to her face that might have been meant as a smile. "There are tunnels all under the castle, passages carved from the rock. And rooms, store-rooms, chambers, cells..." Her voice broke momentarily, but came back stronger. "Some were locked, but not all. Some were empty. Not all. I searched them all, the best I could with an oil-lamp."

"Elisande—what *for*?"

"A way out," she said again.

"What do you mean? I asked at the gate, they said they hadn't seen you."

"They hadn't. I don't want to ask their permission when I leave, so I was looking for another way. A hidden door, a tunnel, stairs that lead to a cave in the rock... There must be one, somewhere. No one builds a fortress this size with only one way out. But I couldn't find it," her voice and shoulders

191

sinking for a moment, eloquent testimony of that long vain search in the shadows.

"Small wonder, if it's meant to be secret."

"It's not meant to be secret from me. I'm good at finding things. Supposed to be." But her dark head lifted, her dark eyes flickered and she sniffed self-mockingly. "I'm just not very good at being faced down and told to be patient. Not by walls, not by anything. Ask my grandfather."

"I'd like to." Julianne grabbed at that, being as obvious as she knew how. "Where do I find him?"

"Oh, you'll find him. I promise. Or your father will. That would be a meeting I'd like to see, I think." She sniffed again, looked at her hands and grimaced, said, "Let me just wash and I will help you with that gown. It's beautiful. And I'll brush your hair out for you, you've got dust in it."

"I expect I have. We'll need two gowns, though. You can choose the other. The knights are entertaining us tonight." Deliberately, she didn't mention the jongleur. Let him be a surprise; a pleasant one, if the man could sing decently. If Elisande were still keeping secrets, then so might she. She only hoped that her friend's were no more sinister than her own. Elisande had been with the Sharai, after all; she could be spying for them. Indeed, the djinni had told her to go back—but no. Ignore the djinni, forget the djinni, she would have nothing of the djinni. She would do her own duty by her own will and in obedience to her father's, and there would be no credit owed for that to any djinni.

IT TOOK NOT long at all for them to decide or discover that they were both too dirty for a single ewer of water to improve matters much. It was Elisande who ran down, determinedly playing the dutiful companion, to waylay a passing brother; shortly afterwards a small procession brought them up a tub, steaming buckets and a box of soap.

Once they had bathed, put on clean shifts and dressed each other's hair—an unequal task, Julianne had thought that would be, but Elisande's short curls were so tangled the girl was yelping under her hands before she was satisfied—they turned to the chest, and the half-dozen rich gowns it held. Elisande demurred, Julianne insisted; then they argued cheerfully about this one or that, which colour would suit best. The great bell interrupted them, but Julianne decreed that they had no time to go to prayers tonight, even if they'd been decently attired. The bell reminded her, though, that the light was failing; she lit all the lamps and candles in the room, before going back to urge the crimson once more.

THE BROTHERS WHO brought up their supper an hour later found them gorgeously robed and decorously veiled, still giggling a little when they caught each other's eye. Those same brothers carried the tub and the buckets away; as soon as they were gone Julianne tossed her veil aside, served Elisande, served herself. And must have eaten herself because her trencher in the end was as empty as the other, but she had no memory of chewing or how the food had tasted. All her focus had been on Elisande, and she'd felt triumphant with every mouthful she saw swallowed. Clearly her adventures this day had shaken the girl deeply, surprisingly deep for one so insouciant and worldly. Julianne felt proud—justifiably proud, she thought—to have distracted her so far into clothes and toilet that her appetite came back.

SUPPER OVER, THEY waited; and Elisande it seemed had more than her appetite back, she had her curiosity also. She wanted to know who they waited for and where they were going, how the knights proposed to entertain them and why the invitation tonight when they'd been ignored by all but Sieur Anton hitherto?

Julianne smiled her best mysterious smile, and refused to say.

A T LAST THERE came a scratching at the curtain; Julianne called permission, and Marron came through.

In his good hand he carried a flambeau, still burning. No sore-footed shuffling this time, but that reminded her. "Marron, you left your sandals behind last night," with altogether a different kind of smile. "Where did we put them, Elisande?"

"In the corner. Over there."

"That's right. I'm afraid one is half burned through, though."

"Er, yes, my lady." He blushed, as she'd been sure that he would. "It, it doesn't matter. I have a new pair..." He even twitched back the hem of his habit, to show her. He had a clean habit too, she was glad to see. But there hadn't really been any doubt of that.

"Good. How are you feeling?"

"Oh, quite well, thank you, my lady."

"Really?" He didn't look well, nor sound it. His voice was as thin and pale as his body had been in the infirmary, those parts the sun had not toasted. "Does your arm hurt much?"

He shook his head, but his whole stance betrayed the lie. With the flambeau in the other, he'd used that arm unthinkingly to part the curtain, and to show his sandals; now it was cradled against his chest, and she thought it hurt exceedingly.

"Well. Mind you are careful with it, or it'll bleed again. Have they fed you properly?"

"Oh yes, my lady. Mutton broth."

This time, she did believe him. His artless smile said that was better food than he might have expected in the refectory. It might well have been a meatless day for his brothers, but not for him.

"Come, then. Take us to wherever it is that we are going."

"The lesser hall, my lady. If you will follow me..."

He moved towards the doorway, but she forestalled him, reaching the curtain first and drawing it back to save his arm. He blushed again and ducked through, watchful not to bring his blazing flambeau too near the fabric. Julianne smiled and let him lead down the stairs, reaching back for Elisande's hand as she went.

ACROSS THE COURT from their little private tower, and into the vast darkness of the castle proper. Economy, perhaps, that left no lights burning here, but also it must help discipline, keeping the brothers to their dormitories at night. There were so many stairs and angles, even a man who knew his way would surely hesitate to take it blind. She was lost already, and glad of the squeeze of Elisande's hand in hers as they trailed behind the bright fire of Marron's flambeau and the shifting shadow of his back and his turning head, his face a white blur that came and went and came again as he reassured himself constantly that he had not lost them yet.

AT LAST HE brought them to a high double door with one leaf standing open, flickering yellow light and a muted roar of voices and laughter beyond. Here he set his flambeau into a bracket on the wall, and gestured them within.

"No, we'll follow you still, Marron," Julianne said, chuckling. "Presumably Sieur Anton is among the throng in there; do you find him for us. I have no mind to push my way among men I do not know."

"My lady would not need to push."

195

"Meaning that you will?" Elisande put in. "I doubt it, Marron. The quality of the master's guests reflects upon his squire. Courtesies due the lady Julianne will clear a path for you also, depend upon it."

Or in other words, Julianne thought wickedly, sharing a glimmering glance with her friend, *the knights will keep their distance as readily as the brothers, albeit for different reasons.* Well-trained gentlemen would bow and step back from sheer force of manners; well-informed gentlemen would be wary of approaching the daughter of the King's Shadow, for fear that some of the rumoured power of that mysterious office might be heritable in the female line. Any gentlemen of Elessi—and there were sure to be some here, so close to their own country—would be jealously protective of her honour. Which last might lead d'Escrivey into difficulties, actually, only that she thought that particular gentleman well capable of protecting both her honour and his own.

Marron didn't look convinced; but then, Marron didn't look as though he wanted to go through the door at all, either leading or following behind. Likely he only wanted his bed and a full night's sleep. Well, he was in the wrong dress, the wrong place and the wrong position for that. Neither brothers nor squires could sensibly expect the rest their bodies hankered for. She sympathised, but he was young; he'd recover. He'd had mutton broth tonight.

She waited, and after a moment he recognised her implacability, bowed and stepped through the open door.

HERE INDEED WERE men she did not know: dozens upon dozens of them, perhaps a hundred white-clad knights. Perhaps more. They stood in groups by pillar and wall, they lounged and spread themselves on benches and table-tops, they murmured and talked and shouted and gesticulated to the imminent danger of the squires and servants who wormed between them with jugs full and empty.

Following Marron made little difference; he obviously knew no better than she where his master might be found in all this chaos. D'Escrivey ought to be watching for them—but then, d'Escrivey really ought to be waiting for them here, by the door, and he was not.

Ah, well. She'd faced worse than this at court, every year since she was six years old and had first walked into a reception hall alone, in search of her father. Facing down the impertinent curiosity of strangers was second nature to her now. Straighten the shoulders, straighten the spine, walk forward firmly but not stiffly, be graceful and gracious and above all be open; look for whom you seek and don't try to hide it, move the head and not only the eyes, and bow to anyone whose eye catches yours in the process...

She wondered how Elisande would cope, beside her. Differently, she guessed, but well enough.

Stand on a table and cry d'Escrivey's name, perhaps, though the God grant not.

TWO PACES INTO the hubbub, and already the silence had begun. A stone dropped into slow and heavy water, she thought their arrival was; the silence spread out from them like unseen ripples washing through the room. Or like a circling knife that cut the strings of tongue and arm, killing every conversation and leaving each knight unmastered for a moment, slack and staring.

D'Escrivey might have told them, Julianne thought irritably. He might at least have told some of them, and let the whisper spread.

They recovered quickly, though, these young gentlemen. Those nearest to the door, nearest to the girls smiled and bowed, made way, gestured them on. Others, too polite to stare, watched none the less with a sidelong eye. Talk picked up again after the wave of silence, though softer and less raucous than before.

THROUGH TO THE very centre of this hall they came, and she had given up by then on strangers' faces, all but given up expecting d'Escrivey's. She was looking more at the pillars, gazing up towards the roof that arched so high the light of the flambeaux couldn't reach it, thinking that in any lesser castle this would not be a lesser hall. Here, though, the name was right: it was little more than a cubby by the standards of the Roq, a place for children to play, except that here there were no children and so it had been given over to the young men for their games, of which it seemed that she was the butt tonight.

Thinking so, she brought her eyes down from that dark and distant roof to find herself before a great chimney breast. The fireplace stood as tall as any door in the castle; its stones were black with soot, but no fire burned there in this hot summer. Instead there was a small table set inside, with chairs around it and a lamp in a niche above. There was wine, there were familiar silver goblets; behind the table stood Sieur Anton d'Escrivey. He made his bow as her eyes met his, and straightened up smiling.

"Welcome, my lady. My lady Elisande," with another, slighter bow. "Will you join me? I thought perhaps you might prefer to sit a little out of the hurly-burly; my confrères can be boisterous at times."

"Sieur Anton," as her displeasure melted into laughter, "I apologise. I had begun to think that you had failed our engagement."

"Not I, my lady." He drew back a chair and she settled herself into it; Elisande sat opposite her, d'Escrivey between them. At a sign from him Marron hastened to fill the three goblets, and then stood back against the wall.

"Where is your, ah, promised entertainment, Sieur Anton?" She still didn't want to say the word "jongleur," to keep the surprise for Elisande.

"I think he comes now, my lady. Listen."

Indeed, another silence was settling on the hall, of a very different quality. Through it she could just hear the soft strumming of a mandora.

There was sudden movement all around, as the knights who had been standing jostled for places at the long tables. She stretched to see over their heads, the same way they were all looking. Yes, there he was: a bearded man in his middle years, dressed in gaudy colours, picking chords from his mandora as he made his slow way between the benches and towards the cleared space before the hearth. Towards her, that was to say; d'Escrivey had had more than his declared reason, she thought, to seat them here.

Elisande also was peering around, looking for the source of this unexpected music. Julianne watched her, to see the results of her little surprise; and was more puzzled than gratified, was almost startled by the depth of her friend's startlement.

Elisande seemed to go quite rigid for a moment, when her eyes found the jongleur. Then she turned and straightened slowly, sat quite still with her hands in her lap and her gaze fixed on the table before her. Her veil hid her face, but there was no hint of pleasure in her pose. Something else, something private, another mystery. Perhaps jongleurs had an unwelcome place in her history? Or perhaps this particular jongleur: perhaps they had met on the road somewhere, and the encounter had not gone well for Elisande?

Well, whatever the truth of that, Julianne could discover it later. She was sorry her surprise had failed of being a happy one, but people who kept so many secrets had no cause to complain if they were obliged in all innocence to confront one. She sipped her wine, lifting the goblet decorously beneath her veil to save affronting any sensibilities, and tried to turn her mind away from Elisande and her shadows.

In honesty, that was not hard. The jongleur might have no known name, but he had a gift of magic in his fingers and his voice. He struck a martial beat and began a song familiar to all, even to Julianne. Not much in the way of music came from Outremer to Marasson; the Empire had sophisticated tastes, and thought itself the heart's home and birthing-place of all art. This was an old tune, though, and one that every battle-hungry boy could hum, from the homelands to Ascariel itself. The words spoke of the great war that won the Sanctuary Land and established Outremer; the jongleur led in a clear baritone, but he soon had the knights singing along with him in a massed chorus, deep male voices and a pulsing rhythm that set Julianne's skin tingling.

The song ended with a triumphant cry of victory. The applause was loud and long, though she thought they applauded themselves as much as the jongleur. Indeed he applauded them also, turning and clapping, bowing, smiling.

Then he lifted his arms for silence, and had it at the gesture. "Sieurs, my ladies," with a particular bow towards the chimney breast which had Elisande's hand clenching around the stem of her goblet, and yes, surely these two had met before. "A song may stir a brave man or a coward to a fight; it may turn a woman's heart to love—yes, or a man's," to general laughter. "But music has much to teach us, and not all of that is joyful. If I may, I will sing you a *pastorela* of my own composing: a small thing, a sorry thing, but one you will not have heard before. It is called 'La Chanson de Cireille'."

Its name brought a gasp from Elisande. Julianne's attention leaped to her friend but found her still once more, only that her head had moved to face the jongleur. Her eyes glittered: with fury, Julianne thought, though that damned veil disguised it.

200

The jongleur was aware of her. He bowed, low and slow, towards their table.

"It is called 'La Chanson de Cireille'," he said again, and his eyes moved no more than Elisande's, "and I, I am called Rudel, who made it."

Then his fingers plucked at the strings of the mandora, calling forth strange, sharp chords that rang bitterly in Julianne's ears as he began to sing.

I came to a border, a land of my choosing,
I followed a river through towering mountains,
I passed a great castle, its walls long abandoned,
Its gates gone to dust and its towers in ruins.
Beyond was an orchard with fruit in abundance,
But all of it fallen with no hand to pick it.
I was young, I was foolish, with no hand to stay me;
I stooped for an apple and bit of its sweetness.

Birds sang about me, the water sang softly,
And all the same music, a murmuring rhythm
That drew me on deeper through woods to a garden,
Its walls high above me, its gate locked against me.
Through bars in the gate I saw poppies and roses,
A maiden among them who sang as she picked them.
Her voice gave a voice to the birds and the river,
Her words were a burden of grief and of sorrow:

"Oh where have you gone to, and why did you leave us?
Your heart must be stone, to betray and bereave us.
Faithless and faceless, all promises broken,
Your name is a curse which may no more be spoken."

I called to the maid but she seemed not to hear me.
I swore faith eternal, and meant her no treachery.
Her own love was lost, she was fair beyond measure;
I wanted no more than to love and to keep her.

The wall might be high but not too high to climb it;
By the grace of a tree I had soon o'erleaped it
And stood among tangles of brambles that tore me
And cried out again, but no voice came to answer.
No poppies lived in this garden, no roses,
No birds could feed of the thorns that possessed it.
Here was no maiden, but true desolation.
I sang with the voice of her own love returning:

"Oh where have you gone to, could you wait no longer?
I had duties elsewhere, and no one vow is stronger.
I left you my name, now I cannot reclaim it.
Thief of my honour, what's love when you shame it?"

Julianne wanted more, another stanza, surely there must
be some resolution, some answer to such terrible questions;
but he gave one last long resonant sobbing stroke to the
strings, stilled them with the palm of his hand and bowed his
head to the silence.

She looked at Elisande again, and again saw how her
friend's eyes glittered, and wondered this time if it were
anger or tears that made them so shine.

THE LOW MURMUR of voices through the hall only
emphasised the quiet. This time there was no applause,
nor did Rudel seem to expect or want it. After a while he
raised his head—and was that a glint of water on his cheeks
also, above the dark of his beard?—and set his hands to the
strings once more.

This time it was a ballad that he sang, an old tale of brothers who loved and fought till they had destroyed each other over a matter of honour. Briefly Julianne felt nothing but relief, that this would give Elisande time to collect herself. But there seemed to be a devil in the man's choices, or else there was a devil lurking in this cold fireplace; she saw d'Escrivey stiffen and pale till his eyes were no more than dark pits fixed on the jongleur. Behind him Marron too seemed discomfited, staring at his master and then turning away. The air in that black chimney felt suddenly unbreathable. Julianne wanted to jump up and leave, to sweep Elisande out with her and take them both away from these strong undercurrents that she couldn't understand.

There was no way to do it, though; they were trapped by their situation. Instead she tipped her empty goblet and tapped its base lightly on the table, to draw Marron's attention. He followed her thought quickly, and came bustling around to serve them all. That at least afforded some distraction. From the corner of her eye Julianne saw d'Escrivey take a slow, deep breath and shake his head slightly, as though denying some unspoken suggestion that he had made to himself.

THAT SONG ENDED with death and disgrace, a broken sword and a man condemned to nameless wandering. As its echoes died away in the great space above them, Rudel passed immediately into an epic lay that seemed much more to the taste of his audience, that had them again singing with him in the chorus. D'Escrivey did not sing, but this time the relief was genuine; Julianne felt the tension ebb from him and so from her too, though Elisande was still looking tight and strained.

She'll answer my questions tonight, Julianne thought grimly. *Willing or otherwise, she shall.*

203

AND FOR A while, for a little while she did. After the jongleur had begged a second period of rest for his ragged voice; after Julianne had seized that chance to retire and been immediately and eagerly supported by Elisande; after d'Escrivey had sent the flagging Marron to bed also and himself lighted the girls back to their chamber, while they helped each other to undress, Julianne posed questions and Elisande answered them. For what little good that did either one of them.

"You know that man. Don't you?"

"Rudel? Yes."

"And he knows you."

"Yes."

"How?"

"Oh, Julianne, everyone knows Rudel."

"Sieur Anton doesn't."

"No, perhaps not. Or not by that name, at least. But then, a man with Sieur Anton's history..."

"What history is that?"

"Don't you know about him either? You told me your father had made you learn all the families in the kingdom."

"I thought he had. I know who the Earl d'Escrivey is, but I know nothing about Sieur Anton. What is there to know?"

"It would be better if you learned that from him."

"Perhaps; but as he has not told me...?"

"Perhaps because you have not asked. Ask him how he came to join the Order. You are such friends, I'm sure he'll tell you. It is his shame, but not his secret."

Were they friends? Not as Elisande meant to imply, at least. Julianne liked him, he interested her—and she him, she was sure, in much the same way. But she was also sure that Elisande was trying to force a quarrel, to save herself any further questions.

"Well, perhaps I will, then. How do you know Rudel?"

"I've known him for years. All my life," with a savage edge to it. "He has not always been a jongleur."

"What else, then?"

"What would you like him to be?"

"Someone who answers questions straight, for a start. That song he sang, 'La Chanson de Cireille' he called it..."

"What of it?"

"If it hadn't been for you, I would have thought it just a melancholy pastorela. A strange one, and unfinished, but no more than that. But it made you angry, and it made you cry. Why?"

"If it hadn't been for me," she echoed harshly, "he would not have sung it. I didn't want to hear it, which is why he did sing it. Which made me angry. The song makes me sad, which is why I cried; which was why I didn't want to hear it."

"What does the song mean?"

"It means that people go away. When they shouldn't."

"Elisande, who *is* he?"

"He is called Rudel, seemingly, for the moment. He has had other names. He is a wanderer who denies his home. He has been a soldier, a farmer, a magician, a merchant, a messenger. Other things. Now he is a jongleur, and he's very good at that too."

And who are you? was the next question Julianne wanted to ask, but that she'd tried before, with Elisande in a more peaceable mood, and had received no answer that satisfied. Tonight she was sure it would be waste of breath.

So, "What is it that lies between you two?"

"A lifetime," she said, on a sigh. "And a death," bitter again. "One that can't be forgiven. He should not have done what he did tonight, it was a coward's act." She flung herself down on her bed and went on hastily, "Julianne, no more questions now. Let me sleep."

JULIANNE ASKED NO more questions; but she didn't sleep, and neither she thought did Elisande. She lay listening to the other girl's fretful silence and felt herself trapped within it, lost in a maze of mystery where every answer only baffled more. For once in her life she wished, she really wished she could have slept this one night alone.

« ¤ »

THEY CROUCHED IN shadows at the foot of a greater shadow, and this was what they had come for, if they had not come purely to kill. Jemel could reach out and touch the upthrust of rock, could feel it gritty and cool and almost damp against his fingers' ends although the heaviest dewfall would not come till just before the dawn, hours away yet. He could tilt back his head and gape at half the sky, and see how the other half was occluded by the massive scarp with its massive castle atop. The castle itself he could not see from here. He and the others had watched all day from close cover, and he knew how it was set back on the height, above a steep talus of faced stone.

Jazra stood suddenly at his side, stretched up, set his hands to the rock and began to climb, swiftly and easily. After a count of five his feet were higher than Jemel's head, though Jemel had stood up also. Further along others were also testing themselves against the rock, shadows moving on black shadow.

"How far are you going?" he called up in a whisper.

206

A soft laugh from above, and his friend jumped down again beside him.

"We can climb this," he said. "Even with no moon and no stars, we could climb this; and we will have both."

"With weapons," a voice asked behind them, "and in silence?"

They turned quickly, to find Hasan with them.

"Yes, and yes," Jazra said.

"Good. But put a stone on your tongue, each of you, when the time comes. If any man should fall, he must not cry out."

They nodded. He had said as much already. A stone in the mouth was better than a gag.

"The rock we can climb," Jemel said slowly, "there are many holds for hands and feet. The talus will be harder."

"When we come to the talus," Hasan said, "we will have help. They will be ready for us. Not tonight, and not tomorrow night, but they will be ready when we come." His eyes moved, up and up, towards the invisible castle. "If we take it," he murmured, "we can keep it, and their grip on our land will be the weaker. But more than that, they do not know the value of what they hold here. The castle is strong, but that is the least of it. If we take the Roq, we take the Tower also; and then, if it is needed, the Ghost Walker comes to our people again."

"Would you carry that?" Jemel asked, on a breath.

"If it is needed," Hasan said again.

Not by you, Jemel wanted to say, *you of all men need nothing more than what you are.* But Hasan had turned and gone, was making his way along the rock and talking to others of their party, men of other tribes. Jemel wanted to follow at his heels like a dog, only that his pride would not allow it.

Neither was it needful after the first moment, the first pang of loss. Jazra's hand touched his, and spoke in silence:

fingers against the beat of blood in his wrist, and then knuckles touched to knuckles. *Whom I love, him do I fight for.*

Jemel turned his own hand and made answer, knuckles to knuckles and fingers to wrist. *Whom I fight for, him do I love.*

NINE

Brothers in Arms

FRA' PIET THOUGHT Marron had faked his swoon on the road and his sick giddiness after, purely to escape the penance laid on him: for the sake of mutton broth, a night in the infirmary and another day's rest after.

Not that he said so, exactly. All he said was, "I had not thought you so weak, Fra' Marron, nor so foolish," but he made it very clear what he meant. Aldo particularly seized on what had not quite been said and said it himself, loud enough for Marron to overhear: "A brother who is afraid of discipline," he said, "will be afraid in battle also. He can't be trusted. Like a brother who seeks his own pleasure, rather than sharing the duties of his troop."

It wasn't true, none of it was true, but it was telling. Marron had to clench his jaws, not to shout or plead or scream his innocence; he had to hide fists in sleeves and hunch his shoulders tight inside his loose habit, to stop himself flinging punches. That would see him in the cells for sure. *Cool enough down there,* he could hear Fra' Piet's cracked voice now, *it'll do you good, little brother. And the time to consider your sins, your many sins, that will be good for you also; and the flogging that will follow, oh my brother, that will be best of all.*

Injuring a brother, weakening the arm of the Church Militant was almost the gravest possible offence against the Rule, and the penalties were correspondingly severe. Marron remembered asking about that once, when they were being catechised at the abbey to test their knowledge. Did it not weaken the Order more, he'd asked, to inflict a penance so harsh that there would be two brothers in the infirmary, where there had been one? Father Prior had smiled and shaken his head, and said that such a brother unchastised would weaken the Order every day, simply by living within it. He must make his peace with his superiors and with his brethren, he must repent before the altar of the God; and that repentance must be marked out on his flesh, in stripes.

So no, no punches. Marron filed obediently with his troop from prayers in hall to the refectory, enduring in dutiful humility all the way; once there he bit hard into his breakfast bread, tearing it between hand and teeth as he couched his wounded arm in his lap and feeling glad as he never used to be, as he seemed always to be glad now for the rule of silence while they ate. At least he was spared taunts at the table.

Despite his wolverine technique, ripping and gulping, Marron was none the less slow to finish; he was still chewing when a single chime from the bar that hung on high table had them all scrambling to their feet for grace. He stilled his jaws desperately, breathed through his nose and prayed for a chance to empty his mouth unnoticed as they cleared the tables after.

The God was not listening to him, that morning as so many others recently; or else the God really did find it an offence to see a man swallow after grace had been said. He could feel Fra' Piet's eyes on him, though he dared not glance up at the table's end to be sure. The half-chewed lump of bread was heavy on his tongue, too big to swallow whole;

he worked it cautiously between his teeth, wished he could draw his hood up just for a moment, looked desperately for some other way to hide his face and saw none.

"Brother Marron." That was Fra' Piet's voice, a summons he couldn't ignore. He turned compliantly towards the confessor, sensing doom—and as he walked past the line of his brothers, it seemed that the God was listening after all. Aldo's elbow jabbed at him maliciously, catching his wounded arm; Marron doubled up around the stabbing pain of it, but still had wit enough to turn his grunt of shock into a coughing fit. He coughed into his hand, spitting out the bread. Squeezed it between his fingers and straightened, letting his long sleeve fall down to hide it; lifted his innocent face to meet Fra' Piet's glare, and said, "Yes, brother?"

"Your manners at table are unfitting to one of our Order. Mend them."

"Yes, brother."

"Meanwhile, your folly of yesterday has left you once more unable to share the work of your troop. Go, and find some service you are fit for."

"Yes, brother."

SENT AWAY, DISMISSED from his brothers—and dismissed by his brothers also, by Aldo's sneer and several shrugging shoulders—Marron knew only one place else to look for some service he could offer, one-handed and inept.

Forbidden hunting they might be, but some of the knights had brought their dogs with them regardless. There was a kennel in the small court between the knights' and squires' quarters; this wasn't the first time that Marron had paused briefly to bid them good morning. This time, though, the first long brindled nose that snuffed at his hand had its reward, if a sodden mass of bread were a prize worth having.

It seemed that it was, the way it was accepted with a gulp and a nudge and an insistent whimper for more.

Marron grinned, fondled silky ears, spread his fingers in apology and hurried away.

Up the steps and along the passage, a polite scratch at a closed door that for once brought no response. He scratched again, then opened the door and peered inside.

The room was empty. Sieur Anton was gone, and so were his sword and his armour. Briefly Marron felt bereft, unwanted here also. But he had perhaps not been expected here, and Sieur Anton was not a patient man, to wait on the chance of his coming. Marron went inside anyway, hoping to find some task he could do unasked to justify himself against Fra' Piet's later questions, how he had spent his day.

The rugs on the floor were dusty, but carrying them out into the air and beating them clean was no work for one hand. Casting about for something, anything else light but useful, Marron saw a small book lying on the window-shelf. He'd seen it before, packed at the bottom of the chest; now a touch of curiosity made him reach for it. He'd seen books, some here and many, dozens and dozens in the abbey's library at home, but never one in private hands before.

The cover was plain stiffened leather; when he opened the volume at random and spelled out the rubric at the head of the page, he realised that it was a missal. He was reading one of the prayers from the midday service.

The book was finely made, good paper well sewn into its binding, but the writing was strangely clumsy: the letters ill-formed and unadorned, the rubrics done simply in red ink with no gilding, some lines not of the straightest even to Marron's unaccustomed eye.

It puzzled him that Sieur Anton of all men should choose to keep—to treasure, indeed, because he kept so few things, each one of them must be a treasure—something so poorly crafted. As he went to close it, though, the pages fell down before the cover, and he saw that there was an inscription on the fly-leaf.

He lifted the cover back again to see, and read it out slowly:

> *This book of true wisdom is a gift of love*
> *to Anton d'Escrivey on his birthday*
> *made by me Charol d'Escrivey*
> *by the God's grace brother to Anton*

Marron took a little longer to understand, even then; but that dedication was written in the same crabbed hand as the text on all the pages of the book. Sieur Anton's brother hadn't only given the volume, he had made it first: penned the words and sewn the pages too, cut and shaped the leather for the binding, done it all.

Marron knew his letters, but he knew too how much pain he had in writing them out, how he would sweat to produce four lines not half so well inscribed as these. The thought of copying out a whole book, so many pages so tightly crammed with words, made his fingers ache in sympathy while his mind gaped in awe. Monks did such work, they gave their lives to it by the orders of their superiors and in honour of the God; but there must have been months of labour even in so simple a volume, and for a nobleman's child to do it for love alone...

And this was, must have been the brother whom Sieur Anton had killed, or said he'd killed. The brother for whom the sword Dard had been made, which Sieur Anton said was Marron's now.

Oh, it was too much, too bewildering. Marron let the book fall shut, and then heard footsteps and voices in the passage beyond the open door; and took a hasty pace backwards and knew even as he did so that it was too short and too late because for sure that would be Sieur Anton coming now to catch him prying here, that was the way his life worked these cruel days, and he had not a word to say in defence or denial,

He was wrong, though. Not Sieur Anton, but two of his confrères; and Marron wasn't trying to overhear but he couldn't help listening when he caught the knight's name mentioned, when he heard, "D'Escrivey's left his door ajar. Not like him. Is he in?"

"Not he," the other replied on an unkind laugh. "He'll be off playing knight-and-squire with that pretty young brother he's taken—Oh. No..."

They stood for a moment, two knights in white gazing in, while Marron stared mutely back at them. Then they walked on, and he heard them convulse with laughter; and felt his face flush furiously, while his hands clenched at his sides and he wanted to snatch up dead Charol's sword and go after, challenge them both, call them liars, call them to account...

And of course he did nothing so stupid, so fatal. He only stood and sweated, stood and hated until the trembling passion passed, until he was sure the passage was safe, was empty. Then he glanced around the chamber to check that he'd moved nothing that he'd not replaced, he'd left no sign of his presence; then he slipped out and closed the door firmly behind him; then he hurried away.

His mind surging with anger and confusion, he could focus only on one thing, the need to justify his day. *Find some service you are fit for,* Fra' Piet had said; *afraid of discipline,* Aldo had said, meaning that he had dissembled yesterday to escape his penance. All he could think of was to go back to the stables, to beg Magister Raul for some work a one-handed brother could do, to show his confessor and his former friend and all his troop that it was not so.

At least he might win himself a smile there, if Mustar were in sight. With Aldo so poisonous against him suddenly—and he still didn't understand quite how that had happened, he could name it jealousy but it made no sense to him—and Aldo and Fra' Piet between them poisoning the troop, with Sieur Anton heedless or forgetful of him this morning, he felt the want of a smile.

He'd have run in search of that smile—or else to seem more eager, more obedient, heedless himself of dispensations—only that jolting hurt his arm as much as using it. Everything hurt his arm, today. He carried it as best he could, cradling his left elbow in his good right hand; but he still winced on every flight of steps up or down. Maybe the stables were not such a good idea after all. There was no virtue in begging for work he was clearly unable to do.

But he could think of nowhere else to go, and the anticipation of that smile drew him down through the castle to the brightness of the stable yard; where he found neither Magister Raul's scowl nor Mustar's sun-dazzling smile but the jongleur Rudel's clever hands making a dazzle of their own from hard light and harder steel, as he stood bareheaded on the cobbles and juggled three blades that flashed cold fire as they turned and twisted in the glare.

He had perhaps only been practising or only passing time, but like any master of his particular trade he knew himself observed. He didn't glance around to acknowledge Marron, but he did straighten his back a little and set his feet more firmly, and he did nip a fourth knife from his belt and send that spinning into the shimmering cascade above his head. His hands seemed hardly to move at all, there was no need; the knives fell handle-down into his palm and leaped high again apparently of their own will.

Marron watched, fascinated and forgetful. After a minute Rudel tossed yet one more knife into the dance of light and steel, but that was one too many for his skill. His hands were suddenly snatching, his feet had to move to follow the dance, and soon two blades clashed in mid-air and fell out of the

215

pattern, skittering away across the cobbles. One slid almost to Marron's feet.

Rudel laughed shortly, caught the other three and held them, then bent to retrieve the one in easy reach. Now at last he looked around, nodded to Marron and said, "Toss that back, would you, brother?"

Marron stooped and stretched without thought. The sudden movement tugged at his injured arm, making him gasp aloud. He heard, "No, wait, are you hurt?" but still fumbled to pick up the knife before he straightened.

"Only a little, sir," he said, not truthfully; his arm ached with a cruel passion. Rudel was right there, taking the knife from him, gazing at him, frowning.

"You're the lad from yesterday, with the dung-cart."

"Yes, sir."

"I'm sorry, I should have looked first. A brother with leisure to stand and watch my juggling? I should have *thought*. How are you feeling?"

"Quite well, thank you, sir."

"Hmm. Then I should hate to see you quite ill. You look— no, not so much drawn, perhaps, as ill-drawn. Apprentice work, and the colours poorly mixed. The arm's bad too, hnh?"

"Only sore, sir."

"Sore enough that you have to hold it on, though. Let me have your girdle, and just slip that habit off for a moment."

"Sir?"

"Do it, lad, don't argue. Here, I'll help, it must be awkward one-handed... What's your name?"

"Marron."

"Good. You were playing servant to the ladies in the hall last night, too, weren't you? When I would have said you should be sleeping. I remember, you were the only brother there."

"Yes, sir. I, uh, I serve Sieur Anton, as he doesn't have a squire, and the ladies were his guests, so..."

"So he routed you out of bed in the infirmary to pour wine for them? Yes, that bears the true stamp of d'Escrivey... Now. If I knot the girdle around your wrist here, see, tight enough to grip but loose enough for you to slip off with your other hand; then I make a loop of the rest and that goes around your neck, so; that'll hold your arm so you don't have to. Comfortable?"

"Er, yes..."

"Good. Now, the habit goes back on over—no, you stand still, I'll do this—and your bad arm's underneath, so you can't use it even if you want to. What were you supposed to be doing this day?"

"I—I'm not sure, sir." *Find some service you are fit for,* but the sling only emphasised what had been clear before, that there was none.

"Will you be my guide, then, Marron? This fortress tangles my mind. And I'm told there's a village down below, but I saw no sign of it from the road?"

"Yes, sir, there's a village. You have to go around the hill to the south, but the track's easy to find."

"Good. You can show me that, then, too. But the secrets of the castle first, I think. It'll give you something to do, at least. I know idleness does not sit well with the Order."

"No, sir."

As he spoke, the jongleur had been crouching over a bright-dyed leather scrip at his feet, stowing his knives within it. Now he stood up, lifting the scrip by its long strap; before he could slip that over his shoulder, Marron had reached out and twitched it from his fingers.

"Eh?"

"You are a guest of the Ransomers, sir, no less than the ladies. I'll be pleased to serve you," *to serve you too, why not? I serve so many masters now,* "but you must at least let me carry your satchel."

"Well, then. Thank you, Fra' Marron, I will. Though most of your Order, I think, would call me and my kind something less welcome than your ladies. You are showing yourself to be somewhat of an unusual brother."

Marron said nothing; Rudel laughed softly, sympathetically, turning his words from a gibe to a simple truth observed.

"That hits home, eh? Well, never mind. There are always some who find it no natural life for them. You must custom yourself to it; custom can be learned. We'll talk of that. But now, will you show me all the dark corners of this citadel? Old places I love, and some parts of this place I think are very old."

"Yes, sir. But I'm new-come myself, I don't know them all."

"Then what you don't know we'll discover together. Lead me, Fra' Marron. Lead me blindly when you must, I'll follow regardless."

IT SEEMED MORE to Marron as though Rudel led and he followed, though that leading was done mostly by questions, *what's down here?* and *where does this go?* and *how do we get up there?*

Nor were those all the questions that Rudel asked. His curiosity ran broader and deeper far than Marron's knowledge: how many brothers were stationed here and how many knights, how many of those made the permanent garrison and how many could expect to be sent elsewhere and how soon, how safe were the lands to the north where no roads ran and for how far did the Order patrol them?

Marron could give him no answers, and the questioning itself made him uncomfortable. He wanted to ask one thing in return, why the jongleur was so interested; but Rudel was a guest and he was only a guide, it was not his place to meet question with question.

"You must ask the masters, sir," was all he said, all that he felt able to say. He wondered if perhaps in duty he should report to one of the masters himself, that so many questions were being asked. He was known to none of them, though, bar Magister Raul, and that man he thought would not listen. Neither would Fra' Piet, he was sure. Sieur Anton might—but still, it was only curiosity after all, perhaps all visitors to the Roq asked such questions.

He felt little easier when Rudel shifted his interrogation onto more personal ground. Why had Marron chosen to come to the Sanctuary Land, and why had he sworn himself to the Order to do so, why not come simply as a yeoman settler and be welcomed? Marron stammered over his father's name, and then could add little more to it; all the old certainties seemed to have abandoned him, so that he no longer knew why he was here or why in this habit.

The harder Rudel pressed, the fewer answers Marron had to offer. He floundered, gestured vainly with his one hand, cast about for some distraction—they were in the kitchens by this time, and if the great kettles of onions and carrots weren't enough to catch the jongleur's eye there were always the massive bread ovens, surely they were worth a word or two?—and saw a miracle instead, or he thought so.

He saw the lady Julianne's companion, Elisande. Running an errand for her lady, perhaps, or else dismissed from duty; whatever the cause she was here, lifting her veil heedlessly aside to munch on an apple. He saw her lick juices from the skin, and his own mouth watered; then she turned her head, and her eyes met his.

He bowed, partly good manners and partly to hide his smile of relief. When he straightened, though, he saw how Elisande was staring, no, *glaring* at his companion; and when he glanced to his side he saw how Rudel was meeting that with a cold gaze of his own. Marron understood this not at all. Perhaps she hadn't enjoyed the man's playing last night, but even so...

"Er, sir, my lady..." He didn't know the order of precedence here, who he should properly introduce to whom, whether a lady's companion outranked a jongleur three times her age.

"It's all right, Marron," Rudel said quietly. "Elisande and I are old friends."

They didn't look to be friends. Even through the veil he could see how Elisande's face twisted at the word. She tossed the fabric aside and took another defiant, crunching bite of her apple; and then, chewing and speaking together in a way that shocked Marron because it would have shocked his aunt and earned him a cuff from his uncle—and the tone of voice another, if ever he could have managed such a mix of vitriol and contempt—she said, "Indeed. He makes songs about the dead. It's a talent that touches us both."

"I'm pleased that something touches you, my lady," Rudel said, quiet yet, though Marron had sensed his sudden stiffening. "Though I might wish that it had been your father's rod when you were younger."

Elisande's veil was still disarranged, enough to show Marron one high cheekbone. Quite white that had gone, at Rudel's first sentence; the second made it red, a fierce flush that mirrored the glowing embers a brother was raking out of the bread oven at her back. Marron watched him, not to watch her; never had he seen the task done so slowly, or so silently.

"You have no right," she hissed, "no right to *say* that! You, of all men..."

"Perhaps not," though there was no hint of apology in his voice. "But I think we ought not to debate what is right or proper or properly owing between us, you and I. It is too late for that."

"Long ago, it was much too late," she concurred bitterly. Then, startlingly, "Forgive me, Marron. I should not have confronted you with this."

Before he could stammer a denial, she had turned away, sweeping past the raking brother in a way that had him staring after her, making public all the curiosity he'd been trying so hard to hide. Nor was he the only one to stare. Elisande was out of sight and gone before Rudel stirred or spoke again.

When he did, it was to pose yet another question, one that had no bearing on what had just passed. "Where does this lead?" he asked, and was already moving towards the doorway behind the ovens before Marron could collect his scattered wits and hurry after him.

"Er, only to the penitents' cells, sir, I don't think you ought..."

Too slow: Rudel had already set his feet on the stairs, and was leading down into the dark. Marron took a breath and followed.

They were not halfway down, though, before a rising sound met them, a low groan that swelled suddenly into a shriek. Marron froze, his scalp prickling coldly. After a moment he heard Rudel's voice just a few steps below him, low and tight.

"No, you're right, Brother Marron. We ought not. Up, I think, back up to the light."

AND ONCE THERE, once far enough from the stairs' doorway that the native noises of the kitchen quelled any other sound that might still be winding its way up from below, Rudel didn't pause; he strode on, leading his hesitant guide with just a glance around and, "Now the village, if you would, Marron."

"Sir, it's simple, turn to your left at the foot of the hill where the track runs, you don't need—"

"Even so. If you would?"

"Yes, sir."

Of course he would, given so plain an order; and glad to have it, glad to get out of the castle for an hour or two. Never had the walls seemed so high, the stones so heavy nor the ways so dark. He thought the echo of a scream—not to be heard now, no, but only in their heads—drove them both, brother and jongleur.

RUDEL WAS GRIM-faced and silent all the long and winding walk down, far from last night's minstrelsy or the curious companion of an hour before. Where the road forked, though, he paused, set his back to the sky-thrusting promontory that overshadowed them and shook his head once, hard. Then he turned his face upward, breathed slowly in and out, and said, "Look, there's a hawk. Do you see?"

Marron squinted into the pale sky. "Where, sir?"

"There." A hand lifted to point. "Come, your eyes are younger than mine."

It took Marron a moment longer to find the dot that hung high in the air above them. Rudel's finger followed it as it wheeled on the wind, marking a slow trail that left no trace behind it, that the finest hunter couldn't follow; then the jongleur laughed abruptly, let his arm fall onto Marron's shoulder and pushed him gently on along the track.

It seemed to Marron as though, in stepping from the rock of the great scarp to the dust of the track, his companion had stepped out of one mood and into another. Or else the hawk's freedom had freed his soul, perhaps. Rudel pointed out and named other birds flitting about the low dry scrub, and imitated their songs in soft whistles; he spotted bright-coloured butterflies on the thorn bushes, and signs of a snake's passage across the path.

Marron's mind found its own freedom, its own content: slipping back past time and travel, years back to long walks with his uncle in a more gentle country, the smells of rich earth after rain and the sounds of a meadow in sunlight, the quiet comfort of an adult voice endlessly patient with a boy's eager questions.

But his uncle had been ever a plain man, not seeing what the boy saw, having the knowledge but feeling none of the enchantment. Marron shook his memories away after a short time, rejecting their easy shelter for what was stronger and more vivid, the present smells of heat and dust and the immediate wisdom of a man who could find life, it seemed, beneath the harshest rock.

They turned one stone beside the track and found a scorpion, dark and smooth and glistening as the mud on a tidal bank. Tiny and deadly, Rudel said, a creature with its own eternal enchantment in its coiled, poised tail.

Marron thought of rocks and things buried beneath rocks, small things, deadly things. To the scorpion, its sheltering stone must have seemed a fortress. Sheltered beneath the fortress that overhung them still, somewhere within that rock was a man who had screamed this morning all unheard by any help, and how small and helpless must he be feeling, and how deadly his host?

But there again Marron's mind chose not to dwell, sliding swiftly on. Small things, deadly things under a weight of rock: the coolth of deep shadow made him shudder, the sun unseen was a candle waiting to be lit, and there burning in his memory was enchantment true, such a small flame and so fatal.

"Sir?"

Rudel settled the rock carefully back in its former place, not to disturb its lethal tenant, straightened and said, "Marron, would it be against your holy Rule if you just called me by my name?"

It was becoming a familiar experience, to be tossed suddenly and unexpectedly into confusion. This time, at least the question had given him a handhold, something to hang on to; he treated it literally, though he wasn't at all sure that it had been meant that way.

Like all his brothers—almost all—he knew the Rule by heart, from beginning to end. To learn it was the first task of every novice, and flagging memories were revived by its being read through once a week in the refectory. From beginning to end, though, was exactly and only how he knew it. He couldn't fillet a neat bone of instruction on demand. There was a great deal, he knew, about respect and obedience, the giving of honour where it was due; but as to the addressing of an older man not of the Order, not of the nobility, not of any rank that either Marron or the Rule could recognise...

"I don't know, sir," he said, nothing more than that.

"You don't know? I thought you all knew every word of it."

"Yes, sir. I'll say it," boldly, "and then you tell me. 'Listen, my son, to the precepts of your Master, and incline the ear of your heart unto them. Freely accept and faithfully fulfil the advice of a loving father, so that you may, by the labour of obedience, return to Him, Whom you abandoned through the sloth of disobedience. To you, therefore, whoever you are, my words are directed, who, renouncing your own will, take up the strong and excellent arms of obedience to fight for the true King, our Lord—'"

"Enough, enough!" Rudel was laughing, even as he clamped a big hand across Marron's mouth to stem the spew of words. "I understand you, lad. And yes, I have heard the Rule before, in all its piety and coarseness; and no, I do not wish to hear it all again. So let us assume, shall we, that it does not forbid your calling me Rudel, and progress from there?"

"Sir—"

"You're thinking that it would be safer to assume the opposite, that the Rule forbids most things and hence quite likely this too? Of course you are, I read boys' minds. Not girls'," and it was as though for a moment a cloud had kissed the sun, casting his face into shadow so that the lines and the pits of it showed only that bleak anger Elisande had woken in him. "But, let me see, in that briefest of introductions you were enjoined two or three times towards obedience, were you not? And there is more, much more later. So how if I *command* you to assume, to believe, to be utterly certain that the Rule not only allows but requires you to follow my wishes in this? How then?"

"Sir, guests are sacred to us; but—"

"Good. You will call me Rudel, then, or I will send you to your confessor in search of a thrashing." Even a jovial reference to Fra' Piet, made in ignorance, could still cause Marron to flinch. If Rudel marked it, he didn't comment. "Now, you had a question for me?"

"I did?"

"I believe so. We were looking at the scorpion..."

"Oh. Yes. Uh," which had nearly come out as a "sir," only changed hurriedly to a grunt as his muddled mind clamped hard down on the habits of his mouth, "have you ever seen magic made?"

"Seen it? Marron, lad, I'm a jongleur. You have heard me singing for my supper, but I do have other skills to trade. I *make* magic. Watch."

He stooped, to pick up three pebbles from the track. All three were smooth and rounded, much of a size, the size of chicken's eggs. He held them up, two in one hand and one in the other, letting his sleeves fall back to show his corded arms bare; then he tossed them into the air and began to juggle.

This was skill, to be sure, but not magic. Marron had seen so much and more at every fair he'd been to as a child. He'd seen men juggle flaming torches, four and five at once. He'd seen Rudel do more this morning, keeping four and almost five knives dancing in the air with never a nick to a finger. He bit back his frustration, though, and watched; and somehow didn't see when the pebbles changed, when they became not pebbles but eggs indeed, gleaming green-white ducks' eggs, twice as big. Neither did he see how Rudel cracked and split them, so that they opened in midair before his eyes with a trill of birdsong and a shower of sparkling silver dust like the soft scales from a butterfly's wing; and briefly he saw bright birds and butterflies rising from the broken shells, before they fell into Rudel's gentle hands and were only gaudy scarves of sheer silk that draped across his stilling fingers.

Rudel laughed, and looped the scarves around Marron's neck; their touch was soft as a child's finger against his skin, a startling change from the rough wool of his habit, and it was a long moment before he moved to pull them off. Silks and colours were certainly very much against the Rule, that he had no doubts about.

He held them out mutely, stiffly awkward; but Rudel only said, "Put them in the scrip, then, if you don't find them easy wearing."

Marron did that, and then, stubbornly, "I didn't mean tricks, or fairground skills. I meant real magic, true wonders."

"Marron, lad," and Rudel was solemn again, at least on the surface, though his eyes still glinted with laughter, "I have lived all my life in this land where your God walked once, and not Him alone. I have lived a year in Ascariel. How could I not have seen wonders? I have seen the djinn in their strength, and other creatures too. Creatures less neutral, more cruelly disposed towards men."

Had seen them, and it seemed wanted not to speak of them. At any rate, he started walking again, briskly along the track. Marron followed quietly, until Rudel glanced back and asked, "So what is it that you have seen?"

Marron wasn't sure that he should say. It might be a secret of the Order, what he had been shown in that damp cold chamber beneath the castle; so he said nothing until Rudel put his question another way.

"Did they show you the King's Eye, lad? Yes, of course they did, they greet you all with that. Well, don't let it hang in your own eye. That's what they want, they only do it to frighten you. Frighten and inspire, I suppose, but frighten mainly."

Frighten him was mainly what the sight had done, to be sure. Frighten and inspire, yes; but awe and terror were so closely matched and so easily confused, and right now everything that the Order touched seemed to make him shudder, like a cold hand laid on him in the heat.

A deep breath that was almost a gasp at his own temerity and then, inevitably, "Have you, have you seen it, sir?"

"I thought you meant to call me by my name."

"I'm sorry, sir. Ru, Rudel, I mean. But," all in a rush now, a frantic burst of honesty, "I don't think I can and I'm really not sure that I should, and I *am* sure that Fra' Piet would say that I shouldn't, he'll make me pay a penance for it if I tell him that I have and I'd have to do that, I'd have to confess, it'd lie on my conscience else and fester there…"

"Gods, what do they *do* to you boys? No, don't answer that. I know what they do, I've seen it. All right, call me as you will. I'd ask you who you think I am, to be deserving of so much respect from a young devout like you, except that I know the answer to that one too. Just a shabby conjuror, a singer of songs and a teller of foolish tales; but a guest none the less, and so honoured. Isn't that right? You'd honour a barefoot beggar and never realise how much honour that does you, though your superiors know it too well. It's this urge to confess that worries me more. Can't you remember what it felt like, *not* to tell your secrets? When you were a child, Marron? I'll wager that nothing festered then."

Yes, he could remember; but all those memories were painful to him now, because all those secrets had been shared with Aldo. Determinedly, Marron came back to what might or might not be a secret, but was apparently shared with the jongleur either way. "Have you seen the King's Eye? Sir?"

"Not as you've seen it, I fancy. How is it for you, shadows and glory buried away in some dark and hidden chamber? Well, let me tell you, lad, it shines as brightly in full sun, in all the noise and sweat and fear of a war."

For a moment Marron thought that was all he'd be granted, a glimpse of another man's secret too soon snatched away. But Rudel sighed, shook his head vainly against the persistence of memory or perhaps against the stupidity of man, and said, "I was down in Less Arvon. Twenty years ago, this was, when all the songs I knew and all the skills I had were violent. I had taken service with the duke; the Little Duke he is called, you'll have heard stories about him. Well, some of those stories, I was there.

"It was a quarrelsome time. The Sharai infested the hills to the east of his country, and there was brutality and treaty-breaking on both sides. Caravans raided, castles taken and retaken. Prisoners slain, of course, that was the governance and practice of the war.

"The duke led an army himself, in the end, when it seemed that he might lose his borders. He drove the Sharai back, but of course he pursued them too far, he was always a hothead. And of course the bulk of the men were left behind, foot soldiers can't keep up with cavalry in a hard chase; and privately I've always believed that some of his own family drew rein deliberately, to let us ride off into trouble. There was always a faction held that the dukedom would be better in younger and less impulsive hands.

"At any rate, there were fewer than two hundred of us with him when we finally got it through his skull that we rode alone. We were a long way into debatable lands, frankly lost, and surrounded by enemies; we couldn't see where the Sharai were regrouping, but of course they would be. That's how they fight, strike and retreat and strike again. Remember that. And they're devils on horseback, those fine-boned little things they ride, faster than you can dream and they turn like dancers. Remember that, too.

"One thing we knew for sure, we couldn't go back as we had come. We sent outriders that way, to see if the army was following; the Sharai returned them to us, strapped into their saddles and missing a few pieces. Tongues and eyes and such. Not dead, though. We had to do them that kindness.

"To be true, I thought we were all of us dead men. White bones walking. Especially when the arrows started coming, out of dead land. We couldn't see the archers. We lost men and horses both; I think we'd have broken if we'd known which way to run.

229

"But we had a troop of brothers among our number. They'd been first in the field, as always; and their elder, their confessor took a twisted candle and set it on a rock, and lit it. He mumbled some nonsense over it, I was close enough to hear and it was no language that I knew, I thought it some death-rite of the Order to take our souls to glory. Only then he held his hands in the flame, and it burned him not at all; and the light of it outshone the sun, filling the hollow where we were grouped and turning the trees to gold.

"Even the duke was amazed. I was nearest, and first to find my tongue; I asked the brother what this was. 'You stand in the King's Eye, my son,' he said, 'and he will see us safe.'

"And so it proved. No more arrows came, and that was blessing enough; but then he set the candle on his saddlebow and led us back along the valley, and all the land glittered and shone and was empty. We had to walk, the horses were half crazed and would not be ridden; but we met no Sharai and none of our army either, in a march of hours. The candle burned out at last, though one doubled taper should never have lasted so long; and then the brother cupped the last of its flame within his hands, and it burned there as brightly as ever it had and the light flowed out between his fingers.

"Where he led us, where we walked was familiar, and yet not so. Though the hills seemed the same, it had been autumn but the air was hot and crisp, stinging in our throats; and the earth and the rocks too were warm, and their touch tingled on our skin. Where we forded rivers, the water steamed and we could not drink it; it ran slowly, and glittered strangely. There were no birds, no insects.

"At last we came out into the plain, and that too seemed empty of life until suddenly the brother flung his hands up, crying certain words I do not remember. The gold was gone in a moment and it was twilight, there were shadows and movement all around us and that was the bulk of our men, making what camp and what order they could without their officers."

As he told his tale, Rudel's voice had deepened and changed its rhythm, the jongleur's art taking charge of his words to make a small performance of them, to play upon his hearer. That too had Marron shivering.

But it was a performance on the move, on the march; Rudel hadn't stopped walking. Neither had the sun, if that had legs to walk with. Higher than the castle now it stood, its light flowing down over them like the heat, like water, and shadows were fractional. It could lack only a few minutes of noon. Which thought, which memory made Marron glance aside, suddenly conscious of just where they were along the track; and yes, there it was still, the little altar that Mustar had erected. Only one of those blue stones on its slab now, he noticed, vaguely puzzled: who would take a stone, two stones, and leave the altar standing? Thrushes, perhaps, to break open a snail's shell. If there were thrushes in the Sanctuary Land, if there were snails.

He could ask Rudel, of course, that man seemed to know everything about the world of life they walked through; but it was only a brief curiosity, and he had something of more moment, much more moment to override it.

He would need to pray, and wasn't sure that Rudel would pray with him. Wasn't sure if he should ask, even. *Your God*, Rudel had said, and that was blasphemy, and he'd been so casual about it. Hadn't even noticed what he'd said, perhaps.

Marron had made his prayers with only one man head to head, only with Sieur Anton. That was a special experience every time and he didn't want it tainted, overlaid by memories of another man's voice and his own doubts about that man's faith.

Neither, of course, could he walk aside to pray alone. But there was a third way, if they hurried. The village was not far ahead now, no distance at all to quick determined feet; and there was a temple there. Listen, soon its thin bell would be calling its people in. Never mind the unfamiliar rite and the press of strangers' bodies, better to hide his questions in a crush. Better far to stand or kneel or prostrate himself in a place where he understood nothing, where he felt a stranger himself.

So hurry, hurry went his feet, and Rudel kept pace with him as the deep tones of Frater Susurrus impelled them both, it seemed, tumbling down from the high castle and pushing at their backs while the temple's bell drew them forward.

And so they came to the village and through the village as the bells hushed, to the village square before the temple; and there they found confusion instead of order, high-pitched voices raised against the proper silence, fear where there should have been peace.

They found the people of the village, the old men and the children all in a pack, not filing into the temple to pray but babbling and staring. They found the priest in his beard standing before the open temple door with one arm out-thrust to bar it and the other lifted high as he called down the God's anger, it seemed, on the little group that stood huddled before him, a man and a woman with a baby in her arms.

Worse—worst, almost, of all the things that Marron could imagine to make this scene worse—they found his own troop of brothers gathered together in the square, all on foot around a single fretful horse, murmuring between them-selves as Fra' Piet paced towards the temple steps, his hand already on the haft of his axe.

M ARRON HESITATED, WANTING to run to his broth-ers to ask what this was about but shy of their contempt or rejection, knowing how poisoned they were against him now.

There was no matching hesitation in Rudel. The jongleur cursed under his breath and hurried forward, close to running before he reached Fra' Piet. The confessor had his hood up, so Marron couldn't see if he spared Rudel so much as a glance; but the two men reached the steps side by side, and matched their paces as they climbed.

Marron followed uncertainly, with many sidelong glances of his own. His brothers were mainly watching the priest and Fra' Piet, those who weren't cautiously watching the horse as it shied and sidled in their midst. Only Aldo was watching him.

He stopped before he'd set foot on the lowest of the broad flat steps. Up there was no place for him. He could hear well enough from down below, he could learn the cause of all this.

"WHAT IS THE matter here?"

That was Fra' Piet, naturally. Rudel seemed content now to stand back a little, perhaps merely to witness.

There was spittle on the priest's beard; more flew from his white-flecked lips as he said, "Holy brother, most welcome come! See these dogs now, they are not of the faith, see..."

And he wrenched at the man's rough robe, where already it was torn open at the neck; and true, there around the man's throat was a leather thong with a blue bead threaded onto it, which was the sign of a heretic Catari anywhere throughout the Sanctuary Land. The Sharai scorned those beads, Marron had heard, the Sharai said that they knew each other and they knew their god as their god knew them, they needed no other sign between them; but all the tamed and conquered peoples wore them. By their new masters' edict, as much as their own will: it was useful to tell heretic from believer at a glance.

As now. The man couldn't deny it, and Fra' Piet's axe had already left his belt when Rudel's hand clamped suddenly around its haft, just a finger's-breadth below the confessor's grip.

The axe stilled, as did the two men and everyone who watched them. It was a stillness born of terrible tension; Marron thought the axe might snap, he thought unseen muscles heaved and strained and matched each other strength for strength, he thought something had to break and neither man would.

Neither did, but no more did the axe. Fra' Piet chose another path, too proud to wrestle for his weapon under the eyes of his men.

"You imperil your soul," he said.

"Not I. There is a law, the king's law, that says such as these are as free as any in the kingdom, if they pay their taxes and do no harm."

"There is law," Fra' Piet rasped, "the Church's law, that says such as these may enter no church, no temple, no chapel nor any place dedicated to the God, on pain of the Order's justice."

That was true too, or so Marron had heard it. Neither did Rudel dispute it.

"And is this the Order's justice," he demanded, "an axe on the temple steps and no one to speak for them, no one even to name them before they die? The husband, the wife and the baby too?"

"The penalty is death," Fra' Piet said, "for such as they. They would have polluted the God's temple with their presence."

"It usually is death," Rudel agreed, and how was it that his voice sounded so measured and at the same time so sardonic, so condemning? "For such as they. Whatever the offence. But their death is not yours to deliver, Brother Confessor. Your masters must have a word in this. The priest too, and the village headman. Who are these people, and why did they seek to go in to prayers to a god they do not follow?"

Fra' Piet hissed—*be careful,* Marron thought urgently, *or he'll charge you too, jongleur, before the masters*—but said only, "Spies. They are spies who seek to hide among the faithful."

"The baby too? More likely they were afraid, under the shadow of your castle, and therefore sought to hide. Where is the headman?"

The headman was perhaps one of the dozen men who pushed past Marron then and hurried up the steps, all of them talking at once to the priest, to Rudel, to Fra' Piet and to each other. Through the babble Marron could hear nothing but the baby's wailing, which chimed cruelly with another baby's crying in his head, and the dreadful sound of that baby's silence after.

THE DEBATE ON the temple steps came to a resolution, of a sort. The man was bound to a pillar and the woman also, though her hands were left free to hold her baby. They would all three be taken up to the Roq after worship, to face the preceptor's judgement.

The villagers filed into the temple; the troop followed at Fra' Piet's word. Rudel beckoned to Marron and they too went inside to kneel at the back, almost in the doorway, all the space there was.

Fra' Piet led the prayers himself, to spare his doubts about the native rite. Let the villagers doubt and misunderstand, murmur and fall silent in the face of unfamiliar responses here in their own temple, so long as his troop was kept pure.

Marron, who could school his mind to the words and his mind's eye to the God—most of the time—when he prayed with Sieur Anton, could do nothing like it when Fra' Piet said the prayers. For all the confessor's own devotion, he had no gift to share it. His voice and manner made this a duty only, to spend the middle hour of a hot day kneeling among hot bodies and chanting words by rote.

Marron's arm ached, his eyes shifted, his mind barely registered when his mouth was speaking and when it was not. All his attention was out through the door at his back and focused on the world there, the three lives forfeit to his earthly masters. He had no doubt of their deaths; he had seen Fra' Piet's fierce righteousness work its madness on the whole troop, and he was sure the confessor's cold condemnation would do the same in the preceptor's court. Even the babe would die, for its parents' stupidity. And Marron had seen, heard, felt, made one baby die for Fra' Piet, and he couldn't bear another. He owed the world restitution, his own death or another's life to quiet that constant silence in his head. No matter what the God might make of such a bad bargain, every choice that came his way was soured now; he had little left to lose that he could care for.

IT STILL TOOK him a long time to find the nerve, to make the first small movement: still on his knees but shuffling backwards, reaching blindly for the light. Only Rudel's head moved to track him; no one else could see except Fra' Piet, if he could peer over all those massed bodies and make out one that shifted against the sun's glare beating in at the open door.

Marron met Rudel's questioning gaze with what he hoped was a telling look, a face that could carry several messages at once: *I have to do this,* and *don't make a sound,* and *thank you, I really enjoyed your company today.* He wouldn't, he thought, be having any more of it. No solace now, no hope of anything but loss ahead, and he'd lost so much already. Brave this might be; stupid it surely was.

Still, once moving, he wasn't going to stop. On his knees but stretching up, he saw Fra' Piet prostrate himself before the crude stone block that made the altar.

Now...

Quiet as he could, swift as he could manage, Marron stood and turned and stepped outside. From sticky shade to the dry burning glare of the sun; from company to solitude; from obedience to rebellion he went in a single pace, and never felt its moment.

F EELING NOTHING BUT urgency, Marron hurried along the temple wall to where the two prisoners stood bound to wooden pillars that supported the overhanging roof. The baby was asleep now, in the woman's arms; that was some relief, at least. Dark eyes watched him questioningly, and he pressed a finger to his lips, *be as silent as the babe, for your own lives' sakes...*

He fumbled inside Rudel's satchel, where it still hung on his shoulder; his fingers found the keen edge of a knife, gripped the handle and drew it out.

He saw the man's eyes widen, wondering, but he went to the woman first. Cut the thong that bound her throat to the pillar, stooped to free her waist and ankles. Quickly from her to the man and cut again, at throat and wrists and ankles; and then with a gesture led them down the steps to where Fra' Piet's horse was hobbled in the square.

Two strokes of the knife cut the hobble away. He straightened, gripped the bridle against the horse's prancing and beckoned the freed prisoners forward.

Can you ride? Oh, tell me you can ride... He had no language to ask them, but no need. The man swung himself up easily into the saddle and the woman followed, awkward only

237

because of the baby. A touch of the man's hand on an arching neck, a murmur close to a flicking ear, and the horse quieted. For a moment the riders gazed down impassively, then the man reached to brush back Marron's hood, to see more clearly. His eyes narrowed and he nodded, *I have your face now, brother.* The woman smiled thinly, as a twitch of the reins turned the horse's head away. Neither seemed much awed now by how near to death they'd stood, though they'd been craven before the priest.

MARRON WATCHED THEM leave, glad to see the horse walked till they were out of sight and out of hearing, not to make a noise that might be heard within the temple.

With them free and gone, though, the enormity of what he'd done descended on him in a rush. His hand was trembling as he stowed the knife carefully with its brothers in the scrip, as he slipped that from his shoulder and set it aside. There were other things than knives inside that scrip; a purse, for one. Forsworn already, outcast by his own choice, he could take it and run, abandon his habit before it was stripped from him and save himself the pains that must come soon; but no. He'd be a traitor to his oaths, his Order and his God, but he would not be a coward.

So he stood and waited there in the square, in the sun, until the soft sound of the responses ceased to murmur through the temple's open door. He stood and faced that dark square until he saw a figure move there, saw Fra' Piet emerge, stiffen, turn his head in search; saw his confessor all but run down the steps towards him, and moved not a muscle.

Met Fra' Piet's cold stare with his own, and answered his questions.

"Where are they?"

"Fled."

"On my horse?"

"Yes."

"How?"

"I freed them." *For a baby's sake, that you had me kill,* but he wouldn't say that. Not here, not to him. To the preceptor, perhaps, or to anyone who might choose to ask why.

Fra' Piet hissed air between his teeth and asked one more question, while his hand reached down to the axe in his girdle.

"Is there another mount anywhere in this village?"

Marron blinked, and answered honestly. "Only a camel, that I have seen; and that is old, and blind."

The axe came free of the girdle then, and swung. The last Marron noticed was that the head of it lay tight against Fra' Piet's wrist.

TEN

In the Dark

DARK. COLD AND dark.

Hunger, cold and dark.

Fear and hunger, cold and dark.

Pain also, he was hurting and frightened and hungry and cold; but all of those could slip away and be lost or forgotten as he lost or forgot himself, as his body came and faded, as his life did, jags and snatches. The dark was ever present, never lost. Even when they brought the light to see him by—twice they'd brought it now, brought it and taken it away and each time left a token to remind him, *here it was and now it's gone again*—even then the dark remained, lurking in all the corners, pressing in scornfully against that little light and rushing back like water at its tail.

Like us, he'd thought, *like us all, that little light: holding the Sanctuary Land but barely, sure of the God's purpose, sure of our doom or we should be, so little a light and the dark all around us, so strong and so constant, pushing, pushing.*

That had been a rare, a rational thought. Mostly he considered the dark, no more than that.

240

Memories came to him unsought, unwanted, unwel-
comed. He found them like seeds in the darkness whether
his eyes were open or closed, and they grew and burned and
consumed themselves like blooms of fire, making his eyes
sting, open or closed.

Nothing of his childhood, nothing of who he had been
though he might have welcomed that as a field to walk in,
smells and textures and voices that had loved him, anywhere
other than here.

All he remembered was moments, flashes, each of them
limned in that absent light:

—the axe, Fra' Piet's axe and how he held it, a moment of
stilled time: hand gripping just below the head so it was the
haft, only the haft that cracked on Marron's skull, and was
that cruelty or kindness?

—Aldo's face, so close: like waking up, that was, like waking up used to be when they could share a bed, when they
used to share everything or tried to. But his face so close and
so sad, this was not how it used to be; and his mouth saying
something that his eyes were not, "No, brother, he's stupid
still," while his eyes said *Oh my brother, where have we come to,
you and I?*

—the face of Master Infirmarer and no charity in it today,
only harsh assessment: fingers waking fire in his skull and in
his arm, voices that swirled and met like waters in a stream,
now running fast, now spreading wide and slow. "...No, not
well, but well enough. He'll do for you. How comes this to be
open again? I sewed it yesterday, and see, my stitches have
been cut."

"Likely he opened it himself," Fra' Piet's voice booming
and whispering, "to escape work another day. No, leave it,
Magister, I pray you. He is none of ours now, or will not be
tomorrow. Let him bleed tonight, as a reminder."

"He will bleed enough, though not I think tomorrow. A man must walk to judgement. Bind it up, brother, I will not sew again. Some we lose, and this one is small loss. One night in my cots here, I think, Fra' Piet, though he deserves it not; one night a penitent, as the rule is; he'll be hungry when he makes that walk."

—not the walk they spoke of, but a walk he remembered, a stumbling rather, hard hands to drag him and steps going down: lamplight swinging, a corridor, a cell with an open door and a body, his body on its knees now and shivering already in a loose white tunic and where had his habit gone, had someone taken it and must he do penance for the loss?

—no face but a body, another body in white and not his because it was moving and he was not. There was light in the corridor, they had brought light and would not let him see; but he smelled dung and familiarity and heard a voice, a whisper, "Here is bread, eat it slowly, slowly." A hand guided his to find it, where he could not see despite the light. "Here is water, drink it slowly. And here," the hand pressed something into his, hard and round and cool it was, "here is for tonight. Show it when they come, it will keep you safe..."

—no face but a body, and this one white and still and still not his. The lamp burned behind the visitor's shoulder and shadow cloaked all but the robe, but the robe and the voice were Sieur Anton's and he said, "Stupid, stupid! Even I cannot help you this time, Marron. You have been condemned. The judgement is that you must be flayed tomorrow before the Order, and then cast out naked into the world."

That judgement is right, the knight's voice said, *I cannot dispute it;* but as his robe swirled to fill the cell and block all light from what his hands did, a weight dropped silently into Marron's lap. *For tomorrow,* the silence said, *if you should choose it. If you cannot bear what must come else.*

As Sieur Anton stalked away, a last fall of light from the warder's lamp showed a soft blue gleam in Marron's palm, where he still held what Mustar had left with him.

Time was a creeping thing, with little to mark it. There had twice been light, brought and taken; three times now there had been sounds. Twice Frater Susurrus had called to him, midday and sunset he thought those must have been; once he had heard a screaming that echoed down the passage and drove the chill deeper into his bones. That too had brought its memory, he and Rudel on the steps above, driven back by another man's agony.

SLOWLY, TIME HAD taken the numbness and confusion from him. He knew now who and where he was; he was Marron, Fra' Marron for one more night and no more than that, by Sieur Anton's word. He knelt in the dark in a penitent's cell, and felt not at all penitent: only hurt and afraid, cold and hungry and very much alone. Sometimes he felt saved, that also, he felt justified: a life for a life, he had repaid the debt, and the voice of a wailing babe was stilled now within him. But that inner peace was fragile, too easily swamped or broken, he dared not touch it often for fear of losing it altogether.

He nibbled at bread and sipped water that he should not have, that Mustar had slipped to him; he stood to use the bucket and staggered, hastily knelt again and used it kneeling; and betweentimes he played with the two tokens he had been so carefully, secretly gifted, and understood only one of them.

Sir Anton's gift was a blade, and the second such the knight had given him. Not a sword this time; a misericorde, a knife slender and short as a girl's finger but wide enough, long enough to serve. If the fear grew through the hours of the night, if the memory of a man's flesh ripped from his living bones proved too terrible, if he could not face those leather straps with their iron barbs or the shame that came after, if anything but death came after—well, he had a way to escape them. That was kindness, he supposed. Of a sort.

Mustar's gift was a bafflement. He knew what else it was, he'd seen it, it was heresy: a blue bead worn at a man's throat, a blue stone laid on a makeshift altar, the sign of their false god. Too large, too heavy for a bead, this was a stone like those he had seen Mustar set out in a pattern of three. For tonight, Mustar had whispered. He didn't know what that meant.

He rolled the stone between his palms, frowning. Mustar was a boy and a believer, still practising his religion despite the dangers; but would even he believe that a little stone might turn a man from one god to another? *For tonight*, he'd said. *Show it when they come*, he'd said. When who came? *It will keep you safe*, he'd said, but safe from what? Not from the Order, that was sure. If they found it on him, if he showed it when they came for him, he'd face worse than a flaying. He'd face the questioners first, it would be his screams that filled the ears of the penitents and their warders tomorrow. Mustar must know that. He'd taken a terrible risk himself, to bring it here.

For tonight. Show it when they come, it will keep you safe.

A blue stone, three blue stones and a blue bead... Marron thought again about the boy kneeling at his little altar, laying out his stones and saying his prayers. What did a slave boy pray for, a captive taken from his people?

And then yesterday, with Rudel, he had seen the altar still standing but only one stone left. A bird, he'd thought; but stones this big, this heavy were too much for any thrush. A crow might take one, he supposed, but a man could do it easier. Or a boy. But any man who followed the God would have scattered all the stones and destroyed the altar.

A man with a blue bead, come from somewhere, for some reason. With a woman and a baby, true, but not like peasants. They'd ridden like masters. Like Sharai, perhaps? *Spies,* Fra' Piet had said, and he might have been right.

For tonight. Show it when they come, it will keep you safe.

Three stones could be a message. *Three days,* they could say; that day, the next day, and this. A man, a spy could take one, and that could be a message too: *we are ready.* A boy could take one, *we too are ready. For tomorrow.* And today that same boy could have taken the last, *come tonight*; and that boy could give it to a friend as a token, a sign to keep him safe.

DARKNESS AND COLD, hunger and fear and pain could make a young man's mind act strangely, see truth in nonsense. Marron shook his head, and winced at the soreness in it; he laid the stone down and tried to think clearly, to see that he was being foolish. He was weaving fantasies, no more than that.

But there had been three stones, and then one; and now he had a stone, and these stones were rare and dangerous, how many could there be?

For tonight. Show it when they come, it will keep you safe.

Marron groaned, in a whisper. His arm was aching badly after even so little exercise, rolling a stone in his palms; when he touched the bandage, he found it sticky. He must be bleeding once again. Well, that didn't matter. He'd bleed worse tomorrow. If he had a tomorrow, if he didn't use Sieur Anton's gift to escape it.

No. Not that. That was a knight's trick which would ill become a knave. Or a brother. It might suit Sieur Anton's sense of honour; for Marron it was not even a question.

Frater Susurrus beat out the hour again; that must be midnight. All his brothers bar the watch would be before the altar now; like those of a true penitent his own lips started moving, saying the office in an unvoiced whisper, though it meant nothing to him. Broken oaths and a love that failed, a faith that faded as the days turned rancid in the heat: the Order would flay him and reject him tomorrow, it had no claim any longer on his loyalty or his soul. But the words came regardless, and with the words came a picture in his mind, one man he knew who would not be praying with the brothers. And there was a count in his head, *three stones to one, and a bead at a man's throat, a stone here now for me and all the garrison praying*; and there was a tremor in him that was more than a starved lad's fancy, a vision of some evil worked against the castle now and he the only one to know or guess it, and was he to know or guess it and do nothing? How many lives this time, to set with those he'd taken against those he'd saved?

H E WAS MOVING almost before he'd taken the decision to move. He stood, and the darkness seethed around him. He grabbed at nothing and scored his palm on rock, leaned against it until the weakness eased, though it did not pass. Then he scabbarded the little knife in the bandage on his arm, where it could be held and handy; he gripped the stone tightly in his other hand like a token, a talisman, *oh, keep me safe, then. If you can.*

And he stepped without permission from his cell into the passage, which perhaps no penitent had done before him.

To one side he saw light, dimmed by distance but bright enough to his starved eyes; that must be the chamber where the lamp burned in its niche in the wall, where the warders stood on guard. Or knelt in prayer, he hoped, he prayed.

He turned the other way, not hopeful, walking slowly with his fingers trailing the wall. Closed doors meant empty cells; and then at the end of the passage one door both closed and bolted. For the questioners' guest, he supposed. No possible exit this way, though in honesty he hadn't expected to find one, he'd only hoped.

So he tracked back towards the light, ghosting past all the opened doors, knowing that even in the dark he'd shine in his white to any penitents' eyes that were looking. Luck: some slept and the rest prayed, and none glanced up to see him.

He came to the chamber at the end, and was lucky again. Two warders there as before, but knowing themselves redundant—what man of the Order, however strayed, would challenge the authority that had sent him penitent here?—they prayed as properly as their wakeful charges, side by side and hooded, on their knees and turned towards the light.

Marron watched them from the passage, waited breathlessly until the rite had them bowing heads to ground and chanting softly; then he slid one cautious foot out into the chamber, and then the other.

His bare toes made no sound on the rock of the floor, his shift didn't rustle, not even the stench of his fear betrayed him. He reached the stairway, and took a moment to bow himself towards the light in gratitude before he slid on upward, still placing each foot with care and doubly so after the staircase turned and he was blind again.

INTO THE KITCHEN, and suddenly warm; he paused for a moment by the bread ovens, just to feel the waft of hot air on long-chilled skin.

Out past the latrines, and this way led to the great hall and his gathered brethren but he turned the other, not so very stupid; what, should he burst in and cry danger to them all, with no more proof than a blue stone in his hand, betraying Mustar and himself?

No, he ran out into the open, where the breeze felt as warm as the air by the ovens, and up steps onto the high wall that circled the castle. By the God's grace the moon was high, giving him light to see by. Light to be seen by, also; but he knew where the guards were stationed, he should be safe enough here and he needed to be sure.

Movement caught his eye, where no one should be moving. He stilled, crouched, stared without breathing and saw white figures in the moonlight, others, darker, swarming over the wall.

That was his proof, his confirmation. He turned to go back down—and there was a man in front of him, dark-robed and deadly, a knife glinting light along its edges.

Marron gasped, flung his hand up desperately, and the man held his stroke. "Show me," he hissed.

Marron held his hand out flat, and the man took the stone from his palm. Looked at it, nodded, sheathed his knife.

"Come…"

The man half turned, and that half-turn was enough. Marron slid the misericorde from his bandage and thrust blindly, felt a moment's grating resistance and thrust harder. There was a rush of warm wetness, the man made a quiet choking noise and slumped heavily, dragging the slippery knife from Marron's grasp as he fell.

NO MORE CAUTION now. Marron sprinted down the steps and through the castle, his arms flying as wildly as his feet, shoving at the walls to push him on faster.

At last the court, the final climb, the corridor he sought; he all but fell against Sieur Anton's door, shoved it open and stumbled inside.

"Marron! What in the world…?"

Sieur Anton was in his nightgown, had been on his knees. Now he was on his feet, stepping forward and then checking suddenly, standing very still.

"Marron, what have you done?"

Marron had blood on his hands, he saw, as they twitched in his sight, beckoning like frantic claws. Blood on the once-white shift, too; the fabric was heavy with it, clinging. He hadn't known a man would offer such a gift of blood to his killer. Or he'd forgotten, rather. In the village they had bathed in blood, but he'd been hot mad then. Now he was cold, chilled, desperate as he gathered his shift and wiped his hands like a madman.

Sieur Anton, he realised, thought he'd used that little knife—as he had—but didn't know on whom. Didn't know, and doubted. He'd seen the warders, after all, who were placed to watch the penitents in their cells.

"Sharai," Marron gasped. "There are Sharai, climbing the north wall. I, I killed one..."

The knight needed no more than that. He seized his sword, drew breath for a bellow—and then held it, shook his head. "All at prayer, yes? They'll not hear us from here. Marron, can you run to the hall?"

Marron shook his head. "Not me, sieur."

"Not...?" A momentary frown, which cleared quickly. "Oh. In the circumstances, no, not you. But I must go to the wall and hold them, if I can."

"Me too, sieur." Bold as he'd ever been, Marron ducked across the room and snatched up the sword Dard from where it lay in its white sheath on the chest. "You gave this to me, sieur, it is mine to use."

"Surely, take the sword—but if ever you practised obedience, do it now. Run to the bell, rouse the castle. If two can hold the wall, perhaps one alone can do it also—but neither can do so for long."

MARRON WASNT SURE that he did still practise obedience, in anything or to anybody. This time tomorrow he would be dead to the Order, so why not this time tonight? He'd likely be dead for real in an hour's time, so why not in five minutes' time instead, and fighting with the knight?

But he didn't truly believe in death, or not his own; and he did still believe in duty, and in hope.

Sounding the bell, rousing the castle was sensible. Nor was there anyone to do it bar himself.

Side by side, the two ran together. They met no one, saw no shadow shift; when Sieur Anton's hand moved in a chopping, urgent motion, *you go that way now,* Marron had no choice but to leave him and run on alone.

H E'D NEVER VISITED what they all called Frater Susurrus' Cell, but he knew where to find it. Up and up, as high up as he could go, the highest point in the Roq and in any of the country round about. At the top of the tallest tower was a bell-shaped chamber of stone with windows cut wide and high at every quarter, open to each and any of the winds; and the shape bespoke the purpose, for there hung the bell that spoke the Great Hours and called the Ransomers to prayer.

Oddly, there was no watch kept from that chamber, or none official. *Brother Whisperer keeps his own eyes open,* they said; but if that were true he must be blind or mute at night, for he spoke no warning now. Marron leaped up the last of the stairs and plunged across the flat roof, tumbled into the bell-chamber and came up short against the awesome presence of the bell.

In the moonlight he saw it more as shadow than substance, but it was shadow with a voice, shadow that chose silence just for now; and even that silence pulsed at a level way below hearing, as the night breeze stroked the great bronze flange of the bell and so light a touch still drew a humming from it.

It hung from a frame wrought of timber and steel and stone, and high as that frame was—perhaps three times Marron's height—the bell's rim was still only knee-high above the floor. He couldn't imagine the weight of it.

Neither could he see how it was sounded. The bells he knew, from chapel or temple or abbey, all hung high in a tower and were rung by pulling on a rope; no rope could topple this massive thing, to make an unseen tongue cry against it. He reversed Dard in his hands, still sheathed, and struck at the great bell's flank with its pommel.

The bell sang, but softly: Brother Whisperer indeed, a throbbing chord that made his bones shake because he stood so close, made the stone floor tremble beneath his bare feet but would never reach down to where the Order prayed in the great hall so far below.

Still he hammered at it, twice and three times, desperately, uselessly, or so he thought. But there was suddenly another noise in the stillness of the chamber, a scuffling sound and then a figure moving against the moonlight, a small man in the robe of a brother stumbling out of the bell's shadow to confront him.

"Who strikes, who strikes my brother? It is not the hour!" His voice was loud, flat and slurred; his eyes were wide, his hands hard and calloused as they pawed and thrust at Marron, pushing him away.

"Brother, make it sound, there are Sharai below…"

"Who? Who strikes? It is my duty, mine, and this is not the hour…"

"Don't you hear me? There are Sharai on the walls!" But no, the man did not hear him, he only slobbered and shoved. Deaf, Marron realised, stone deaf and perhaps half mad also after years of tending the bell too closely.

Marron backed off until he stood outside the chamber, on the tower's roof with his face full in the moonlight; he gripped the man's shoulder in his one free hand, his bad hand, and mouthed the words carefully. "Sharai! Sound the bell, wake the castle!"

Still no reaction, and Marron was half crazed himself now, frustrated and enraged by this stupid twist of fortune. He pushed the man back into the chamber, though it hurt his arm to do it; he slipped Dard free of its sheath and held its blade to the man's throat, screaming. "Sound it! Sound the bell!"

Whether he understood at last, or whether he was only trying to call help to himself in the face of a lunatic penitent with a sword in his hand and blood on his robe, Marron never knew; but the man stooped, and straightened after with a rope in his grip. He hauled on that frantically, let the rope slide away between his hands and hauled again, and Frater Susurrus cried out full-voiced beside them.

No wonder the man was deaf. Marron gasped and staggered out into the night, pursued by the bell's roar. It made the air shiver, again and again; he thought his ears must be bleeding as his arm was, as he stumbled blindly down the tower's stairs. The terrible weight of sound shoved at his back and flowed around him in the darkness like falling earth or water. It could pick him up, he thought, and carry him down, roll him over and over and crush him utterly if once he lost his feet on these narrow steps.

SAFELY DISTANT WHEN he reached the tower's base, for a moment he felt stupidly safe.

Then he heard the mutter and rush to his left, brothers hurrying—all in order, though, in their well-drilled troops— running from the hall in response to the bell's alarum. To his right he heard faintly the clash and grate of steel on edged steel.

"Swords, swords! Sharai!" he cried to his left, to where the masters came pushing through the throng. "Sharai on the north wall! Fetch swords!"

And stayed not to see that he was understood, but turned to his right and ran with his own sword light in his hand, shimmering like cold flame under the moon; ran to the foot of the stair that led up to where he had killed his first Sharai.

That man's body or another's lay sprawled across the steps now. Above, atop the wall, he saw Sieur Anton like an angel of war, robed in gleaming white and shifting, dancing, all grace and strength as his sword leaped and spun, as he fought for his life and the castle's safety.

All along the wall, dark figures moved and massed. Only space up there for one at a time to cross swords with the knight, but others were descending, swarming down the same ropes they must have used to scale the height of the wall. The ropes that Mustar and the other boys must have let down for them—but no time to think of that now. Marron saw half a dozen dark-robed men drop down into the court, with others right behind them; and he left them all for his brothers, ran up the steps to fight beside Sieur Anton.

ELEVEN

The Living Bleed

EVERY NIGHT THE bell woke her with its sonorous, jarring call, but it had done that once tonight already. She'd muttered a brief prayer and gone to sleep again. Not a dream. That had happened, she was certain.

But now here came the bell again, thudding into and through her body, startling her up from the bolster; and not the regular call to prayer, three slow strokes and silence before another three. This was rapid, almost racing, a juddering incoherent cry from a man in a panic, she thought. She'd never seen a brother in a panic, except perhaps that lad Marron trying to pour wine with Elisande flirting at him around her veil. Certainly they didn't panic without reason. This must be an alarm, *wake! wake!*

That was reason enough to have her out of bed and running to the window, trying to look through the carved screens and seeing nothing. Working the latches with a grunt and swinging the panels back to lean out, and still she could see nothing. Ink-black, soot-black shadows, silver lights where the moon touched a glint from the stone of wall or

254

ward, nothing more than that. No torch, no running man, no hint of threat.

Elisande was beside her, hanging out so far Julianne snatched anxiously at her shoulder. The other girl only glanced at her glitter-eyed, twisted her head awry in a vain attempt to see around corners and said, "What is it?"

"I don't know. The bell..." It still went on, making the air thrum, making her teeth ache, setting her every small hair arise.

"Yes, Julianne," with a hint of humour yet in her oh-so-patient smile, "but why?"

"I can't see..."

No more could Elisande; but, "Listen," she said.

She was right. Dominant though it was, the bell's disordered voice was so bass that it didn't drown out other noises. Straining, she could just make out faint sounds of battle, the clash of weapons and men's voices crying loud.

Elisande was gone from her side before she realised. Julianne spun around to see her fumbling in the shadows beside her bed, hauling something from the pack that held all she chose to travel with.

"What are you doing?"

"Well, I can't go out like this," and her fingers twitched hurriedly at the ties of her nightgown, tangled the bows into knots and gave up; she grabbed at the fabric and yanked it over her head like a child, wriggled and tugged and tossed it aside.

"Out where?"

"To see what's happening, of course. Do you want to sit and fold your hands and wait to be instructed? You're not married yet, Julianne."

That told, that was the killer blow. Julianne turned towards her own bed, her own clothes; but Elisande was already dressed in the same peasant burnous she'd been wearing when they met, was jamming her feet into boots and obviously wanted to be gone. Every dress that Julianne had brought would be too slow in the donning for Elisande's impatience, and hopelessly awkward if they found trouble out there, if they had to run or hide.

"Have you got another one of those?"

"Of course," with a full smile this time, showing white in the gloom.

ELISANDE HELPED HER with her own bows, dropped the burnous over her head and belted it with a length of rope. The stuff felt coarse and scratchy against her skin, and riding boots ridiculous beneath, but the choice lay between those and slippers, nothing more suitable.

"One thing else," Elisande said. "Take a knife," and she held one out on her palm, handle foremost.

Julianne grinned mirthlessly. "Keep it," she said, turning back to her trunks and boxes. "I have my own," in this at least her father's daughter and no man's quiet wife, not yet.

Jewel-handled knives she carried, costume pieces with blunted silver blades, pretty adornments for a pretty wife if young Baron Imber should think her pretty or care for her adornment. But those were not the extent of her armoury. When a girl, any girl ran wild in the streets of Marasson, she did well to carry a blade or two, to prick men into manners. When that girl was the daughter of the King's Shadow, she had need and duty to protect herself. Julianne had been grateful more than once for the feel of a good sharp knife in her hand, and the knowledge of how to use it.

She pulled two now from their travelling-case, and couldn't resist flicking them neatly hand to hand in a jug-gler's shuffle before she thrust them into the rope girdle.

Elisande nodded approval, and stowed her own blades the same way.

The lamp outside the door had burned out; they held hands on the darkness of the stair, and still for a while longer as they slipped through the castle, towards the sounds of fighting. Ghost-footed, the two girls made no more noise than the breeze, or so Julianne imagined. She couldn't hear their steps, and if not she, then who? Amid the row, the cries and clatter of the fighting up ahead?

Nor would they be spotted soon, she thought, if they were careful. These dun-coloured robes they wore, light enough to blend with parched earth and dust in the daytime, were dark and dull enough not to shine at night. Even with the moonlight full on them, and both girls were being wary to avoid that.

SO THEY CAME as spies to where the battle was, in a long outer ward below the north wall. Elisande taught Julianne in dumbshow how to turn her knife in her hand so that the blade lay inward, against the soft flesh of her forearm and within the loose sleeve of the burnous, where it could be hidden but ready, ready but hidden, gleaming in no stray beam of light. Then they scuttled and crouched, crouched and scuttled until they found a place to settle, against the buttress of a tower wall from where they could see easily but not easily be seen: deep shadow would guard them better than their knives might.

At first, crouching and scuttling, all that Julianne saw was a mêlée, a swirling chaos of dark robes, bright blades, pale faces and others not so pale. This close, the sounds were still no clearer: the great bell had stopped its booming at last, but the battle was all clash and grunt, gasp and hack and scream.

Once in the shelter of the buttress, though, where she could squat and be still in the squeeze between cool stone and warm Elisande, she pulled her long hair down like a veil of shadow across her face and gazed out through the tresses. Now she could see more clearly: she could distinguish the brothers in their shapeless habits from the men they fought, who wore a different style of robe and used curved scimitars, whose jaws were often dark with beards, whose heads were always covered. *Sharai,* she thought. Dozens of them, but no more than dozens; doomed, she thought they were. They must be, surely. A raiding-party, and what could be the point? There were hundreds of brothers in the castle, and a hundred knights also. She could see knights in the throng, standing out in their white dress and also in their swordsmanship, their strength and skill: meeting the Sharai on equal terms or better, it seemed to her, where the brothers only blocked and thrust in simple, well-drilled movements. Blocked and thrust and fell, that too, injured or dying or dead. Individually, Brother Ransomer against Sharai, this would have been a slaughter, she thought, and herself and Elisande only the least part of the prize; but fear ebbed quickly, as she saw no real danger. Even without the knights, sheer weight of numbers must have won this battle for the brothers.

Discipline was asserting itself after the shock of the sudden attack, she thought; or else she was beginning to understand what she watched, to see order where all had seemed random before. She saw how senior brothers, troop-leaders marshalled their forces around them, and how the knights did the same, urging men forward or calling them back, taking control. The Sharai had their own discipline also, but they were falling back, although there was nowhere they could run to. *Disciplined to die,* she thought, and hoped they thought the fighting had been worth it.

Elisande nudged her with an elbow, pointed with her chin. Up, up on the wall above the ward: Julianne raised her eyes, saw black and white in motion against the stars. A man in a white gown, nightgown, another knight he must be, fighting at the head of the steps there almost alone; only a boy at his side and a step or two below him in a stained white shift, his squire surely, and the two of them facing off half a dozen or more. The narrow measure of the wall made that almost a single combat, though, or two single combats side by side when a Sharai leaped from wall to steps to take on the boy.

Julianne wondered why the nudge from Elisande, why the gesture, unless it was simply to call her attention to some pretty swordplay; the boy and his master both were elegance itself against the more brutal hack and thrust in the ward below. Though they had space enough above, and there was none down here...

No. Slowly, watching, Julianne recognised knight and squire. They were known, they were friends, or nearly so: that was Sieur Anton d'Escrivey, and the boy was Marron. Marron in white because he was under sentence, a penitent in the cells or meant to be, or did the Order free all its defaulters at the call to arms? Perhaps they did, though no one else was fighting in a like loose shift. Neither in a nightgown, as d'Escrivey was.

Nor was anyone else, knight or brother, climbing the steps to help them. Julianne had been observing with her father's eye, analytical, judgemental, as he would expect of her; suddenly she was herself again, watching people she knew and worried for.

She looked around, and there was the preceptor himself, standing aloof from the fray. If she asked, surely he would send men up to help? If the Sharai held the wall, they did after all hold a way of escape or reinforcement, and would remain a threat until they were driven from it.

She nudged Elisande in her turn, to say a silent *come with me, we can help them*; but if the message was understood, it was wilfully misinterpreted. Elisande nodded, rose from where she squatted on her heels, and moved fast in completely the wrong direction. *Towards* the steps...

"Come back! Where are you—?"

Only a whisper, too soft and too late. Elisande didn't check her cautious but urgent progress across the ward, huddling low even as she leaped over bodies and skirted pools of blood, until she had found a new shelter in the shadows below the wall, in the crook where the steps climbed to the walkway.

Invisible she might be—only a pale blur of face against black stone, and that only when she moved—but she was vulnerable too, she must be. Julianne could see the ropes hanging down from the battlements, where the Sharai must have descended the wall; how if more came down, only a few paces from where Elisande was lurking? Or how if those in the ward rallied and fought their way back, to climb up and make their escape...?

Julianne was on her feet by now, and following. Two were twice as easy to spot, of course; but it might be a knight or a sharp-eyed brother who spotted them first, and brought men to their relief. If not, two could fight twice as effectively also. *And die with twice the loss*, but that was a thought for later.

Trying to look in three directions at once—forward to Elisande, left to where the fighting was, right to where the preceptor watched, though he was not watching her— Julianne forgot to look down. Her feet could never have picked their own way through such a carnage; she stumbled over a body's outflung arm, slid when her other foot came down in something greasy and fell with a squawk onto hands and knees. Looked around to see if she'd been heard, decided she'd been lucky—or its opposite, perhaps—and looked ahead to see more clearly what path she should follow to get to Elisande.

And saw Elisande fully, saw her step from shadow into moonlight, saw her arm stretch back and then hurl itself skyward; even saw—or so she thought—the flicker of a rising star that was Elisande's dagger spinning, streaking up from ward to wall.

Julianne stared upward, her eyes dragged behind its flight. A man, Sharai, stood against the stars with his sword-arm raised, frozen as it seemed, not slashing down as it was surely meant to. D'Escrivey it was who moved, whose own sword cut the night; the tip of it cut a throat neatly, the man toppled and fell.

Only for a moment, Julianne's gaze followed that fall, anxious for Elisande beneath it. Then a savage scream wrenched at her, jerked her attention up once more. Not the falling man who had screamed, he only thudded mutely to ground. She saw another Sharai—young by his cracked voice, though his face was just a beardless smudge in moonlight—crouched on the wall and staring down, then twisting to stare at d'Escrivey. And standing, trying to push through his companions towards the knight; and being blocked, hauled back, thrust to where someone was pulling up one of those dangling ropes.

Enough of watching. Julianne scrambled to her feet and hurried over to the wall's base, to find Elisande on her knees beside the body of a Sharai. The one she'd felled, she and d'Escrivey between them. She was pulling her knife from his side, and there were unexpected tears on her face.

"Elisande...?"

The dash of a rough sleeve across her eyes, no more than a shake of her head and a scowl for her friend, and a few hard words squeezed out from a full throat. "No. Leave me. I have to give him grace."

She reached to lay a hand on the dead man's brow, heedless of the blood that had spattered it; she began to murmur, to chant in a soft sobbing voice and a language Julianne didn't know. Elisande seemed not to know it well, either, or not to have used it for a long time. It was more than distress made her tongue pause and stumble and repeat. Her eyes were closed and her body rocked slightly to and fro, and that seemed to be ritual too, enough perhaps to carry her through where her memory failed her.

Julianne backed away, as she'd been asked to. She looked up, and saw that positions on the wall had been reversed; one Sharai was fighting to hold d'Escrivey back, to give his companions time to flee the trap the castle had become. One brave Sharai: he fought well, but she could see he was outmatched, and he'd have no chance to get away himself. At least one rope must be hanging outside the wall now; she watched men scramble through an embrasure and disappear.

D'Escrivey parried, feinted, thrust casually and his opponent fell. The knight stepped across him with Marron still at his back, still watchful. Together they walked to the embrasure, where d'Escrivey lifted his sword as though to cut the rope that Julianne couldn't see, that must be there; but he paused, and held his stroke. Murmured something to his squire and turned, looking down into the ward as he strode towards the stair. Julianne pressed herself back into the shadow of the wall; there could be no danger now, the last of the raiders were penned into a distant corner and she didn't want to be spotted and treated like an errant child, conducted back to her chamber under an unnecessary guard. Neither did she want Elisande interrupted in her quiet chanting. Whatever that rite meant, it meant something important to her.

When knight and squire both were away and out of sight—heading for the infirmary, she hoped, if those dark stains on Marron's shift were what she supposed—she hurried over to the steps and up onto the wall, trying to look purposeful and entitled. Trying to look like herself, of course, nothing more. She most certainly was entitled, she was a guest here and no prisoner; and as to a purpose, she genuinely did have that. She still didn't understand this raid, so few men against a citadel so strong. And she hated ignorance with a passion, especially when it was her own. Her father had instilled that in her early: *always seek to understand, little one, always ask the question. Of yourself, of the world, of a stranger. And remember, the question is always, "Why?"*

So she went high to see far, although heights frightened her; and when she saw the plains move and spark, then she did understand.

ALL AROUND THE great promontory, the upthrusting base of rock where the Roq sat like a guardian bird—great bird, black and red, ill-omened bird, she thought—all around it seethed a shadow specked with light, a mass of men with flambeaux. Mounted men, she thought: too far below to see by the moon and those distant lights, far too far to hear sounds of hooves, but something in the way the shadow shifted said that there were horses under the men who held the brands.

There would need to be. What was she looking at, three hundred men, perhaps? A hundred lights at least, and far from all held flambeaux. There could be many times the number if they circled the scarp, if that was a besieging ring. They couldn't have brought up such an army on foot, not so secretly: however fast they'd marched, whispers of their coming would have run ahead.

Gripping tightly, staring down despite her terror at the drop, she made slow sense of what she saw, as with the battle, finding shape and pattern and meaning in what at first seemed chaotic. Although those faint specks of light moved this way and that, although the river of shadow that bore the light bulged and broke and rippled at its edges, still like any river it had its flow; and that was north, away. This was an army in retreat that she was watching. Not in defeat, not in any hurry, but on the march.

There would be no siege, then. They'd meant to take the Roq with a sneak attack, so much was clear. A small party must have made the climb up the north face of the hill and then the talus and the outer wall, hoping to fight their way through to the gate and let the main force in. At midnight, while the brothers were at prayer and the watch perhaps less watchful.

With the failure, the army was retreating. Good generalship, not to risk further loss on hope or improvisation: Julianne's father would approve, undoubtedly. So did she. Plan and strike, hold if you win and withdraw if not, to make another plan. Looking somewhere else she hoped, she fervently hoped. If the Sharai had taken Roq de Rançon, they no less than the Ransomers could have held it indefinitely; and that would have been the northern border broken, the shield-arm of Outremer. All of Tallis open to raiding or worse, Elessi as good as cut off... It could have meant the slow death of the kingdom itself, or possibly not so slow. The Roq was the key, or so she thought it that night, and if such a key should turn...

Though she'd never so much as travelled let alone lived anywhere within the Sanctuary Land, still she was her father's daughter, she had his restless love. Tonight she had visions, a Sharai horde sweeping down all the length of the country, through Tallis and Less Arvon and even hidden Surayon till it came to the gates of Ascariel itself, by which time there would be no man left to defend them. All terror and grief her vision was, all blood and fury: and all for such a small thing, a mark on a map, one castle lost from a land of a hundred, a thousand castles.

Only that the Roq was no ordinary castle, which must be why the Sharai were so keen to take it, sending so many men so far for a single fling of the dice; which was certainly why the king had given it to the Ransomers to defend. The best troops and the most of them, almost the only troops in Outremer who had no other role than to watch and guard and be ready to fight.

Watch and guard, fight and pray, she shouldn't forget the praying. Their enemy the Sharai general had not forgotten the praying. It took a cold mind, a cunning mind to come to people at prayer, she thought, with a sword in your hand. Cold and cunning the Sharai were, though, or were said to be: people with hidden hands. Desert people, those were the attributes they had to set against their hot and open country.

Patient people, also. She stood and watched them ride away, shadow and light and silence, and knew they would come again. And again and again, until her vision was a true seeing and Outremer was overrun. Even her father didn't believe they could be held back forever.

Despite the height she wanted to stand and watch for an hour, two hours, however long it took until they were quite gone, their little glimmer quite lost against the dawn. But men would be coming soon, she knew: brothers to clear the bodies from the wall, masters perhaps to see what she was seeing, an enemy departed. She still wanted to avoid that encounter, cold words and a silent escort to her room. Besides, Elisande was in the ward below and shouldn't be left alone too long, had perhaps been left too long already.

One last look and she turned to go; and as she picked her way across the fallen on the wall, one slumped figure reared up suddenly in front of her. His teeth gleamed behind his beard, his blade glittered in his hand, his eyes were white and shining; his pain was written on his body but his purpose too, that he meant to pave his way to paradise with one more infidel life.

She felt the haft of a knife cool against her hand, and
didn't know what to do with it. All her training failed her, in
one fatal moment. She stood utterly still before him, almost
lifted her chin to make his stroke the easier, to say a swifter
farewell to her father's plans and her own weary fears; saw
the sword's fall almost as relief, a liberty unlooked-for.

And was hurled back by a blast of air made solid, an
impossible fist of wind. Fell into an embrasure with a longer
fall only a hand's breadth behind her, gasped and grabbed at
the merlon to deny it—and no, she did not after all want to
die yet, it seemed, or not by falling—and hung there gasping,
staring.

Staring at a whirling rod of light and darkness, a spinning
black rope that drank moonlight and sparkled gold, that
stood not on the wall but a little aslant in the air between her
and the Sharai.

She knew of course what it was, and was still startled
beyond measure at its appearing, too bewildered to be grateful yet.

So too did the Sharai know what it was. He let go his
sword, which dropped with a dull clatter that was still
resoundingly loud amid their silence. She wasn't breathing,
neither she thought was he, and if the djinn breathed she had
never been told so.

The Sharai dropped to his knees, which forced more than
a breath, a grunt of anguish from him. Julianne thought,
that's enough, leave him, he won't harm me now. And heard
herself gasp again at the implications of that thought, the
certainty this time that the djinni was watching over and
protecting her. Even from her own foolishness.

The djinni—*Shaban Ra'isse Khaldor* it had named itself, she
remembered—either couldn't hear her unspoken thought, or
else chose to ignore it. It moved slowly, drifting, she might
almost have said, except that it moved against the wind and

266

with definite purpose; towards the Sharai it went, cruelly unhurried, and his eyes bulged with terror. He flung his arms up—*don't*, she thought uselessly, *don't touch it*, remembering the boy who had done that, who had lost his arm in its spinning coils—and he opened his mouth to plead or scream or maybe just to make a sound against this silent doom, and never had the chance to do any.

The djinni touched him, only a little, only the tail of its twisting body touched his chest. So little but enough, more than enough. She heard a tearing, wrenching, snapping sound, and briefly saw the gleam of bone and then a rush of what was dark and wet. The man leaped, no, was snatched high into the air, simply by the force of what had touched him; for a moment he seemed to hang there spread-eagled, crucified in air.

Then he fell, struck a merlon and fell again. Would be rolling, had she cared to look, down the steep talus below the wall; and then no doubt falling once more, a longer fall all the way to the plain. No matter. He was dead before the falling started. No doubt of that, there had been a scooped-out hollow where his heart and lungs should have been working behind their cage of bone, where instead the ribs had been splayed like open fingers, empty hands.

Steady. It's waiting to hear you scream, she thought, *so do not.*

It was waiting for something, certainly, or else it had simply chosen to spend some few minutes of its eternal time standing or floating in the air there, slightly asquint to the world unless it was the world, as she felt, that stood slightly asquint to it. Waiting, she thought, more likely. Waiting for her. Not to scream, not now, the moment had passed. To speak, then. To speak to it. *What do you want of me?* perhaps, or any other question forced by the moment, a scream in little, a cry without thought. *Never ask a djinni a question,* she remembered. Advice taken too late to heart, but she wouldn't repeat the folly, if folly it had been.

Neither would she kneel, nor curtsey, nor bow. Not if it had tricked her before, as Elisande claimed.

Guile was an invaluable tool, but it earned no respect.

So she stood erect and faced it; and she said, "I am grateful, djinni: though," just to make the point clear, "I did not ask for aid."

It laughed, that same cold silvery sound with nothing human in it. "Neither do I claim a debt for it. Lady."

"I must suppose, then," treading oh so carefully through the tricks and traps of language, "that your concern for me springs from some concern of the djinn, that is not clear to me."

"Indeed you must. And it must remain unclear to you, daughter of the Shadow. Only this, I charge you: go where you are sent, and marry where you must."

"You said that to me before. I do not forget. But," daughter of the Shadow indeed, with all that that implied as evident as she could make it in her stature and in her voice, she said, "it is my father's will that I obey in this." *Not yours, spirit,* written boldly in her thoughts and she hoped on her face and in her voice also.

"For the present, perhaps. I will say it to you a third time, Julianne de Rance, and also a fourth. Be ready. And remember, you stand already in my debt."

Not for tonight, it had said that; neither for its last appearance on the plain, before her galloping horse. Only for the first time, for those careless questions of hers and its unresponsive answers. She was not sure she was prepared to acknowledge a debt for so little given or taken, such a small exchange. She was certainly prepared to say so, here and now, only that it gave her no chance to do so. Sparks of gold flew from its rope of a body, faster and further, till she flinched back for fear of being burned; it spun itself into a cord, a twine, a thread of black, and then it was nothing at all.

Nothing except a whisper, at least, a voice in darkness, thin as the wind: "Tell Lisan there is one below she should also say the khalat for. The carrion-eaters will have his body and not leave a bone to be prayed over. His name was Kamaal ib' Shofar."

"Do you know *everything*?" she demanded furiously—and choked, too late, and bit her tongue in penance. And waited for the djinni's laugh, its answer yes or no, its casual assumption of another debt; and heard only the wind and distant voices calling on the walls, softer voices closer, mingling with grunts and groaning, the occasional sharp cry as brothers carried their wounded to the infirmary.

What did they do with wounded Sharai? she wondered; and thought probably that there would be none, that a knife's silent work would relieve that problem wherever it occurred.

Thoughts of the Sharai fallen reminded her of Elisande, down there among those labouring brothers. Alone and grieving over the body of an enemy, chanting what the Order would surely call heresy, and within their own walls too...

She went down the steps far more quickly than she had come up them and found Elisande not chanting now but still kneeling beside the body, too weary or too distressed to move. And she so active usually, so determined to see things done...

"Elisande?"

This time at least she wasn't sent away; the smaller girl lifted her head to look at her and even so much was an effort, her nod was exhaustion.

"I have, I have a message for you," which she didn't dare not to deliver.

"A message? How?"

"From the djinni," and never mind how, she didn't want to say. "It called you Lisan again, and said, it said there is

269

another you should say the, the khalat for, is that right? A man who fell from the wall, whose body will be lost, it said. It said his name, but I can't remember it now."

"It doesn't matter," Elisande murmured. "They are all lost, here. They will get none of the rites that their deaths deserve. I will say khalat for them all. This one was special," *this one I killed myself,* "but so were they all."

"They were brave," Julianne said hesitantly, "but they would still have killed us, probably, if they had won the gate and let their army in."

"Was that it? I wondered. And perhaps you're right, perhaps they would. There might have been a very great slaughter. Their codes forbid it, and so does their religion, but there have been so many killings now, on every side... These people were my *friends,* Julianne. I was their guest, they fed and sheltered me for a year, they visited me at my home..."

Where is your home? she wanted to ask, it seemed the obvious question; but what was more obvious yet, Elisande did not want to be questioned. Not now, not with tears running down her cheeks. Vulnerable she might be, feeling too much to keep her guard; but she was Julianne's friend also. So no, no prying questions yet. Besides, Julianne thought she might already have some answers and she didn't want to hear them just now, certainly didn't want them overheard.

"Not these men, surely?" she asked instead, innocently, stupidly.

"Their cousins, then. Men and women both, they gave me greater freedom than they give their own. And there are men here from so many tribes," she said, her mind sliding off suddenly, sliding back to the blood and bodies that she knelt among. "Beni Rus I have seen, Kauram and Ashti and the Ib' Dharan. This one is Saren, by his dress. These men should not be fighting together, it's so strange."

"Come back to the chamber, Elisande. Come now, before there's trouble. You can say your prayer there, can't you? Where we're private?"

"Oh, yes," she said. "I don't *need* their blood on my hands."

But she still made no effort to wipe it off; and Julianne had to help her to her feet, and support her across the blood-washed stones of the court until inevitably a brother did see them, and come to them, and escort them firmly back to their quarters in the guests' tower.

« ¤ »

JAZRA WAS DEAD, and the tribes were in retreat. The night and Jemel's heart had turned to bitter shame, and he hated Hasan more than he hated even the infidels in their high castle, more than he hated any man save one.

Jazra was dead, a blood-brother lost in blood, and all their oaths were broken. They had sworn their lives and bodies to each other, in public by the fire and in private again and again, in their single shared blanket and their bodies' heat against the desert chill; but the fight, the night had made a treacher of him. Of them both, because Jazra had gone ahead where he should have waited, Jazra had fought and fallen because he was alone. A knife had come from below, and the man in white had swung his sword, and so Jazra fell. Because he was alone where he should not have been, where there should have been another blade to guard him.

This blade, his blade, sworn to that. It had been Hasan, Hasan himself who had held Jemel back from just revenge; and all oaths were broken, and if Hasan had ridden with the Saren tonight Hasan would have died for that, this blade would have found out his heart.

Hasan was away, ahead, leading this withdrawal. That too was shame, and he should die for it. And would not, because the old men of every tribe and every fire stood with him in this, said yes. *We came, we failed,* they said, *we pull back. At least for tonight. We will take fresh counsel in the morning.*

And so they rode away and left their dead like a badge of their shame, for the infidels to display or disgrace as they chose; and still each tribe's oaths were holding—for this night, at least—and he couldn't believe that it was happening this way. His body twitched and sweated as though he had fever, coldly, as he would sweat cold he thought every night now, without Jazra.

THERE HAD BEEN such pride, such hope when they rode out, those weeks ago. The Sharai united, again and at last: all tribes together for this first great strike against the greatest of the infidels' castles. That would fall, they swore, and they would hold it. One try, an hour's unlucky fighting and all oaths were forgotten, it seemed, as dead as his own.

HASAN HAD ORDERED torches lit as soon as the climbing party was seen to have breasted the walls, to show that the Sharai did not skulk in victory or defeat, he'd said. To draw the guards' eyes outward from the walls was the general belief, not to let them see the blades at their backs. But that was before, that was when the strike was certain and defeat was a word for the infidels to learn at the scimitar's point or else perhaps in the collar of a slave, those few who were let live. So great a castle, there were bound to be some who hid or were just overlooked until the blood-debt was well paid. *There's a time,* the old ones said, *when everyone wearies of killing. No matter the offence, to us or to our holy places; comes a time when there has just been blood enough.*

He didn't believe it, himself. He couldn't imagine blood enough to pay this debt, though that man in white and every infidel in the land were wrung dry of it and Hasan too, and all the tribes of all the men who stood by Hasan this calamitous night.

Jazra was dead, and he wanted to kill and kill until these watery lands were as dead as the high desert wastes; and then at the end, when he was the last man moving under the sun—*like the Ghost Walker*, he thought, and shivered, and spat superstitiously into the dust, giving water to the land to buy its favour, not to meet the Ghost Walker this night—he wanted to kill himself and be dead also, to seek Jazra in whatever paradise there might be.

TWELVE

The Lights of Judgement

O N HIS KNEES again, hungry and confused and afraid again. Marron remembered that it had not always been like this, his life; there was a time when he had been comfortable and content, warm and fed and certain.

Only then had come his oaths, the fulfilment of a life-long promise, to follow his dead father to the God's war in the God's own land; and since then—*since Fra' Piet* his mind said, as though one man, any man else but himself could be to blame—nothing had gone easy or as it was meant to go. Blessed he'd felt once, but no longer.

Cold and afraid, hurt and hungry and very much in the dark, for all the sun that fell through high and narrow chapel windows to make a pool of light around him.

This time he was not alone, though, at least he had that to cling to. This was his judgement, he faced his accusers and each man's face was hard and set against him; but one man stood at his back, and gave his voice to Marron.

L AST NIGHT, AFTER the fighting was over, Sieur Anton had led Marron quickly, directly to his own chamber. "Now, while my confrères are hot for a chase," he'd said, "before wiser heads preach caution and daylight and send them to their beds to wait for it. I don't want questions," he'd said, "or even questioning looks."

"Sit on the bed," he'd said once they were there; and himself had fetched water in a bowl, cloths and bandages from Marron knew not where.

"Sieur, should you not go to the infirmary? You're hurt."

"And so are you; and no, neither one of us should go to the infirmary. I have everything we need. Show me your arm."

Actually, Marron had not been hurt on the wall, bar a few nicks and bruises. Fighting beside and behind Sieur Anton, he'd been largely protected by the knight's reach and skill. Only his arm had bled badly, and in the strange exultant giddiness afterwards he'd felt that to be normal, almost a part of him now, a sign he carried from the God or perhaps from Sieur Anton: a brand of ownership that he could mar but not mend.

Marred it was when Sieur Anton unwrapped it from its sticky bindings, a far cry from the clean cut it had been once, that should have healed quickly and left only a white seam for a scar. Now it was a fat and ragged mouth of red wet flesh, half grown over before it was torn again and yet again, with a margin of pricked scabs where Master Infirmarer's stitches had sewn it closed and then been cut away to let it gape again.

Sieur Anton had hissed softly as he wiped the blood away, had murmured, "Best not have it stitched this time, lad, for fear the flesh should rot within and poison the whole arm. It'll not be pretty when it mends, mind, but keep it clean and mend it should."

Strong fingers had held it firm against Marron's flinching as the wound was washed and dabbed with salve from a clay pot. *Horse-liniment?* he had wondered and not asked, biting back the giggle that the question carried with it. Then when the arm was bound again and the binding tied, Sieur Anton had stripped off his own blood-marked robe and it had been Marron's turn to wash and salve what cuts the knight had taken. No great hurt on him either; his own swordsmanship and Marron's blade at his shoulder had mostly guarded him. One bandage on his upper arm and one around his ribs suf- ficed. That done and over with, Sieur Anton had tossed furs onto the floor in a corner and told Marron to slip out of his soaked shift, lie down and sleep.

"Sieur, I should go back to the cells."

"Probably you should, but I forbid it. Come the morning, we will worry what you should or should not do. If you can- not obey your masters, try to obey me."

SO HE HAD; and had slept, though he'd thought he would not. Come the morning, wrapped in a fur for decency, he had prayed once more at the knight's side and then served him breakfast in his chamber, fresh bread and milk fetched by another knight's squire. Marron had refused to eat him- self, sick with nerves and giddy with memory and trying to make a point also, unless he was only giving a gloss of virtue to the sour-stomached truth. "No, sieur, I am meant to be fasting. I can fast," if he couldn't keep any other one of his vows, it seemed.

Sieur Anton had left him after that, ordered him to finish the milk if he would not eat, and then to lie quietly on the bed for an hour. Marron had dozed again, despite the pain in his arm and his restless mind; then the knight had returned, had him dress again in the stained and filthy shift, and brought him here. And now he knelt in the knights' chapel before the preceptor himself and half a dozen masters, the consistory court that would pass judgement on him.

SIEUR ANTON HAD told him little, only that scouts had ridden out at dawn to see if the Sharai had truly withdrawn or if they meant to attack again. And that Marron's trial was not postponed, that Fra' Piet had been required to stay within the castle to testify against him.

That testimony, Marron thought, had been damning. In truth, he had no defence. He had broken the Rule, acting in gross disobedience to save the life of a man who very likely was the spy Fra' Piet had named him, the woman and baby only a disguise.

But Sieur Anton stood behind him, and spoke for him: said, "Masters, there is no dispute of this. Fra' Marron has been foolish, wilful and disobedient since he came to this place, and his acts of yesterday imperilled the castle and every man in it. Every man, and every woman who guests here," which was twice damning.

"But Fra' Marron's acts of last night saved the castle, its garrison and its guests. That too cannot be disputed. The Sharai prisoners would not have told of the impending attack, even under question; they guard their tongues fanatically. If Fra' Marron had not understood what signs he had seen that day, if he had not broken his oaths again to leave his cell and give warning, if he had not alerted us all with his ringing of the bell, that raiding party would have won through to the gate and the Sharai would have ridden in among us."

Marron shook his head slightly; that wasn't quite right. There was no proof after all that the prisoner had been Sharai, or a spy; it was only his own mazed mind seeing patterns where perhaps none lay to be seen. The man might have been quite innocent, a wanderer trying to keep faith with his god and protect his family both at once in difficult

277

lands, difficult times. And it was Sieur Anton who had sent Marron to the bell—and the deaf brother there who had sounded it, but that was a quibble—and Sieur Anton who had delayed the raiders on the wall until more help could come.

But it was Sieur Anton too who had whispered one brief command to Marron before they came into the chapel here. "You say nothing, boy. On your obedience, on your soul, keep silence!" He knelt with head bowed, held his tongue and hoped that twitch of honesty hadn't betrayed him. He was sworn to tell truth to these men, if they called on him to answer.

"Masters," Sieur Anton went on, "I know Fra' Marron cannot stay within your Order. He has broken your Rule too often, and too grievously. He cannot keep his oaths, it seems, and he will never make a Ransomer. But I plead with you, on my knees," and the proud knight did indeed kneel beside Marron, "be generous. He is a young man, a foolish boy; but he is a brave boy also, he proved that fighting at my side on the wall. And he is an avowed enemy of your enemies, although he lacks the discipline to remain as one of your brotherhood. Cast him out from among you, but do it gently. Do not punish him, more than the shame of expulsion is a punishment; respect his courage for his father's sake, whom Marron has tried and failed to emulate. His failure is not his fault. You ask much of your brothers; no man should be blamed for being too weak to meet your standards. Cast him out, but give him to me, whole and unharmed. I am in need of a squire, and Marron needs a discipline less exacting than your own. I can teach him that much. Let me have him, and he may yet serve the God and the king in these dangerous times. I beg you, do not make a waste of his life, more than he has wasted it already."

Sieur Anton fell silent then, rising to his feet; Marron risked a glance up, to see the preceptor glance to one side and then the other, gathering the masters with his eyes.

"Thank you, Sieur Anton. We will withdraw," he said, "to discuss this. Remain here, each of you."

That meant Marron, and Sieur Anton, and Fra' Piet; and that last meant that Marron had to stay as he was, penitent and silent, not a word of gratitude or question. He glanced across to where Fra' Piet stood, quite still except for his thumb which stroked the keen edge of his axe, thrumming across it again and again, like a man giving rhythm to his prayers. To see even so much, Marron had had to turn his head a touch, enough to bring a warning finger on his shoulder from the knight who stood behind him. Sieur Anton was right, he had no discipline, no strength to deny even the least whisper of temptation...

THE CHAPEL FLOOR was cold and hard, his stomach churned and all his bones were aching. He wanted to raise his eyes to see the colours of light and paint around the chapel, and could not; he wanted to lean back against Sieur Anton's legs, and of course dared not.

He was trembling before the masters filed back in, and only hoped that Fra' Piet could not see it, that Sieur Anton would not think it fear. The court arrayed itself before him, and the preceptor said, "Fra' Marron."

He jerked, as though a whip had licked his back. He had been whipped as a child, as a youth; this lash of voice, he thought, was worse.

"Your faults are many, your offences grave. If you had done what you did and had not been of the Order, you would have died for it ere now. As a brother, you are sanctified to the God and we may not kill His servants; as a brother, you have betrayed the God and we owe you no duty except your life, if you were strong enough to keep it. His vengeance also He delegates to us, and neither He nor we are easy with a treacher.

"But as Sieur Anton d'Escrivey has said, you served Him well last night, though it cost another act of disobedience to do so. Because of that—because this reminds us that there can be virtue outside our discipline, for which humility we thank you—we are minded to accede to Sieur Anton's request. You must leave the Order, that sentence cannot be remitted nor should it be, you have no place with us; but you need not leave the castle, if you are able to stay and serve Sieur Anton with a better will than you have shown in serving us."

Was that a question, was he meant to speak? Marron opened his mouth, ready to say *yes, your grace* and whatever more might be required of him; and was forestalled, Fra' Piet's cracked voice insistent, incredulous, crushing his first faint breath of hope.

"Your grace, masters, he must pay his penance. The Order, all the brothers must see him pay—"

"You want to see him flayed, Fra' Piet?" That was Sieur Anton again, with a cold, condemning smile in his voice. "Then say so, don't blame it on your brethren. And yes, flay him by all means. Strip the flesh from his back, leave him useless to me or any man else. Why not? Let's sacrifice a skilled young fighter to your offended pride, that would surely please the God unendingly."

"He is only one man," chill matched with chill, only that Fra' Piet was not smiling, probably could not remember how. "The God calls us all to sacrifice. The penance must be paid, or all discipline will be lost. His troop saw what he did, so every troop will know by now. If there is no punishment, how can we look for obedience the next time a heedless, arrogant fool thinks he knows better than his confessor?"

"Marron is only one man, true; and yes, you can make an example of him if you will, to frighten others into a thoughtless obedience. But let word of that go back to where he came from, *he saved the castle and they flogged him half to death*, send his bones back maybe because of course you do not kill but sometimes brothers die regardless, and see how many more recruits that wins you. Do you know how desperate our case is, how few of us there are to guard this land? We have enemies on every border, and heretics within; we can ill afford to lose even one man, and if that loss means that we lose a dozen others, then it's a bargain that may cost us dear next year, or the year after. We fight for the God, we fight the Sharai; we should not fight each other."

"Enough!" The preceptor, not shouting but making the chapel echo. "You both forget your places. Fra' Marron is not the only one here who owes a duty of obedience; nor it seems is he the only one who forgets that, or finds it inconvenient. Sieur Anton, your rank does not set you aloof from punishment; neither does yours, Fra' Piet."

The knight at Marron's side bowed low; on the other side and farther off, Fra' Piet dropped to his knees. Marron couldn't see, but he heard the sullen sound of it, and knew.

"Nor is this court entirely foolish, Sieur Anton, to be moved to mercy by the sight of a warrior unwashed. You could, I think, have brought the boy before us in a clean shift. It might have seemed more appropriate, given where we stand. However, I was saying, we are minded to an unaccustomed leniency in this matter. Other voices than yours, Fra' Piet, have called for punishment, for the due measure of the Rule's prescription to assuage the righteous wrath of the God; but it seems to me presumptuous to assert the God's anger, where the consequences have been so beneficial. I have opened the King's Eye to see, and the army sent against us now stands some miles to the north and east. Magister Ricard has ridden out in force to harry it further, and I have hopes he may scatter it completely; he rides in secrecy, in the Eye, and will come upon them unannounced. However that may fall out, it is all but certain that this castle is in no danger now. None can say that would have been the case, had Fra' Marron prayed with his brethren last midnight and not been watchful in a penitent's cell.

"This, then, is my judgement: that having failed in your service to the Order but yet served the God well, Fra' Marron, you shall lose that title and the habit that signifies it. You shall lose the brotherhood of the Society of Ransom and be cast out from our number in the sight of all, never to be accepted again. But our gates shall not be closed against you, for so long as you serve the Knight Ransomer Sieur Anton d'Escrivey who has spoken for you. Are you content?"

"Your grace, I am content." Easy to say, hard to find a voice to say it with, relief was choking him; but he did manage a whisper, enough.

"Very well, then. It shall be done this evening, after prayers. Meantime, you will return to the penitents' cells to wait and pray this last day in our company."

"Your grace, is that necessary?"

"Oh, yes. Very necessary, Sieur Anton. One final day of our discipline, I think, before he must submit himself to yours. He is ours yet, until we relinquish him; and as Fra' Piet says, that must be done in the sight of all."

BACK IN THE dark, the cold, the hunger. This time, though, he had a bubble of warmth in his chest, the promise of hope realised. That was enough.

He also had a clean shift, tossed to him with mute disdain by one of the warders. It was a single length of worn white stuff, so thin it was near-transparent in places. The head went through a tear at the midpoint, and a length of coarse white cord tied around the waist held front and back together. Or was meant to. Marron had used hand and teeth to knot the cord into a double loop, a sling for his aching injured arm.

Probably that was disobedience, he thought, not to use the cord as girdle, as it was meant to be used. He didn't care. He had only a few hours of hungry patient waiting now, shivering with chill and anticipation. And no, he was not going to pray as the preceptor had told him to. He had spent a long lifetime, it seemed to him, on his knees and only a moment last night on his feet, Dard in hand, his skin wet with blood and sweat and fear like a live thing in his gut, the battle like a storm all around him, making the very air shriek; and he knew which had thrilled him, which his heart had leaped to like a creature coming home. Not like the slaughter in the village, when he had been mad, made mad. Last night had been trained muscles and a sharp mind balanced behind a sharp eye, fear but not terror, thrill but not frenzy.

Last night had been what he wanted, what he'd thought he could find in his father's legacy, in his father's life. What he thought now he would find at Sieur Anton's heel, like a good dog rewarded: the chance to fight for the God he might still, might yet believe in, without the poison of dead babies and friends turned unkind, confessors too ready to kill.

So he'd whispered the due prayers at noon, and had allowed himself a smile in the dark at the thought of Sieur Anton doing the same, equally alone in his room. He thought the God would not begrudge the smile.

And he had not prayed since, neither dwelt on what was to come at evening prayers. That was hours away yet, and would last only minutes. After that a new life under a new master, a new chance, bitterness set aside...

TROUBLE CAME BACK to Marron with the soft glow of lamplight and the soft sounds of feet approaching slowly, the daily delivery of bread and water, the emptying of buckets. Late today, he thought, but no wonder in that, given what had happened overnight.

The brother with the light and basket passed him by. No wonder in that either: he was disgraced, under doom of exile from the Order. Fasting was the least penance he could expect.

The brother came a second time with water, and again there was none for him. A third time the brother passed, and came not into Marron's cell even to empty his bucket. This time Marron was startled to recognise him as one of the warders from yesterday. Doing his own penance, apparently, for having been so slack last night, not seeing a penitent slip from his cell, under that man's very eye...

That made Marron smile again, briefly, when he was again left in darkness. But the smile was lost too soon, as he remembered that it was usually one of the Sharai boys who did this duty. Mustar had done it yesterday. A blue stone, *this will keep you safe...*

There had been nothing to keep Mustar safe. They had betrayed the castle, Mustar and others, he had seen them on the walls.

What had happened to them, to him? Marron didn't know, no one had said. Nothing good, though, surely. They might have died with the warriors, on the walls or in the court below; they might have snatched swords from the fallen and fought, and died with honour. Or they might be here, he thought, not penitents but prisoners awaiting the Order's harsh justice.

He had to know. Nothing he could do if he found them—in a cell with the door bolted, perhaps, they wouldn't be trusted as the brothers were—but he couldn't simply kneel here in patience waiting and not know. Mustar who had tried to save him might be just the other side of the rock wall there. Mustar who had saved him, who had stupidly saved the castle with a blue stone for warning, protection to a friend.

Marron stood up slowly, groping for balance against the dizziness of hunger and darkness. He shuffled forward, feeling with his one arm for the doorway while the shift swung light and loose against his skin. Found it, and peered cautiously out. These warders might be more watchful, having seen their brother doing penance for his carelessness. It might be an order, even, *trust no more.*

But there was only the light at the end of the passage, a dim glow in the chamber beyond and no figure outlined against it. He took a slow, wary breath and slipped out, turned his back to the light and felt his way along to the next cell. The door stood closed but not bolted, as before, he found that with his fingers; this time he opened it and the cell felt empty, smelled empty too. No sounds of breathing, no response when he hissed a greeting.

Out again, and on; the next was empty, too, and the next after that. No point now in going further, he thought; but he went further regardless, only because it felt good to be moving, to be one last time defiant. All the way to the end of the passage he went; and here once more he did finally find a door that was bolted against him.

And drew another cautious breath, took a grip on the bolt and moved it slowly. It slid from its bracket with never a squeal of metal on metal; neither did the hinges make a sound as he eased the door open.

What he hadn't expected, at this darkest end of a dark passage where he couldn't see his fingers' tips an inch in front of his eyes, he hadn't expected light. There hadn't been a glimmer or a hint of it squinting through cracks in the planking or slipping between door and jamb.

It was a curtain which prevented that, the heavy, dusty black curtain that he sidled straight into because he couldn't see it, black against black in this dead darkness. But it billowed just a little when his shoulder caught it, as he stilled;

285

and in its movement he could see it after all, or the edges of it as they spilled light.

He stood and breathed nervously in that narrow space between door and curtain, bewildered now. Only one solid, rock-sure thought in his head, and that was *don't let the warders see, if either one of them should look.* He pulled the door to at his back before gripping the felted curtain and twitching it aside, chancing a glance around it.

A cell, a larger cell: but more than that. Here was where the questioners did their work; their implements hung on the walls, their machines of wood and steel sat below.

No boys, but here was the man whose scream had met them on the stair, Marron and Rudel, whose screams he had heard again yesterday. Surely it must be him, that bruise-blackened and filthy figure sprawled near-naked on a rank pallet in the corner, his back to Marron, his face turned to the wall. The man who had come, been brought here in a barrel, they said, though Marron had not seen it.

Neither had he seen instruments of torture before, but not they nor the man could hold his eyes quite yet. Not in this light, not when the light was there to stare at, to seed wonder and terror in his fuddled mind like sparks from a dull flint.

He'd thought that he knew magic, that magic was the King's Eye, lines of hot gold which branded pictures deep inside his skull. That must be holy magic, he thought now, sanctioned by the God like the preceptor's light at midnight; and this must be its opposite, devil's magic, witchlight. If this man came from Surayon as the rumour was, and Surayon was anathema, then nothing good could it breed. Which meant that the soft warm glow pulsing gently from a globe the size of a big man's fist must be something cursed, malevolent; and he should be afraid to stand in its creamy light, he should dread to look upon it for fear of the taint entering his own soul and damning him forever.

But it hung in the air without strings or wires and burned nothing at all if it burned at all; and it didn't seem to him to burn, it only shone, light without fire. How could he help but stare?

Or move? Before he knew it, he had come all the way through the curtain and was standing heedlessly in the cell, directly under that ball of light with his head tipped back as if he were checking for those absent strings or wires; and he must have stirred the air or made some soft barefoot sound to declare himself, because the man on the pallet grunted and turned his head, and then cried out with the pain of that small movement.

The light died. Marron sighed softly, then whispered, "I'm sorry. Do not fear me."

"No? Why should I not?" The voice was a broken reed, as cracked and hoarse as Fra' Piet's, only that it kept yet some echo of humour in it; and despite the words the light came back, a little: a faint and pearly ball now, motionless and further off, where it would show Marron's face more clearly. "Even boys can be fearful, and I am a fearful man."

A man willing to play, it seemed, at least with words. Marron thought him not at all afraid, once recovered from that first moment of discovery, a stranger standing in his cell, in his surely forbidden light.

The light showed both their faces, and they both gazed in silence for a while, assessing, guessing.

Marron saw an old man gaunt and strained, unshaven and little fed; what the man saw, he didn't say.

What he did say, he whispered through swollen, broken lips. He said, "Well. You're not the boy, you're not any of the boys whom they allow to wash and water me, sometimes. You're certainly not the boy who slipped me an ayar-stone yesterday. But you don't choose to dress like a brother either," with even a hint of mockery, he could manage so much, to say that he knew Marron was not dressed this way from choice. "Perhaps you're right, perhaps I shouldn't fear you. I'll try not. At any rate, you don't look like a boy who'll run to tell your masters of my wicked light. Or am I wrong? Should I burn you where you stand? Who are you, boy?"

And the light flared fiercely, too bright to look upon; Marron twisted away and saw hard shadows shift across the floor, as if the light had followed his movement. He was the one who was afraid, as he was meant to be.

He straightened, turned back to face the man and said, "My name is Marron. I am, I am a brother here," though for only a few hours longer, "and I do not believe your light can harm me," or surely the man would never have come to this, starved and tortured in a hidden cell, surely he would not have let it happen?

The man laughed wheezingly, and the light faded to a comfortable glow once more. "No? Well, perhaps you're right again, Fra' Marron. Perhaps it is only a toy, though it could damn me; but likely I'm damned already."

As Marron was likely damned also, if anyone should hear of this. Sieur Anton he thought would be no more forgiving than the preceptor, if he heard that his squire blinked at devilry.

But blink he did, deliberately stepping forward under the globe of light. Mustar had given this man a stone also, an ayar-stone, that must be what he meant; it had to be significant. *My friend's friend*, he thought, trying to understand it.

He knelt beside the filthy pallet and said, "Sir, can I help you? In any way?"

The man's mouth twisted, something like a smile it made. "You're a strange brother, Fra' Marron, and not only in your dress. If you're not a trick of those questioners of yours, more subtle than their usual. You could pass me a drink of water."

"Sir?"

"Over there." A nod towards a flask and a goblet, little more than an arm's reach away; the man lifted an arm to show how it was shackled to the wall, a clinking chain which made that reach impossible. "This is as subtle as they can manage ordinarily, to leave it just a finger's length beyond me."

The wit was as dry as the mouth must be. Talking clearly pained him, but he talked none the less. In these past days the man must have screamed a lot, but talked hardly or not at all. Marron poured water into the goblet and held it out— then looked again at the state of the man's hands and held it to his lips instead, tilted a little, watched how eagerly, how greedily the throat gulped the water down. He refilled the goblet and helped the man to drink it, then used the hem of his shift to wipe up what had been spilt on chin and bare chest.

Dabbing gingerly with the damp cloth at stains of blood and sweat on the man's face, he said, "What's your name, sir?"

"Ah. No. No questions, Fra' Marron. You might yet be a trick." The voice was stronger now, but no less caustic.

"No, sir. I am, I am under a doom, to be expelled from the Order."

"Indeed? Even so. No questions, please. You can call me Jonson. You're not supposed to be in here, I take it?"

"No, sir. I was looking for someone else..." And hadn't found him, or any of them; and was trying not to worry about that, not to see Mustar and the other boys dead in a pit. Perhaps they'd climbed down the ropes and fled to freedom?

Perhaps not. It was as much to distract his mind as to allay the man Jonson's suspicions, certainly not at all from curiosity or any genuine wish to know, that Marron asked, "Sir, your hands—what happened to your hands?"

Jonson lifted them, gazed at them more dispassionately than Marron could, seeming to consider exactly how twisted they were, how bent the fingers. "Clever men, Fra' Marron, they have made for themselves clever machines. But they are still stupid about people, they still believe pain can overmaster anyone, if there is enough of it for long enough. They are wrong. I have told them that, but they will not believe me, you see."

Marron did see, and had no trouble believing. Men like Fra' Piet, the questioners must be. They would be confident; *just a little more, another day and he will break, he must.* Especially with a prisoner, a victim like Jonson, a man not ashamed to scream. Screaming was weakness and weakness meant victory, tomorrow if not today. It was cruel ignorance, but constant failure, constant deaths still would not show them so.

"What can I do, sir?"

"Go away. If they find you here, they'll have another to try their machines on. You taint your soul by speaking to me. Infection spreads, and must be cauterised."

It was true. A Surayon witch might corrupt the holiest brother with honeyed words and secret spells; heresy at the heart could destroy the Ransomers and all Outremer from within, the worm in the apple, poisonous and deadly. Cast out or not, if they thought him tainted they would never let him go. He might have escaped a flaying in the hall above only to encounter what was worse and far worse down here in the cold, where all that was warm was the betraying witch-light.

"May I give you one more drink before I leave you?" He wanted to do more, but there was no way that he could see.

"No—but leave the flask within my reach. That will explain the missing water. With luck they'll blame it on their own carelessness."

And would never stop to think that he couldn't have poured from a flask nor gripped a goblet, however close they left it? Well, perhaps. *People believe what's easiest,* his uncle used to say. After midday service sometimes, as they went back to food and the fields. Marron's aunt would shush him then, and glance around anxiously for priests or listening neighbours.

Marron set the flask where he'd been told to, rose to his feet and made his way to the curtained door. He wanted to leave good wishes, but that was stupid, pointless. This man was going to die—soon, and in terrible pain—and they both knew it. The best he could manage was a warning, "Sir, that light you make," *that magic you make, in defiance of the God and the law,* "you should take more care..."

"I do, ordinarily. You surprised me; you work that door very quietly, Fra' Marron. The questioners are not so careful. Even though that curtain muffles sound. That's what it's for, to keep me from disturbing your prayerful duties."

If so, it didn't work too well, Marron thought, remembering the cries in the stairwell. But then, without it, perhaps those cries would have scoured the kitchens also, and soured the soup.

He bade the man Jonson a respectful farewell—he might be Surayonnaise and heretic, he was certainly a witch, but he was still a man; he hid a great courage behind his craven screaming, and that spoke to Marron far more forcefully than even his long-trained soul could recoil from—and backed out of the cell as cautiously as he had entered, through the curtain first and then through the door, letting

no fall of light betray him. Neither any sound: he took slow
pains with the bolt, to be sure it whispered into its bracket.
All but blind then, he counted off the empty cells till he
came to his own, confirmed it by the smell from his bucket,
and knelt quietly in his place as though he had never strayed
a little inch from his due obedience that day.

HIS MIND STRAYED, further than his body had; his
mind was up in the castle and down on the plain,
seeking Mustar. And further, far further, looking for hidden
Surayon: looking to see if anyone there wept and wailed for
an absent man, a wonder-worker lost to cold Ransomers,
unransomable to them or anyone.

And found nothing, of course, except his own doubts
and dreads; and so settled back into chill and hunger once
more, into the sharp aching of his never-mending arm, into
unhappy anticipation of what was to come.

BROTHERS CAME TO fetch him out, before the great
bell sounded for evening service. Not to take him to the
hall, not yet: only to an antechamber where they stood silent
guard over him, making no comment even about his sling
and his flapping shift, until the call to prayer pushed them
all to their knees, sound made solid.The brothers recited the
prayers in a soft chant. Marron joined them in a whisper, not
to add to his known faults, but it was all rote. Today he could
feel only bitterness towards the God and all men who wor-
shipped Him, who tortured and killed and called it worship.

When they were done they waited, once more in silence.
At last the high doors to the hall swung open; the preceptor,
masters and knights filed out. Magister Rolf and Magister
Sewart, the two Masters Confessor stepped aside from the
procession and stood in the doorway to the antechamber,
not deigning even to glance at Marron.

Then it was time to stand, to follow them back into the great hall; to walk all the length of the aisle between the gathered brothers, to feel their hidden eyes on him, to stand and then kneel before the steps to the altar with his head uncovered, a public sign of his disgrace.

The masters between them declared his faults, gross disobedience that amounted to treachery against the kingdom, the Order and the God; then his mitigation, that his later understanding had perhaps saved the castle, and that he had fought well and bravely on the wall. Justice condemned him, justice reprieved him. He was to be stripped and cast out from the Order, to make what way he could in the world unblessed by brotherhood.

The two brothers who stood watch behind him ripped the shift from his body, tearing it in two between them; they took the girdle also, that had made his sling. Naked, cradling his bad arm, he made that long walk again the other way, head as high and feet as steady as he could manage.

And so out of the hall and all the way through the castle, and no sign of Sieur Anton to succour him; only the harsh silence of the brothers at his back, and the sidelong glances of those who stood watch on the walls.

In the wide yard before the stables was a vast pile of wood, with small kegs beside. He didn't understand that, but his curiosity was almost dead within him, drowned by dread. Sieur Anton had changed his mind or the court had changed its sentence: he was not to serve as squire after all, only to be thrust out alone, afraid, anathema...

THE GUARDS AT the gate opened it, still with no word spoken. He walked through, heard it slammed behind him; and lifted his eyes to face this new world, wondering who he was now, where he could go, what he might do to survive in this unkind land.

And saw the knight some few paces off, standing waiting for him.

CHAZ BRENCHLEY

ABOUT THE AUTHOR

Chaz Brenchley spent his childhood in Oxford, generally with his nose in a book. At the age of twelve he met J R R Tolkien in a theatre dressing room, and his fate was sealed.

He sold his first stories at the age of eighteen, and has been a professional writer ever since. His work ranges from science fiction to epic and urban fantasy, from mysteries and thrillers to romance and horror. He's published upwards of forty books, and many hundreds of short stories.

A decade ago he moved from bachelordom to marriage, from Newcastle to California, along with 120 boxes (115 of which were books), two squabbling cats and a famous teddy bear.

http://www.chazbrenchley.co.uk/
@ChazBrenchley

THE DEVIL IN THE DUST

CPSIA information can be obtained
at www.ICGtesting.com
Printed in the USA
LVHW040253170422
716398LV00008B/250

9 781913 892326